Philothea

by

Lydia Maria Child

The Echo Library 2007

Published by

The Echo Library

Echo Library
131 High St.
Teddington
Middlesex TW11 8HH

www.echo-library.com

Please report serious faults in the text to complaints@echo-library.com

ISBN 978-1-40684-550-1

PHILOTHEA:

A Grecian Romance.
BY L. MARIA CHILD.

AUTHOR OF LETTERS FROM NEW YORK, FLOWERS FOR CHILDREN, ETC

The intelligible forms of ancient poets,
The fair humanities of old religion,
The Power, the Beauty, and the Majesty,
That had their haunts in dale or piny mountain.
Or forest by slow stream, or pabbly spring,
Or chasms and watcry depths, all these have vanished—
They live no longer in the faith of Reason!
But still, the heart doth need a language—still
Doth the old instinct bring back the old names.
COLERIDGE.

A Spirit hung,
Beautiful region! o'er thy towns and farms,
Statues, and temples, and memorial tombs,
And *emanations* were perceived.
WORDSWORTH.

A NEW AND CORRECTED EDITION.
To
MY BELOVED BROTHER,
Dr. Francis,
OF HARVARD UNIVERSITY,

To whose Early Influence I owe my Love of Literature

THIS VOLUME
IS RESPECTFULLY AND AFFECTIONATELY INSCRIBED.

PREFACE

This volume is purely romance; and most readers will consider it romance of the wildest kind. A few kindred spirits, prone to people space "with life and mystical predominance," will perceive a light *within* the Grecian Temple.

For such I have written it. To minds of different mould, who may think an apology necessary for what they will deem so utterly useless, I have nothing better to offer than the simple fact that I found delight in doing it.

CHAPTER I.

Here let us seek Athenæ's towers,
The cradle of old Cecrops' race,
The world's chief ornament and grace;
Here mystic fanes and rites divine,
And lamps in sacred splendour shine;
Here the gods dwell in marble domes,
Feasted with costly hecatombs,
That round their votive statues blaze,
Whilst crowded temples ring with praise;
And pompous sacrifices here
Make holidays throughout the year.
                    ARISTOPHANES.

The moon was moving through the heavens in silent glory; and Athens, with all her beautiful variety of villas, altars, statues, and temples, rejoiced in the hallowed light.

The white columns of the lofty Parthenon stood in distinct relief against the clear blue sky; the crest and spear of Pallas Promachos glittered in the refulgent atmosphere, a beacon to the distant mariner; the line of brazen tripods, leading from the Theatre of Dionysus, glowed like urns of fire; and the waters of the Illyssus glanced right joyfully, as they moved onward to the ocean. The earth was like a slumbering babe, smiling in its sleep, because it dreams of Heaven.

In the most ancient and quiet part of the city, not far from the gate Diocharis, was the modest mansion of Anaxagoras; and at this tranquil hour, the grand-daughter of the philosopher, with her beloved companion Eudora, stood on the roof, enjoying the radiant landscape, and the balmy air.

Philothea's tall figure was a lovely union of majesty and grace. The golden hair, which she inherited from a Laconian mother, was tastefully arranged on the top of her head, in a braided crown, over the sides of which the bright curls fell, like tendrils of grapes from the edge of a basket. The mild brilliancy of her large dark eyes formed a beautiful contrast to a complexion fair even to transparency. Her expression had the innocence of infancy; but it was tinged with something elevated and holy, which made it seem like infancy in Heaven.

Eudora had more sparkling eyes, lips more richly coloured, and a form more slender and flexile. Her complexion might have seemed dark, had it not been relieved by a profusion of glossy black hair, a portion of which was fastened with a silver arrow, while the remainder shaded her forehead, and fell over her shoulders.

As they stood side by side, with their arms twined around each other, they were as lovely a sight as the moon ever shone upon. Totally unlike each other, but both excellent in beauty. One might have been a model for the seraphs of Christian faith, the other an Olympian deity.

For a few moments, Philothea stood in earnest silence, gazing upon the bright planet of evening—then, in a tone of deep enthusiasm, she exclaimed:

"It is a night to feel the presence of the gods! Virgin sister of Phoebus, how calm thou art in thy glorious beauty! Thou art filling the world with music—silent to the ear, but audible to the heart! Phidias has embodied the unbreathing harmony in stone, and we worship the fair proportions, as an emanation from the gods. The birds feel it—and wonder at the tune that makes no noise. The whole earth is lulled by its influence. All is motionless; save the Naiades of the stream, moving in wreathed dance to the voiceless melody. See how their shining hair sparkles on the surface of the waters! Surely there is music in this light! Eudora, what is it within us, that listens where there is no sound? Is it thus we shall hear in Elysium?"

In a subdued and troubled voice, her companion answered, "Oh, Philothea, when you talk thus, my spirit is in fear—and now, too, all is so still and bright, that it seems as if the gods themselves were listening to our speech."

"The same mysterious influence impresses me with awe," replied the contemplative maiden: "In such an hour as this, Plato must have received the sublime thought, 'God is truth—and light is his shadow.'"

Eudora drew more closely to her friend, and said, timidly: "Oh, Philothea, do not talk of the gods. Such discourse has a strange and fearful power, when the radiant daughter of Zeus is looking down upon us in all her heavenly majesty. Even the midnight procession of the Panathenæa affected me less deeply."

After a few moments of serious silence, she continued: "I saw it last night, for the first time since my childhood; for you know I was very ill when the festival was last celebrated. It was truly a beautiful and majestic scene! The virgins all clothed in white; the heifers decorated with garlands; the venerable old men bearing branches of olive; the glittering chariots; the noble white horses, obeying the curb with such proud impatience; the consecrated image of Pallas carried aloft on its bed of flowers; the sacred ship blazing with gems and gold; all moving in the light of a thousand torches! Then the music, so loud and harmonious! It seemed as if all Athens joined in the mighty sound. I distinguished you in the procession; and I almost envied you the privilege of embroidering the sacred peplus, and being six long months in the service of Pallas Athenæ. I have had so much to say since you returned, and Phidias has so many guests, that I have found little time to ask concerning the magnificent sights you saw within the Acropolis."

"The night would wear away, ere I could describe all I witnessed within the walls of the Parthenon alone," rejoined her companion: "There is the silver-footed throne, on which Xerxes sat, while he watched the battle of Salamis; the scimitar of Mardonius, captured at Platææ; a beautiful ivory Persephone, on a pedestal of pure gold; and a Methymnean lyre, said to have belonged to Terpander himself, who you know was the first that used seven strings. Victorious wreaths, coins, rings, and goblets of shining gold, are there without number; and Persian couches, and Egyptian sphynxes, and—",

"What do you find so interesting beyond the walls?" asked Eudora, smiling at the earnestness with which her friend gazed in the distance:" Do the slaves, bringing water from the Fountain of Callirhöe, look so very beautiful in the moonlight?"

"I marvel that you can speak so lightly," replied Philothea: "We have as yet heard no tidings concerning the decision in the Court of Cynosarges, on which the fate of Philæmon depends; and you know how severely his high spirit will suffer, if an unfavourable sentence is awarded. Neither of us have alluded to this painful topic. But why have we thus lingered on the house-top, if it were not to watch for the group which, if I mistake not, are now approaching, on their return from Cynosarges?"

"Then it is for Philæmon's sake, that you have so long been looking wistfully toward the Illyssus?" said Eudora, playfully.

"I will not deny that Paralus has had the largest share of my thoughts," replied the simple-hearted maiden; "but for Philæmon, as your betrothed lover, and the favourite pupil of my grandfather, I feel an interest strong enough to keep me on the watch during a less delightful evening than this. I think it must be Paralus who walks in the centre of the group; we have been separated many months; and courtesy to the numerous strangers under his father's roof has prevented our having much discourse to-day. For his sake, I am glad once more to be in my own happy home. He is none the less dear to me because I know that he can never be my husband."

"And why should he not?" exclaimed Eudora: "The blood of princes flowed in the veins of your ancestors. If Anaxagoras is poor, it is because he has preferred wisdom to gold."

With a faint sigh, Philothea answered, "Had the good old man preferred gold to wisdom, I should have loved him less; nor would his instructions have made me such a wife as Paralus deserves; yet Pericles would have better liked the union. He has obtained from his son a solemn promise never to speak to me of marriage. The precaution was unnecessary; for since this new law has passed, I would not marry Paralus, even with his father's consent. I would never be the means of bringing degradation and losses upon him."

"If you still love Paralus, I wonder you can be so quiet and cheerful," said Eudora.

"I wished him to make the required promise, because obedience to parents is our first duty," replied Philothea; "and had I thought otherwise, the laws compel it. But the liberty of loving Paralus, no power can take from me; and in that I find sufficient happiness. I am bound to him by ties stronger than usually bind the hearts of women. My kind grandfather has given me an education seldom bestowed on daughters; and from our childhood, Paralus and I have shared the same books, the same music, and the same thoughts, until our souls seem to be one. When I am very happy, I always see a peculiar brightness on his countenance; and when I am powerfully impressed by any of the fair sights of this beautiful world, or by those radiant deities who live among the stars, often, before I can speak my thoughts, he utters my very words. I sometimes think the gods have united human beings by some mysterious principle, like the according notes of music. Or is it as Plato has supposed, that souls originally one have been divided, and each seeks the half it has lost? Eudora, if you consider how generally maidens are bestowed in marriage without consulting their affections, you must confess that you have reason to feel deeply grateful for your own lot."

"Yet this new law against those of foreign parentage, renders marriage with me as dishonourable as with you," rejoined the maiden: "Nay, it is much more so; for I am a slave, though, by courtesy, they do not call me one."

"But Philæmon has no parents to forbid his choice," said Philothea; "and if the court decide against him, he will incur no fine by a marriage with you; for he himself will then be a sojourner in Athens. The loss of his paternal estates will indeed leave him poor; but he has friends to assist his own energies, and in all probability, your union will not be long delayed. Ah, now I am certain that Anaxagoras approaches, with Paralus and Philæmon. They perceive us; but Paralus does not wave his hand, as he promised to do, if they brought good tidings."

Without appearing to share her anxiety, Eudora carelessly inquired, "Did you witness the Festival of Torches, while you were within the Acropolis? The swiftness of the runners, moving in the light of their own torches, making statues and temples ruddy with the glow as they passed, was truly a beautiful sight. I suppose you heard that Alcibiades gained the prize? With what graceful celerity he darted through the course! I was at Aspasia's house that evening. It is so near the goal, that we could plainly see his countenance flushed with excitement and exercise, as he stood waving his unextinguished torch in triumph."

"I am sorry Phidias considers improvement in music of sufficient consequence to encourage your visits to that dangerous woman," answered Philothea: "It was an unpropitious day for Athens when she came here to invest vice with all the allurements of beauty and eloquence."

"I think women should judge kindly of Aspasia's faults, and remember that they are greatly exaggerated by her enemies," rejoined Eudora; "for she proves that they are fit for something better than mere domestic slaves. Her house is the only one in all Greece where women are allowed to be present at entertainments. What is the use of a beautiful face, if one must be shut up in her own apartment for ever? And what avails skill in music, if there is no chance to display it? I confess that I like the customs Aspasia is trying to introduce."

"And I should like them, if I believed they would make the Grecian women something *better* than mere domestic slaves," said Philothea; "but such as Aspasia will never raise women out of the bondage in which they are placed by the impurity and selfishness of man. Your own confessions, Eudora, do not speak well for her instructions. Why should a true-hearted woman wish to display her beautiful face, or her skill in music, to any but those on whom her affections are bestowed?"

"It is natural to wish for admiration," replied the handsome maiden: "The goddesses themselves contended for it. You, at least, ought not to judge Aspasia harshly; for she has the idea that you are some deity in disguise; and she has the most extravagant desire to see you."

"Flattery to ourselves does not change the nature of what is wrong," answered Philothea. "Pericles has more than once mentioned Aspasia's wish that I should visit her; but nothing short of my grandfather's express command will ever induce me to do it. Our friends are now entering the gate. Let us go to welcome them."

Eudora hastily excused herself under the plea of duties at home; and Philothea, supposing it might be painful to meet her unfortunate lover in the presence of others, forebore to urge it.

A paternal blessing beamed from the countenance of Anaxagoras, the moment Philothea appeared. Paralus greeted her as a brother welcomes a cherished sister; but in the earnest kindness of his glance was expressed something more deep and heart-stirring than his words implied.

Philæmon, though more thoughtful than usual, received his own and Eudora's friend, with cheerful cordiality. His countenance had the frank and smiling expression of one who truly wishes well to all men, and therefore sees everything reflected in forms of joy. His figure was athletic, while his step and bearing indicated the promptitude and decision of a man who acts spontaneously from his own convictions.

Paralus, far from being effeminate, was distinguished for his dexterity and skill in all the manly sports of the gymnasium; but the purity of his complexion, and the peculiarly spiritual expression of his face, would have been deemed beautiful, even in a woman. The first he probably derived from his mode of life; for, being a strict Pythagorean, he never partook of animal food. The last was the transparent medium of innocence, through which thoughts and affections continually showed their changing forms of life.

In answer to her eager questions, Philothea soon learned that her fears had prophesied aright concerning the decision of the court. Philæmon had been unsuccessful; but the buoyant energy of his character did not yield even to temporary despondency. He spoke of his enemies without bitterness, and of his own prospects with confidence and hope.

Philothea would have immediately gone to convey the tidings to her friend, had not Philæmon early taken his leave, and passed through the garden into the house of Phidias.

Paralus remained until a late hour, alternately talking with the venerable philosopher, and playing upon his flute, while Philothea sung the songs they had learned together.

In the course of conversation, Anaxagoras informed his child that Pericles particularly urged her attendance at Aspasia's next symposium. "I obey my grandfather, without a question," she replied; "but I would much rather avoid this visit, if it were possible."

"Such is likewise my wish," rejoined the philosopher; "but Pericles has plainly implied that he should be offended by refusal; it is therefore necessary to comply with his request."

The maiden looked doubtingly at her lover, as if she deemed his sanction necessary; and the inquiring glance was answered by an affectionate smile. "I need not repeat my thoughts and feelings with regard to Aspasia," said Paralus, "for you know them well; but for many reasons it is not desirable that an estrangement should take place between my father and Anaxagoras. Since, therefore, it has pleased Pericles to insist upon it, I think the visit had better be made. You need not fear any very alarming innovation upon the purity of ancient manners. Even Aspasia will reverence you,"

Philothea meekly yielded to the opinion of her friends; and it was decided that, on the evening after the morrow, she should accompany her grandfather to Aspasia's dwelling.

Before proceeding farther, it is necessary to relate the situation of the several characters introduced in this chapter.

Anaxagoras had been the tutor of Pericles, and still retained considerable influence over him; but there were times when the straightforward sincerity, and uncompromising integrity of the old man were somewhat offensive and troublesome to his ambitious pupil. For the great Athenian statesman, like modern politicians, deemed honesty excellent in theory, and policy safe in practice. Thus admitting the absurd proposition that principles entirely false and corrupt in the abstract are more salutary, in their practical manifestation, than principles essentially good and true.

While Pericles was determined to profit by diseases of the state, the philosopher was anxious to cure them; therefore, independently of personal affection and gratitude, he was willing to make slight concessions, in order to retain some influence over his illustrious pupil.

The celebrated Aspasia was an elegant and voluptuous Ionian, who succeeded admirably in pleasing the good taste of the Athenians, while she ministered to their vanity and their vices. The wise and good lamented the universal depravity of manners, sanctioned by her influence; but a people so gay, so ardent, so intensely enamoured of the beautiful, readily acknowledged the sway of an eloquent and fascinating woman, who carefully preserved the appearance of decorum. Like the Gabrielles and Pompadours of modern times, Aspasia obtained present admiration and future fame, while hundreds of better women were neglected and forgotten. The crowds of wealthy and distinguished men who gathered around her, were profuse in their flattery, and munificent in their gifts; and Pericles so far yielded to her influence, that he divorced his wife and married her.

Philæmon was at that time on terms of intimacy with the illustrious orator; and he earnestly remonstrated against this union, as alike disgraceful to Pericles and injurious to public morals. By this advice he incurred the inveterate dislike of Aspasia; who never rested from her efforts until she had persuaded her husband to procure the revival of an ancient law, by which all citizens who married foreigners, were subjected to a heavy fine; and all persons, whose parents were not both Athenians, were declared incapable of voting in the public assemblies, or of inheriting the estates of their fathers. Pericles the more readily consented to this, because such a law at once deprived many political enemies of power. Philæmon was the son of Chærilaüs, a wealthy Athenian; but his mother had been born in Corinth, though brought to Athens during childhood. It was supposed that this latter circumstance, added to the patriotism of his family and his own moral excellence, would prevent the application of the law in his individual case. But Alcibiades, for reasons unknown to the public, united his influence with that of Aspasia; and their partizans were active and powerful. When the case was tried in the court of illegitimacy at Cynosarges, Philæmon was declared a sojourner in Athens, incapable of holding any office, and dispossessed of his paternal inheritance.

Eudora was a mere infant when Phidias bought her of a poor goatherd in Phelle. The child was sitting upon a rock, caressing a kid, when the sculptor first saw her, and the gracefulness of her attitude attracted his attention, while her innocent beauty touched his heart. She and her nurse had been stolen from the Ionian coast, by Greek pirates. The nurse was sold into slavery, and the babe delivered by one of the pirates to the care of his mother. The little creature, in her lisping way, called herself baby Minta; and this appellation she retained, until Phidias gave her the name of Eudora.

Philothea, the orphan daughter of Alcimenes, son of Anaxagoras, was a year or two older than Eudora. She was brought to Athens, at about the same period; and as they resided very near each other, the habitual intercourse of childhood naturally ripened into mature friendship. No interruption of this constant intimacy occurred, until Philothea was appointed one of the Canephoræ, whose duty it was to embroider the sacred peplus, and to carry baskets in the grand procession of the Panathenæa. Six months of complete seclusion within the walls of the Acropolis, were required of the Canephoræ. During this protracted absence, Aspasia persuaded Phidias to bring Eudora frequently to her house; and her influence insensibly produced a great change in that young person, whose character was even more flexile than her form.

CHAPTER II.

"With grace divine her soul is blest,
And heavenly Pallas breathes within her breast;
In wonderous arts than woman more renowned,
And more than woman with deep wisdom crowned.
                    HOMER.

It was the last market hour of Athens, when Anaxagoras, Philothea, and Eudora, accompanied by Geta, the favourite slave of Phidias, stepped forth into the street, on their way to Aspasia's residence.

Loud shouts of laughter came from the agoras, and the whole air was filled with the hum of a busy multitude. Groups of citizens lingered about the porticos; Egyptians, Medians, Sicilians, and strangers from all the neighbouring States of Greece, thronged the broad avenue of the Piræus; women, carrying upon their heads olive jars, baskets of grapes, and vases of water, glided among the crowd, with that majestic motion so peculiar to the peasantry in countries where this custom prevails.

Philothea drew the folds of her veil more closely, and clung timidly to her venerable protector. But neither this, nor increasing twilight, could screen the graceful maidens from observation. Athenians looked back as they passed, and foreigners paused to inquire their name and parentage.

In a few moments they were under the walls of the Acropolis, walking in the shadow of the olive groves, among god-like statues, to which the gathering obscurity of evening gave an impressive distinctness—as if the light departing from the world, stood petrified in marble.

Thence they entered the inner Ceramicus, where Aspasia resided. The building, like all the private houses of Athens, had a plain exterior, strongly contrasted by the magnificence of surrounding temples, and porticos. At the gate, an image of Hermes looked toward the harbour, while Phoebus, leaning on his lyre, appeared to gaze earnestly at the dwelling.

A slave, stationed near the door, lighted the way to the apartment where Aspasia was reclining, with a Doric harp by her side, on which she had just been playing. The first emotion she excited was surprise at the radiant and lucid expression, which mantled her whole face, and made the very blood seem eloquent. In her large dark eye the proud consciousness of intellect was softened only by melting voluptuousness; but something of sadness about her beautiful mouth gave indication that the heavenly part of her nature still struggled with earth-born passions.

A garland of golden leaves, with large drops of pearl, was interwoven among the glossy braids of her hair, and rested on her forehead.

She wore a robe of rich Milesian purple, the folds of which were confined on one shoulder within a broad ring of gold, curiously wrought; on the other they were fastened by a beautiful cameo, representing the head of Pericles. The crimson couch gave a soft flush to the cheek and snowy arm that rested on it; and, for a moment, even Philothea yielded to the enchantment of her beauty.

Full of smiles, Aspasia rose and greeted Eudora, with the ease and gracefulness of one long accustomed to homage; but when the venerable philosopher introduced his child, she felt the simple purity emanating from their characters, and something of embarrassment mingled with her respectful salutation.

Her own face was uncovered, contrary to the custom of Grecian women; and after a few of those casual remarks which everywhere serve to fill up the pauses in conversation, she playfully seized Eudora's veil, and threw it back over her shoulders. She would have done the same to Philothea; but the maiden placed her hand on the half transparent covering, and said, "With your leave, lady, I remain veiled."

"But I cannot give my leave," rejoined Aspasia, playfully, still keeping her hold upon the veil: "I must see this tyrannical custom done away in the free commonwealth of Athens. All the matrons who visit my house agree with me in this point; all are willing to renounce the absurd fashion."

"But in a maiden it would be less seemly," answered Philothea.

Thus resisted, Aspasia appealed to Anaxagoras to exert his authority; adding, in an audible whisper, "Phidias has told me that she is as lovely as the immortals."

With a quiet smile, the aged philosopher replied, "My child must be guided by her own heart. The gods have there placed an oracle, which never misleads or perplexes those who listen to it."

Aspasia continued, "From what I had heard of you, Philothea, I expected to find you above the narrow prejudices of Grecian women. In *you* I was sure of a mind strong enough to break the fetters of habit. Tell me, my bashful maiden, why is beauty given us, unless it be like sunlight to bless and gladden the world?"

"Lady," replied the gentle recluse, "beauty is given to remind us that the soul should be kept as fair and perfect in its proportions, as the temple in which it dwells."

"You are above ordinary women," said Aspasia; "for you hear me allude to your beauty without affecting to contradict me, and apparently without pleasure."

The sound of voices in earnest conversation announced the approach of Pericles with visiters. "Come to my room for a few moments," said Aspasia, addressing the maidens: "I have just received a magnificent present, which I am sure Eudora will admire. As she spoke, she led the way to an upper apartment. When they opened the door, a soft light shone upon them from a lamp, which a marble Psyche shaded with her hand, as she bent over the couch of Eros.

"Now that we are quite sure of being uninterrupted, you cannot refuse to raise your veil," said Aspasia.

Simply and naturally, the maiden did as she was desired; without any emotion of displeasure or exultation at the eager curiosity of her hostess.

For an instant, Aspasia stood rebuked and silent, in the presence of that serene and holy beauty.

With deep feeling she exclaimed, "Maiden, Phidias spoke truly. Even thus do we imagine the immortals!"

A faint blush gleamed on Philothea's face; for her meek spirit was pained by a comparison with things divine; but it passed rapidly; and her whole soul became absorbed in the lovely statues before her.

Eudora's speaking glance seemed to say, "I knew her beauty would surprise you!" and then, with the eager gayety of a little child, she began to examine the gorgeous decorations of the room.

The couch rested on two sphinxes of gold and ivory, over which the purple drapery fell in rich and massive folds. In one corner, a pedestal of Egyptian marble supported an alabaster vase, on the edge of which were two doves, exquisitely carved, one just raising his head, the other stooping to drink. On a similar stand, at the other side, stood a peacock, glittering with many coloured gems. The head lowered upon the breast formed the handle; while here and there, among the brilliant tail feathers, appeared a languid flame slowly burning away the perfumed oil, with which the bird was filled.

Eudora clapped her hands, with an exclamation of delight. "That is the present of which I spoke," said Aspasia, smiling: "It was sent by Artaphernes, the Persian, who has lately come to Athens to buy pictures and statues for the great king."

As Philothea turned towards her companion, she met Aspasia's earnest gaze. "Had you forgotten where you were?" she asked.

"No, lady, I could not forget that," replied the maiden. As she spoke, she hastily withdrew her eyes from an immodest picture, on which they had accidentally rested; and, blushing deeply, she added, "But there is something so life-like in that slumbering marble, that for a moment I almost feared Eudora would waken it."

"You will not look upon the picture," rejoined Aspasia; "yet it relates a story of one of the gods you reverence so highly. I am told you are a devout believer in these fables?"

"When fiction is the robe of truth, I worship it for what it covers," replied Philothea; "but I love not the degrading fables which poets have made concerning divine beings. Such were not the gods of Solon; for such the wise and good can never be, in this world or another."

"Then you believe in a future existence?" said Aspasia, with an incredulous smile.

With quiet earnestness, Philothea answered:—"Lady, the simple fact that the human soul has ever *thought* of another world, is sufficient proof that there is one; for how can an idea be formed by mortals, unless it has first existed in the divine mind?"

"A reader of Plato, I perceive!" exclaimed Aspasia: "They told me I should find you pure and child-like; with a soul from which poetry sparkled, like moonlight on the waters. I did not know that wisdom and philosophy lay concealed in its depths."

"Is there any other wisdom, than true simplicity and innocence?" asked the maiden.

With a look of delighted interest, Aspasia took her arm familiarly; saying, "You and I must be friends. I shall not grow weary of you, as I do of other women. Not of you, dearest," she added in an under tone, tapping Eudora's cheek. "You must come here constantly, Philothea. Though I am aware," continued she, smiling, "that it is bad policy for me to seek a guest who will be sure to eclipse me."

"Pardon me, lady," said Philothea, gently disengaging herself: "Friendship cannot be without sympathy."

A sudden flush of anger suffused Aspasia's countenance; and Eudora looked imploringly at her friend, as she said, "You love *me*, Philothea; and I am sure we are very different."

"I crave pardon," interrupted Aspasia, with haughty impatience. "I should have remembered that the conversation prized by Pericles and Plato, might appear contemptible, to this youthful Pallas, who so proudly seeks to conceal her precious wisdom from ears profane."

"Lady, you mistake me," answered Philothea, mildly: "Your intellect, your knowledge, are as far above mine, as the radiant stars are above the flowers of the field. Besides, I never felt contempt for anything to which the gods had given life. It is impossible for me to despise you; but I pity you."

"Pity!" exclaimed Aspasia, in a piercing tone, which made both the maidens start. "Am I not the wife of Pericles, and the friend of Plato? Has not Phidias modelled his Aphrodite from my form? Is there in all Greece a poet who has not sung my praises? Is there an artist who has not paid me tribute? Phoenicia sends me her most splendid manufactures and her choicest slaves; Egypt brings her finest linen and her metals of curious workmanship; while Persia unrolls her silks, and pours out her gems at my feet. To the remotest period of time, the world,—aye, the *world*,—maiden, will hear of Aspasia, the beautiful and the gifted!"

For a moment, Philothea looked on her, silently and meekly, as she stood with folded arms, flushed brow, and proudly arched neck. Then, in a soft, sad voice, she answered: "Aye, lady—but will your spirit *hear* the echo of your fame, as it rolls back from the now silent shores of distant ages?"

"You utter nonsense!" said Aspasia, abruptly: "There is no immortality but fame. In history, the star of my existence will never set—but shine brilliantly and forever in the midst of its most glorious constellation!"

After a brief pause, Philothea resumed: "But when men talk of Aspasia the beautiful and the gifted, will they add, Aspasia the good—the happy—the innocent?"

The last word was spoken in a low, emphatic tone. A slight quivering about Aspasia's lips betrayed emotion crowded back upon the heart; while Eudora bowed her head, in silent confusion, at the bold admonition of her friend.

With impressive kindness, the maiden continued: "Daughter of Axiochus, do you never suspect that the homage you receive is half made up of selfishness and impurity? This boasted power of intellect—this giddy triumph of beauty—what do they do for you? Do they make you happy in the communion of your own heart? Do they bring you nearer to the gods? Do they make the memory of your childhood a gladness, or a sorrow?"

Aspasia sank on the couch, and bowed her head upon her hands. For a few moments, the tears might be seen stealing through her fingers; while Eudora, with the ready sympathy of a warm heart, sobbed aloud.

Aspasia soon recovered her composure. "Philothea," she said, "you have spoken to me as no one ever dared to speak; but my own heart has sometimes uttered the truth less mildly. Yesterday I learned the same lesson from a harsher voice. A Corinthian sailor pointed at this house, and said, 'There dwells Aspasia, the courtezan, who makes her wealth by the corruption of Athens!' My very blood boiled in my veins, that such an one as he could give me pain. It is true the illustrious Pericles has made me his wife; but there are things which even his power, and my own allurements, fail to procure. Ambitious women do indeed come here to learn how to be distinguished; and the vain come to study the fashion of my garments, and the newest braid of my hair. But the purest and best matrons of Greece refuse to be my guests. You, Philothea, came reluctantly—and because Pericles would have it so. Yes," she added, the tears again starting to her eyes—"I know the price at which I purchase celebrity. Poets will sing of me at feasts, and orators describe me at the games; but what will that be to me, when I have gone into the silent tomb? Like the lifeless guest at Egyptian tables, Aspasia will be all unconscious of the garlands she wears.

"Philothea, you think me vain, and heartless, and wicked; and so I am. But there are moments when I am willing that this tongue, so praised for its eloquence, should be dumb forever—that this beauty, which men worship, should be hidden in the deepest recesses of barbarian forests—so that I might again be as I was, when the sky was clothed in perpetual glory, and the earth wore not so sad a smile as now. Oh, Philothea! would to the gods, I had your purity and goodness! But you despise me;—for you are innocent."

Soothingly, and almost tearfully, the maiden replied: "No, lady; such were not the feelings which made me say we could not be friends. It is because we have chosen different paths; and paths that never approach each other. What to you seem idle dreams, are to me sublime realities, for which I would gladly exchange all that you prize in existence. You live for immortality in this world; I live for immortality in another. The public voice is your oracle; I listen to the whisperings of the gods in the stillness of my own heart; and never yet, dear lady, have those two oracles spoken the same language."

Then falling on her knees, and looking up earnestly, she exclaimed, "Beautiful and gifted one! Listen to the voice that tries to win you back to innocence and truth! Give your heart up to it, as a little child led by its mother's hand! Then shall the flowers again breathe poetry, and the stars move in music."

"It is too late," murmured Aspasia: "The flowers are scorched—the stars are clouded. I cannot again be as I have been."

"Lady, it is *never* too late," replied Philothea: "You have unbounded influence—use it nobly! No longer seek popularity by flattering the vanity, or ministering to the passions of the Athenians. Let young men hear the praise of virtue from the lips of beauty. Let them see religion married to immortal genius. Tell them it is ignoble to barter the heart's wealth for heaps of coin—that love weaves a simple wreath of his own bright hopes, stronger than massive chains of gold. Urge Pericles to prize the good of Athens more than the applause of its populace—to value the permanence of her free institutions more than the splendour of her edifices. Oh, lady, never, never, had any mortal such power to do good!"

Aspasia sat gazing intently on the beautiful speaker, whose tones grew more and more earnest as she proceeded.

"Philothea," she replied, "you have moved me strangely. There is about you an influence that cannot be resisted. It is like what Pindar says of music; if it does not give delight, it is sure to agitate and oppress the heart. From the first moment you spoke, I have felt this mysterious power. It is as if some superior being led me back, even against my will, to the days of my childhood, when I gathered acorns from the ancient oak that shadows the fountain of Byblis, or ran about on the banks of my own beloved Meander, filling my robe with flowers."

There was silence for a moment. Eudora smiled through her tears, as she whispered, "Now, Philothea, sing that sweet song Anaxagoras taught you. He too is of Ionia; and Aspasia will love to hear it."

The maiden answered with a gentle smile, and began to warble the first notes of a simple bird-like song.

"Hush!" said Aspasia, putting her hand on Philothea's mouth, and bursting into tears—"It was the first tune I ever learned; and I have not heard it since my mother sung it to me."

"Then let me sing it, lady," rejoined Philothea: "It is good for us to keep near our childhood. In leaving it, we wander from the gods."

A slight tap at the door made Aspasia start up suddenly; and stooping over the alabaster vase of water, she hastened to remove all traces of her tears.

As Eudora opened the door, a Byzantian slave bowed low, and waited permission to speak.

"Your message?" said Aspasia, with queenly brevity.

"If it please you, lady, my master bids me say he desires your presence."

"We come directly," she replied; and with another low bow, the Byzantian closed the door. Before a mirror of polished steel, supported by ivory Graces, Aspasia paused to adjust the folds of her robe, and replace a curl that had strayed from its golden fillet.

As she passed, she continued to look back at the reflection of her own fair form, with a proud glance, which seemed to say, "Aspasia is herself again!"

Philothea took Eudora's arm, and folding her veil about her, with a deep sigh followed to the room below.

CHAPTER III.

All is prepared—the table and the feast—
With due appurtenance of clothes and cushions.
Chaplets and dainties of all kinds abound:
Here rich perfumes are seen—there cakes and cates
Of every fashion; cakes of honey, cakes
Of sesamum, and cakes of unground corn.
What more? A troop of dancing women fair,
And minstrels who may chaunt us sweet Harmodius.
                    ARISTOPHANES.

The room in which the guests were assembled, was furnished with less of Asiatic splendour than the private apartment of Aspasia; but in its magnificent simplicity there was a more perfect manifestation of ideal beauty. It was divided in the middle by eight Ionic columns, alternately of Phrygian and Pentelic marble. Between the central pillars stood a superb statue from the hand of Phidias, representing Aphrodite guided by Love, and crowned by Peitho, goddess of Persuasion. Around the walls were Phoebus and Hermes in Parian marble, and the nine Muses in ivory. A fountain of perfumed water, from the adjoining room, diffused coolness and fragrance, as it passed through a number of concealed pipes, and finally flowed into a magnificent vase, supported by a troop of Naiades.

In a recess stood the famous lion of Myron, surrounded by infant Loves, playing with his paws, climbing his back, and decorating his neck with garlands. This beautiful group seemed actually to live and move in the clear light and deep shadows derived from a silver lamp suspended above.

The walls were enriched with some of the choicest paintings of Apollodorus, Zeuxis, and Polygnotus. Near a fine likeness of Pericles, by Aristolaus, was Aspasia, represented as Chloris scattering flowers over the earth, and attended by winged Hours.

It chanced that Pericles himself reclined beneath his portrait, and though political anxiety had taken from his countenance something of the cheerful freshness which characterized the picture, he still retained the same elevated beauty—the same deep, quiet expression of intellectual power. At a short distance, with his arm resting on the couch, stood his nephew Alcibiades, deservedly called the handsomest man in Athens. He was laughing with Hermippus, the comic writer, whose shrewd, sarcastic and mischievous face was expressive of his calling. Phidias slowly paced the room, talking of the current news with the Persian Artaphernes. Anaxagoras reclined near the statue of Aphrodite, listening and occasionally speaking to Plato, who leaned against one of the marble pillars, in earnest conversation with a learned Ethiopian.

The gorgeous apparel of the Asiatic and African guests, contrasted strongly with the graceful simplicity of Grecian costume. A saffron-coloured mantle and a richly embroidered Median vest glittered on the person of the venerable Artaphernes. Tithonus, the Ethiopian, wore a skirt of ample folds, which scarcely fell below the knee. It was of the glorious Tyrian hue, resembling a crimson light shining through transparent purple. The edge of the garment was curiously wrought with golden palm leaves. It terminated at the waist in a large roll, twined with massive chains of gold, and fastened by a clasp of the far-famed Ethiopian topaz. The upper part of his person was uncovered and unornamented, save by broad bracelets of gold, which formed a magnificent contrast with the sable colour of his vigorous and finely-proportioned limbs.

As the ladies entered, the various groups came forward to meet them; and all were welcomed by Aspasia with earnest cordiality and graceful self-possession. While the brief salutations were passing, Hipparete, the wife of Alcibiades came from an inner apartment, where she had been waiting for her hostess. She was a fair, amiable young matron, evidently conscious of her high rank. The short blue tunic, which she wore over a lemon-coloured robe, was embroidered with golden grasshoppers; and on her forehead sparkled a jewelled insect of the same species. It was the emblem of unmixed Athenian blood; and Hipparete alone, of all the ladies present, had a right to wear it. Her manners were an elaborate copy of Aspasia; but deprived of the powerful charm of unconsciousness, which flowed like a principle of life into every motion of that beautiful enchantress.

The momentary silence, so apt to follow introductions, was interrupted by an Ethiopian boy, who, at a signal from Tithonus, emerged from behind the columns, and kneeling, presented to Aspasia a beautiful box of ivory, inlaid with gold, filled with the choicest perfumes. The lady acknowledged the costly offering by a gracious smile, and a low bend of the head toward the giver.

The ivory was wrought with exquisite skill, representing the imaginary forms of the constellations, studded with golden stars. The whole rested on a golden image of Atlas, bending beneath the weight. The box was passed from hand to hand, and excited universal admiration.

"Were these figures carved by an artist of your own country?" asked Phidias.

With a smile, Tithonus replied, "You ask the question because you see a Grecian spirit in those forms. They were indeed fashioned by an Ethiopian; but one who had long resided in Athens."

"There is truly a freedom and variety in these figures, which I have rarely seen even in Greece," rejoined Phidias; "and I have never met with those characteristics in Ethiopian or Egyptian workmanship."

"They belong not to the genius of those countries," answered Tithonus: "Philosophy and the arts are but a manifestation of the intelligible ideas that move the public mind; and thus they become visible images of the nations whence they emanate. The philosophy of the East is misty and vast—with a gleam of truth here and there, resting like sunlight on the edge of a dark and mighty cloud. Hence, our architecture and statuary is massive and of immense proportions. Greece is free—therefore she has a philosopher, who sees that every idea must have a form, and in every form discovers its appropriate life. And because philosophy has perceived that the principle of vitality and beauty flows from the divine mind into each and every earthly thing, therefore Greece has a sculptor, who can mould his thoughts into marble forms, from which the free grandeur of the soul emanates like a perpetual presence." As he spoke, he bowed low to Plato and Phidias.

"The gigantic statues of Sicily have fair proportions," said Plato; "and they have life; but it is life in deep repose. There is the vastness of eternity, without the activity of time."

"The most ancient statuary of all nations is an image of death; not of sleeping energy," observed Aspasia. "The arms adhere rigidly to the sides, the feet form one block; and even in the face, the divine ideal seems struggling hard to enter the reluctant form. But thanks to Pygmalion of Cyprus, we now have the visible impress of every passion carved in stone. The spirit of beauty now flows freely into the harmonious proportions, even as the oracle is filled by the inspiration of the god. Now the foot bounds from the pedestal, the finger points to the stars, and life breathes from every limb. But in good time the Lybian pipe warns us that the feast is ready. We must not soar too far above the earth, while she offers us the rich treasures of her fruit-trees and vines."

"Yet it is ever thus, when Plato is with us," exclaimed Pericles. "He walks with his head among the stars—and, by a magic influence, we rise to his elevation, until we perceive the shadows of majestic worlds, known in their reality only to the gods. As the approach of Phoebus fills the priestess with prophecy, so does this son of Phoebus impart something of his own eloquence to all who come within its power."

"You speak truly, O Pericles," replied Tithonus; "but it is a truth felt only by those who are in some measure worthy to receive it. Aspasia said wisely, that the spirit of beauty flows in, only where the proportions are harmonious. The gods are ever with us, but few feel the presence of the gods."

Philothea, speaking in a low tone to Eudora, added, "And Plato rejoices in their glorious presence, not only because he walks with his head among the stars, but because he carries in his heart a blessing for every little child."

These words, though spoken almost in a whisper, reached the ear of the philosopher himself; and he turned toward the lovely speaker with a beaming glance, which distinctly told that his choicest blessings were bestowed upon spirits pure and gentle as her own.

Thus conversing, the guests passed between the marble columns, and entered that part of the room where the banquet was prepared. Aspasia filled a golden basket with Athenian olives, Phoenician dates, and almonds of Naxos, and whispering a brief invocation, placed it on a small altar, before an ivory image of Demeter, which stood in the midst of the table. Seats covered with crimson cloth were arranged at the end of the couches, for the accommodation of women; but the men reclined in Asiatic fashion, while beautiful damsels sprinkled perfumes on their heads, and offered water for their hands in vases of silver.

In choosing one to preside over the festivities of the evening, the lot fell upon Tithonus; but he gracefully declined the office, saying it properly belonged to an Athenian.

"Then I must insist that you appoint your successor," said Aspasia.

"Your command partakes little of the democracy of Athenian institutions," answered he, smiling; "but I obey it cheerfully; and will, as most fitting, crown the wisest." He arose, as he spoke, and reverently placed the chaplet on the head of Plato.

"I will transfer it to the most beautiful," rejoined the philosopher; and he attempted to place the garland on the brow of Alcibiades. But the young man prevented him, and exclaimed, "Nay—according to your own doctrines, O admirable Plato, wisdom should wear the crown; since beauty is but its outward form."

Thus urged, Plato accepted the honours of the banquet; and taking a handful of garlands from the golden urn on which they were suspended, he proceeded to crown the guests. He first placed upon Aspasia's head a wreath of bright and variegated flowers, among which the rose and the myrtle were most conspicuous. Upon Hipparete he bestowed a coronal of violets, regarded by the proud Athenians as their own peculiar flower. Philothea received a crown of pure white lilies.

Aspasia, observing this, exclaimed, "Tell me, O Plato, how you knew that wreath, above all the others, was woven for the grand-daughter of Anaxagoras?"

"When I hear a note of music, can I not at once strike its chord?" answered the philosopher: "Even as surely is there an everlasting harmony between the soul of man and the visible forms of creation. If there were no innocent hearts, there would be no white lilies."

A shadow passed over Aspasia's expressive countenance; for she was aware that her own brilliant wreath contained not one purely white blossom. But her features had been well-trained to conceal her sentiments; and her usual vivacity instantly returned.

The remainder of the garlands were bestowed so rapidly, that there seemed scarcely time for deliberate choice; yet Pericles wore the oak leaves sacred to Zeus; and the laurel and olive of Phoebus rested on the brow of Phidias.

A half mischievous smile played round Aspasia's lips, when she saw the wreath of ivy and grape leaves placed on the head of Alcibiades. "Son of Aristo," she exclaimed, "the Phoenician Magii have given you good skill in divination. You have bestowed every garland appropriately."

"It needed little magic," replied Plato, "to know that the oaken leaves belonged to one whose eloquence is so often called Olympian; or that the laurel was due to him who fashioned Pallas Parthenia; and Alcibiades would no doubt contend boldly with any man who professed to worship the god of vineyards with more zeal than himself."

The gay Athenian answered this challenge by singing part of an Anacreontic ode, often repeated during the festivities of the Dionysia:

"To-day I'll haste to quaff my wine,
As if to-morrow ne'er should shine;
But if to-morrow comes, why then—
I'll haste to quaff my wine again.

For death may come with brow unpleasant—
May come when least we wish him present,
And beckon to the sable shore,
And grimly bid us—drink no more!"

This profane song was sung in a voice so clear and melodious, that Tithonus exclaimed, "You err, O Plato, in saying the tuneful soul of Marsyas has passed into the nightingale; for surely it remains with this young Athenian. Son of Clinias, you must be well skilled in playing upon the flute the divine airs of Mysian Olympus?"

"Not I, so help me Dionysus!" lisped Alcibiades. "My music master will tell you that I ever went to my pipes reluctantly. I make ten sacrifices to equestrian Poseidon, where I offer one gift to the Parnassian chorus."

"Stranger, thou hast not yet learned the fashions of Athens," said Anaxagoras, gravely. "Our young equestrians now busy themselves with carved chariots, and Persian mantles of the newest mode. They vie with each other in costly wines; train doves to shower luxuriant perfumes from their wings; and upon the issue of a contest between fighting quails, they stake sums large enough to endow a princess. To play upon the silver-voiced flute is Theban-like and vulgar. They leave that to their slaves."

"And why not leave laughter to the slaves?" asked Hermippus; "since anything more than a graceful smile distorts the beauty of the features? I suppose bright eyes would weep in Athens, should the cheeks of Alcibiades be seen puffed out with vulgar wind-instruments."

"And can you expect the youth of Athens to be wiser than their gods?" rejoined Aspasia. "Pallas threw away her favourite flute, because Hera and Aphrodite laughed at her distorted countenance while she played upon it. It was but a womanly trick in the virgin daughter of Zeus."

Tithonus looked at the speaker with a slight expression of surprise; which Hermippus perceiving, he thus addressed him, in a cool, ironical tone: "O Ethiopian stranger, it is evident you know little of Athens; or you would have perceived that a belief in the gods is more vulgar than flute-playing. Such trash is deemed fit for the imbecility of the aged, and the ignorance of the populace. With equestrians and philosophers, it is out of date. You must seek for it among those who sell fish at the gates; or with the sailors at Piræus and Phalerum."

"I have visited the Temple of Poseidon, in the Piræus," observed Aspasia; "and I saw there a multitude of offerings from those who had escaped shipwreck." She paused slightly, and added, with a significant smile, "But I perceived no paintings of those who had been wrecked, notwithstanding their supplications to the god."

As she spoke, she observed that Pericles withdrew a rose from the garland wherewith his cup was crowned; and though the action was so slight as to pass unobserved by others, she instantly understood the caution he intended to convey by that emblem sacred to the god of silence.

At a signal from Plato, slaves filled the goblets with wine, and he rose to propose the usual libation to the gods. Every Grecian guest joined in the ceremony, singing in a recitative tone:

Dionysus, this to thee,
God of warm festivity!
Giver of the fruitful vine,
To thee we pour the rosy wine!

Music, from the adjoining room, struck in with the chorus, and continued for some moments after it had ceased.

For a short time, the conversation was confined to the courtesies of the table, as the guests partook of the delicious viands before them. Plato ate olives and bread only; and the water he drank was scarcely tinged with Lesbian wine. Alcibiades rallied him upon this abstemiousness; and Pericles reminded him that even his great pattern, Socrates, gave Dionysus his dues, while he worshiped the heaven-born Pallas.

The philosopher quietly replied, "I can worship the fiery God of Vintage only when married with Nymphs of the Fountain."

"But tell me, O Anaxagoras and Plato," exclaimed Tithonus, "if, as Hermippus hath said, the Grecian philosophers discard the theology of the poets? Do ye not believe in the Gods?"

Plato would have smiled, had he not reverenced the simplicity that expected a frank and honest answer to a question so dangerous. Anaxagoras briefly replied, that the mind which did not believe in divine beings, must be cold and dark indeed.

"Even so," replied Artiphernes, devoutly; "blessed be Oromasdes, who sends Mithras to warm and enlighten the world! But what surprises me most is, that you Grecians import new divinities from other countries, as freely as slaves, or papyrus, or marble. The sculptor of the gods will scarcely be able to fashion half their images."

"If the custom continues," rejoined Phidias, "it will indeed require a life-time as long as that conferred upon the namesake of Tithonus."

"Thanks to the munificence of artists, every deity has a representative in my dwelling," observed Aspasia.

"I have heard strangers express their surprise that the Athenians have never erected a statue to the principle of *Modesty*" said Hermippus.

"So much the more need that we enshrine her image in our own hearts," rejoined Plato.

The sarcastic comedian made no reply to this quiet rebuke. Looking toward Artaphernes, he continued: "Tell me, O servant of the great king, wherein the people of your country are more wise in worshipping the sun, than we who represent the same divinity in marble!"

"The principles of the Persian religion are simple, steady, and uniform," replied Artaphernes; "but the Athenian are always changing. You not only adopt foreign gods, but sometimes create new ones, and admit them into your theology by solemn act of the great council. These circumstances have led me to suppose that you worship them as mere forms. The Persian Magii do indeed prostrate themselves before the rising Sun; but they do it in the name of Oromasdes, the universal Principle of Good, of whom that great luminary is the visible symbol. In our solemn processions, the chariot sacred to Oromasdes precedes the horse dedicated to Mithras; and there is deep meaning in the arrangement. The Sun and Zodiac, the Balance and the Rule, are but emblems of truths, mysterious and eternal. As the garlands we throw on the sacred fire feed the flame, rather than extinguish it, so the sublime symbols of our religion are intended to preserve, not to conceal, the truths within them."

"Though you disclaim all images of divinity," rejoined Aspasia, "yet we hear of your Mithras pictured like a Persian King, trampling on a prostrate ox."

With a smile, Artaphernes replied, "I see, lady, that you would fain gain admittance to the Mithraic cave; but its secrets, like those of your own Eleusis, are concealed from all save the initiated."

"They tell us," said Aspasia, "that those who are admitted to the Eleusinian mysteries die in peace, and go directly to the Elysian fields; while the uninitiated wander about in the infernal abyss."

"Of course," said Anaxagoras, "Alcibiades will go directly to Elysium, though Solon groped his way in darkness."

The old philosopher uttered this with imperturbable gravity, as if unconscious of satirical meaning; but some of the guests could scarcely repress a smile, as they recollected the dissolute life of the young Athenian.

"If Alcibiades spoke his real sentiments," said Aspasia, "I venture to say he would tell us that the mystic baskets of Demeter, covered with long purple veils, contain nothing half so much worth seeing, as the beautiful maidens who carry them."

She looked at Pericles, and saw that he again cautioned her, by raising the rose toward his face, as if inhaling its fragrance.

There was a brief pause, which Anaxagoras interrupted, by saying, "The wise can never reverence images merely as images. There is a mystical meaning in the Athenian manner of supplicating the gods with garlands on their heads, and bearing in their hands boughs of olive twined with wool. Pallas, at whose birth we are told gold rained upon the earth, was unquestionably a personification of wisdom. It is not to be supposed that the philosophers of our country consider the sun itself as anything more than a huge ball of fire; but the sight of that glorious orb leads the contemplative soul to the belief in one Pure Intelligence, one Universal Mind, which in manifesting itself produces order in the material world, and preserves the unconfused distinction of infinite varieties."

"Such, no doubt, is the tendency of all reflecting minds," said Phidias; "but in general, the mere forms are worshipped, apart from the sacred truths they represent. The gods we have introduced from Egypt are regarded by the priests of that learned land as emblems of certain divine truths brought down from ancient times. They are like the Hermae at our doors, which outwardly appear to rest on inexpressive blocks of stone; but when opened, they are found to contain beautiful statues of the gods within them. It is not so with the new fables which the Greeks are continually mixing with their mythology. Pygmalion, as we all know, first departed from the rigid outline of ancient sculpture, and impressed life and motion upon marble. The poets, in praise of him, have told us that his ardent wishes warmed a statue into a lovely and breathing woman. The fable is fanciful and pleasing in itself; but will it not hereafter be believed as reality? Might not the same history be told of much that is believed? It is true," added he, smiling, "that I might be excused for favouring a belief in images, since mortals are ever willing to have their own works adored."

"What! does Plato respond to the inquiries of Phidias?" asked Artaphernes.

The philosopher replied: "Within the holy mysteries of our religion is preserved a pure and deep meaning, as the waters of Arethusa flow uncontaminated beneath the earth and the sea. I do not presume to decide whether all that is believed has the inward significancy. I have ever deemed such speculations unwise. If the chaste daughter of Latona always appears to my thoughts veiled in heavenly purity, it is comparatively unimportant whether I can prove that Acteon was torn by his dogs, for looking on the goddess with wanton eyes. Anaxagoras, said wisely that material forms lead the contemplative mind to the worship of ideal good, which is in its nature immortal and divine. Homer tells us that the golden chain resting upon Olympus reaches even to the earth. Here we see but a few of the last links, and those imperfectly. We are like men in a subterranean cave, so chained that they can look only forward to the entrance. Far above and behind us is a glowing fire: and beautiful beings, of every form, are moving between the light and us poor fettered mortals. Some of these bright beings are speaking, and others are silent. We see only the shadows cast on the opposite wall of the cavern, by the reflection of the fire above; and if we hear the echo of voices, we suppose it belongs to those passing shadows. The soul, in its present condition, is an exile from the orb of light; its ignorance is forgetfulness; and whatever we can perceive of truth, or imagine of beauty, is but a reminiscence of our former more glorious state of being. He who reverences the gods, and subdues his own passions, returns at last to the blest condition from which he fell. But to talk, or think, about these things with proud impatience, or polluted morals, is like pouring pure water into a miry trench; he who does it disturbs the mud, and thus causes the clear water to become defiled. When Odysseus removed his armour from the walls, and carried it to an inner apartment, invisible Pallas moved before him with her golden lamp, and filled the place with radiance divine. Telemachus, seeing the light, exclaimed, 'Surely, my father, some of the celestial gods are present.' With deep wisdom, the king of Ithaca replied, 'Be silent. Restrain your intellect, and speak not.'"

"I am rebuked, O Plato," answered Phidias; "and from henceforth, when my mind is dark and doubtful, I will remember that transparent drops may fall into a turbid well. Nor will I forget that sometimes, when I have worked on my statues by torch-light, I could not perceive their real expression, because I was carving in the shadow of my own hand."

"Little can be learned of the human soul, and its connection with the Universal Mind," said Anaxagoras: "These sublime truths seem vague and remote, as Phoeacia appeared to Odysseus like a vast shield floating on the surface of the distant ocean.

"The glimmering uncertainty attending all such speculations, has led me to attach myself to the Ionic sect, who devote themselves entirely to the study of outward nature."

"And this is useful," rejoined Plato: "The man who is to be led from a cave will more easily see what the heavens contain by looking to the light of the moon and the stars, than by gazing on the sun at noon-day."

Here Hermippus interrupted the discourse, by saying, "The son of Clinias does not inform us what *he* thinks of the gods. While others have talked, he has eaten."

"I am a citizen and a soldier—neither priest nor philosopher," replied Alcibiades: "With a strong arm and a willing heart to fight for my country, I leave others to settle the attributes of her gods. Enough for me, that I regularly offer sacrifices in their temples, and pour libations upon their altars. I care very little whether there be Elysian fields, or not. I will make an Elysium for myself, as long as Aspasia permits me to be surrounded by forms so beautiful, and gives me nectar like this to drink." He replaced the goblet, from which he had drunk deeply, and exclaimed, "By Dionysus! they quaff nothing better than this in voluptuous Ionia!"

"Methinks a citizen and a soldier might find a more worthy model in Spartan, than in Ionian manners," said Anaxagoras; "but the latter truly suits better with the present condition of Athens."

"A condition more glorious than that of any other people upon earth," exclaimed Pericles, somewhat warmly: "The story of Athens, enthroned in her beauty and power, will thrill through generous hearts, long after other nations are forgotten."

"She is like a torch sending forth its last bright blaze, before it is extinguished forever," replied Anaxagoras, calmly: "Where idle demagogues control the revenues of industrious citizens, the government cannot long stand. It is a pyramid with the base uppermost."

"You certainly would not blame the wisdom of Aristides, in allowing the poor as well as the rich, the privilege of voting?" said Pericles.

"A moderate supply of wealth is usually the result of virtuous and industrious habits; and it should be respected merely for what it indicates," rejoined Anaxagoras. "Aristides, and other wise men, in their efforts to satisfy the requirements of a restless people, have opened a sluice, without calculating how it would be enlarged by the rushing waters, until the very walls of the city are undermined by its power."

"But can the safety of the state be secured by merely excluding the vicious poor?" said Plato. "Are there not among us vicious rich men, who would rashly vote for measures destructive of public good, if they could thereby increase their own wealth? He who exports figs to maintain personal splendour, when there is famine in Attica, has perhaps less public virtue than the beggar, who steals them to avoid starvation."

"But the vicious rich man will bribe the beggar to vote as he dictates," replied Anaxagoras; "and thus his power of doing evil becomes two fold."

"Your respect for permanent institutions makes you blind to the love of change, inherent and active in the human mind," said Pericles. "If society be like the heaving ocean, those who would guide their vessels in safety, must obey the winds and the tides."

"Nay, Pericles," replied the old man, earnestly; "if society be a tumultuous ocean, government should be its everlasting shores. If the statesman watches wind and tide only that his own bark may ride through the storm in safety, while every fresh wave sweeps a landmark away, it is evident that, sooner or later, the deluge must come."

The discourse was growing too serious to be agreeable to Pericles, who well knew that some of his best friends deemed he had injured the state, by availing himself too freely of the democratic tendencies of the people. Plato, perceiving this, said, "If it please you, Anaxagoras, we will leave these subjects to be discussed in the Prytaneum and the Agoras. Fair and glorious is the violet-crowned city, and let us trust the gods will long preserve it so."

"Thou hast well spoken, son of Aristo," replied Artaphernes: "Much as I had heard of the glory and beauty of Athens, it far surpasses my hopes. Perhaps I find myself lingering to gaze on the Odeum more frequently than on any other of your magnificent edifices; not for its more impressive beauty; but because it is in imitation of our Great King's Pavilion."

Hermippus looked up, and smiled with ill-natured significance; for Cratinus, the ribald, had openly declared in the theatre, that Pericles needed only to look in his mirror, to discover a model for the sloping roof of the Odeum. Athenian guests were indignant at being thus reminded of the gross allusion to a deformity conspicuous in the head of their illustrious statesman; but Artaphernes, quite unconscious of his meaning, continued: "The noble structure is worthy of him who planned it. Yet the unpretending beauty of some of your small temples makes me feel more as if I were in the presence of a god. I have often marvelled what it is in those fair white columns, that charms me so much more than the palaces of the East, refulgent with gems and gold."

"The beauty that lies *within* has ever a mysterious power," answered Plato. "An amethyst may beam in the eye of a statue; but what, save the soul itself, can give the expression of soul? The very spirit of harmony is embodied in the proportions of the Parthenon. It is marble music. I sometimes think the whole visible beauty of creation is formed from the music of the Infinite; and that the various joys we feel are but the union of accordant notes in the great chorus of the universe. There is music in the airy dance; music in poetry; music in the glance of a beautiful woman; music in the involutions and inflexions of numbers; above all, there is music in light! And what *Light* is in this world, *Truth* is in that glorious world to which the mind of man returns after its long exile. Yes, there is music in light! Hence, Phoebus is god of the Sun and of the Lyre, and Memnon yields sweet sounds to welcome approaching day. For this reason, the disciples of Zoroaster and Pythagoras hail the rising sun with the melody of harps; and the birds pour forth their love of light in song. Perchance the order of the universe is revealed in the story of Thebes rising to the lyre of Amphion; and Ibycus might have spoken sublime truth, when he told of music in the motion of the everlasting stars."

Philothea had listened so earnestly, that for a moment all other thoughts were expelled from her mind. She threw back her veil, and with her whole soul beaming from her face, she exclaimed, "O Plato, I once *heard* the music of the stars! Ibycus"——

The ardent gaze of Alcibiades restored her to painful consciousness; and, blushing deeply, she replaced her veil. Aspasia smiled; but Plato, with gentle reverence, asked, "What would Philothea say of the divine Ibycus?"

The timid maiden gave no reply; and the tears of innocent shame were seen falling fast upon her trembling arm.

With that ready skill, which ever knows how to adapt itself to the circumstances of the moment, Aspasia gave a signal to her attendants, and at once the mingled melody of voices and instruments burst upon the ear. It was one of the enchanting strains of Olympus the Mysian; and every heart yielded to its influence. A female slave noiselessly brought Aspasia's silver harp, and placed before her guests citharas and lyres, of ivory inlaid with gold. One by one, new voices and instruments joined in the song; and when the music ceased, there was a pause of deep and silent joy.

"Shame to the feast, where the praises of Harmodius are not sung," said Pericles, smiling, as he looked toward Eudora. With rapid fingers the maiden touched her lyre, and sung the patriotic song of Callistratus:

"I'll wreathe my sword with myrtle, as brave Harmodius did,
And as Aristogeiton his avenging weapon hid;
When they slew the haughty tyrant and regained our liberty,
And, breaking down oppression, made the men of Athens free.

"Thou art not, loved Harmodius, thou art not surely dead,
But to some secluded sanctuary far away art fled;
With the swift-footed Achilleus, unmolested there to rest,
And to rove with Diomedes through the islands of the blest.

"I'll wreathe my sword with myrtle, as Aristogeiton did,

And as the brave Harmodius his avenging weapon hid;
When on Athenæ's festival they aimed the glorious blow,
And calling on fair freedom, laid the proud Hipparchus low.

"Thy fame, beloved Harmodius, through ages still shall brighten,
Nor ever shall thy glory fade, beloved Aristogeiton;
Because your country's champions ye nobly dared to be,
And striking down the tyrant, made the men of Athens free."

The exhilarating notes stirred every Grecian heart. Some waved their garlands in triumph, while others joined in the music, and kept time with branches of myrtle.

"By Phoebus! a glorious song and divinely sung," exclaimed Alcibiades: "But the lovely minstrel brings danger to our hearts in those sweet sounds, as Harmodius concealed his sword among myrtle leaves."

Hipparete blushed, and with a quick and nervous motion touched her cithara. With a nod and a smile, Aspasia said, "Continue the music, I pray you." The tune being left to her own choice, the young matron sang Anacreon's Ode to the Grasshopper. Her voice was not unpleasing; but it contrasted disadvantageously with the rich intonations of Eudora; and if the truth must be told, that dark-haired damsel was quite too conscious of the fact.

Tithonus expressed an earnest desire to hear one of Pindar's odes; and Philothea, urged by Aspasia, began with a quivering hand to accompany herself on the harp. Her voice was at first weak and trembling; and Plato, to relieve her timidity, joined in the music, which soon gushed forth, clear, deep, and melodious:

"Hail, celestial Poesy!
Fair enchantress of mankind!
Veiled in whose sweet majesty
Fables please the human mind.
But, as year rolls after year,
These fictitious charms decline;
Then, O man, with holy fear,
Write and speak of things divine.
Of the heavenly natures say
Nought unseemly, or profane—
Hearts that worship and obey,
Are preserved from guilty stain."

Oppressed with the grandeur of the music, and willing to evade the tacit reproach conveyed in the words, Aspasia touched her lyre, and, with mournful tenderness, sung Danæ's Hymn to her Sleeping Infant. Then, suddenly changing to a gayer measure, she sang, with remarkable sweetness and flexibility of voice:

"While our rosy fillets shed
Blushes o'er each fervid head,
With many a cup, and many a smile,
The festal moments we beguile.
And while the harp impassioned flings
Tuneful rapture from the strings,
Some airy nymph, with fluent limbs,
Through the dance luxuriant swims,
Waving in her snowy hand,
The leafy Dionysian wand,
Which, as the tripping wanton flies,
Shakes its tresses to her sighs.

At these words, a troop of graceful maidens, representing the Zephyrs and the Hours, glided in and out, between the marble columns, pelting each other with roses, as they flew through the mazes of the dance.

Presently, the music, more slow and measured in its cadence, announced the dance of Ariadne guiding her lover from the Labyrinth. In obedience to a signal from Aspasia, Eudora sprang forward to hold the silken cord, and Alcibiades darted forward to perform the part of Theseus. Slowly, but gracefully as birds balancing themselves on the air, the maidens went through the difficult involutions of the dance. They smiled on each other, as they passed and repassed; and though Eudora's veil concealed the expression of her features, Philothea observed, with an undefined feeling of apprehension, that she showed no tokens of displeasure at the brief whispers and frequent glances of Alcibiades.

At last, Pericles bade the attendants bring forth the goblet of the Good Genius. A large golden bowl, around which a silver grape-vine twined its luxuriant clusters, was immediately placed before him, filled with the rich juices of the Chian grape. Then Plato, as king of the feast, exclaimed, "The cup of the Good Genius is filled. Pledge him in unmixed wine."

The massive goblet passed among all the guests; some taking a deep draught, and others scarcely moistening their lips with the wine. When the ceremony was finished, Pericles said, "Now, if it pleases Hermippus, we should like to see him in the comic dance, for which he is so celebrated."

Philothea looked earnestly at her grandfather. He instantly understood her wishes, and bade farewell to Aspasia; urging the plea that his child was unused to late hours, and too timid to be in the streets of Athens without his protection. Phidias requested that Eudora might accompany them; and Hipparete likewise asked leave to depart. Aspasia bestowed gifts on her visiters, according to the munificent custom of the country. To Hipparete she gave a bracelet of pearls; to Philothea, a lyre of ivory and gold; and to Eudora, a broad clasp for her mantle, on which the car of Aphrodite, drawn by swans, was painted in enamel, by Polygnotus, the inventor of the art.

Alcibiades chose to remain at his wine; but slaves with torches were in readiness at the gates, and Hipparete lived in the Ceramicus, within sight of Aspasia's dwelling.

A rapid walk soon restored the maidens to their own peaceful homes. Philothea, with the consent of Anaxagoras, went to share the apartment of her friend; which, separated only by a small garden, was almost within hearing of her own.

CHAPTER IV.

Much I dislike the beamless mind,
Whose earthly vision, unrefined,
Nature has never formed to see
The beauties of simplicity!
Simplicity, the flower of Heaven,
To souls elect by nature given."
               ANACREON.

As the maidens entered their apartment, Eudora rather abruptly dismissed Dione, the aged nurse, who had been waiting their arrival. Her favourite dog was sleeping on the couch; and she gave the little creature a hasty box on the ear, which made him spring suddenly to the floor, and look up in her face, as if astonished at such ungentle treatment.

Philothea stooped down and caressed the animal, with a slightly reproachful glance at her friend.

"He was sleeping on my mantle," said the petulant damsel.

"His soft, white fur could not have harmed it," rejoined her companion; "and you know that Hylax himself, as well as the mantle, was a gift from Philæmon."

Eudora carelesssly tossed the mantle over her embroidery frame, from which it trailed along the dusty floor. Philothea looked earnestly in her face, unable to comprehend such wayward conduct. "It is evident you do not want my company to-night," she said; "I will therefore return to my own apartment."

The peevish maiden slowly untied her sandal, without making any reply. Philothea's voice trembled slightly, as she added, "Good night, Eudora, To-morrow I hope you will tell me how I have offended you."

"Stay! Stay!" exclaimed the capricious damsel; and she laid her hand coaxingly on her friend's arm. Philothea smiled a ready forgiveness.

"I know I am very petulant to-night," said Eudora; "but I do not believe you yourself could listen to Hipparete without being vexed. She is so stupid, and so haughty. I don't think she spoke ten words to-night without having a grasshopper for one of them. She is so proud of her pure Athenian blood! Do you know she has resolved to employ a skilful artificer from Corinth, to make her an ivory box just like the one Tithonus gave Aspasia; but she took care to inform me that it should be inlaid with golden grasshoppers, instead of stars. A wise and witty device, is't not? to put grasshoppers in the paws of transformed Calisto, and fasten them in the belt of Orion. The sky will be so purely Athenian, that Hipparete herself might condescend to be a constellation."

The talkative maiden laughed at her own conceit; and even her more serious companion could not refrain from a smile, as with untiring volubility she continued: "Then she told me that she herself embroidered her grasshopper robe, and bade me admire the excellence of the pattern. She said Plato could not possibly have mistaken the wreath intended for her; knowing, as he did, that her father and mother were both descended from the most ancient families in Athens; and she repeated a list of ancestors with names all ending in *ippus* and *ippides*. When, in answer to her question, I acknowledged that the ornament in her hair was beautiful, she told me she would gladly give me one like it, if it were proper for me to wear it. I do so detest the sight of that Athenian emblem! I would walk to the fields of Acharnae, on purpose to crush a grasshopper."

"You put yourself in a singular passion for such a harmless insect," replied Philothea, smiling. "I hope there are none of them within hearing. You know the poets say they rose from the ashes of men, who, when the Muses first had existence, pined away for the love of song; and that after death they go to Parnassus, and inform the most ancient Calliope, the heavenly Urania, and the amorous Erato, concerning the conversation of their votaries. If they are truly the children of song, they will indeed forget their own resentments; but your conversation would be so unlikely to make a favourable impression on the tuneful sisters, that it may be well for you the insects are now sleeping."

"If the tattling tribe were all awake and listening," replied Eudora, "I would freely give them leave to report all I say against Astronomy, or Poetry, or Music. If this be the test, I am willing to be tried with Hipparete at the court of the Muses. If she were less stupid, I think I could tolerate her pride. But I thought she would never have done with a long story about a wine-stain that nearly spoiled her new dove-coloured robe; the finest from the looms of Ecbatana; the pattern not to be matched in all Greece; and Aspasia half wild to obtain one like it. She did not fail to inform me that the slave who had spilled the wine, was tied to the olive-tree in the garden, and whipped six days in succession. I never saw her in my life that she did not remind me of being a slave."

"Dearest Eudora," said Philothea, "how can you make yourself so unhappy on this subject? Has not Phidias, from the first hour he bought you, allowed you all the privileges of a daughter?"

"Yes," replied Eudora; "but the very circumstance that I was bought with his money embitters it all. I do not thank him that I have been taught all which becomes an Athenian maiden; for I can never be an Athenian. The spirit and the gifts of freedom ill assort with the condition of a slave. I wish he had left me to tend goats and bear burdens, as other slaves do; to be beaten as they are beaten; starved as they are starved; and die as they die. I should not then have known my degradation. I would have made friends with the birds and the flowers, and never had a heart-wound from a proud Athenian fool."

Philothea laid her hand gently on her friend's arm, and gazing on her excited countenance, she said, "Eudora, some evil demon vexes you strangely to-night. Did I not know the whole tenor of your blameless life, I should fear you were not at peace with your own conscience."

Eudora blushed deeply, and busily caressed the dog with her foot.

In a mild, clear voice, Philothea continued: "What *now* prevents you from making friendship with the birds and the flowers! And why do you cherish a pride so easily wounded? Yes, it is pride, Eudora. It is useless disguise to call it by another name. The haughtiness of others can never make us angry, if we ourselves are humble. Besides, it is very possible that you are unjust to Hipparete. She might very naturally have spoken of her slave's carelessness, without meaning to remind you of bondage."

"She *did* mean it," replied Eudora, with angry emphasis. "She is always describing her pompous sacrifices to Demeter; because she knows I am excluded from the temple. I hope I shall live to see her proud heart humbled."

"Nay, Eudora," said Philothea, turning mournfully away: "Your feelings are strangely embittered; the calm light of reason is totally obscured by the wild torch-dance of your passions. Methinks hatred itself need wish Hipparete no worse fate than to be the wife of so bold and bad a man as Alcibiades."

"Oh, Philothea! I wonder you can call him bold," rejoined Eudora. "He looks steadily at no one; his eyelashes ever rest on his face, like those of a modest maiden."

"Aye, Eudora—but it is not the expression of a sinless heart, timidly retiring within the shrine of its own purity; it is the shrinking of a conscience that has something to conceal. Little as we know about the evils of the world, we have heard enough of Alcibiades, to be aware that Hipparete has much need to seek the protection of her patron goddess."

"She had better worship in the temple of Helen, at Therapne," answered Eudora, sharply: "The journey might not prove altogether hopeless; for that temple is said to confer beauty on the ugliest woman that ever entered it." As the peevish damsel said this, she gave a proud glance at her own lovely person, in the mirror, before which a lamp was burning.

Philothea had often seen her friend in petulant moods; but she had never before known her to evince so much bitterness, or so long resist the soothing influence of kindness. Unwilling to contend with passions she could not subdue, and would not flatter, she remained for some moments in serious silence.

The expression of her countenance touched Eudora's quick feelings; and she said, in an humble tone, "I know I am doing wrong, Philothea, but I cannot help it."

Her friend calmly replied, "If you believe you cannot help it, you deceive yourself; and if you do not believe it, you had better not have said it."

"Now you are angry with me," exclaimed the sensitive maiden; and she burst into tears.

Philothea passed her arm affectionately round her waist, saying, "I am not angry with you, Eudora; but while I love you, I cannot and ought not to love the bad feelings you cherish. Believe me, my dear friend, the insults of others can never make us wretched, or resentful, if all is right within our own hearts. The viper that stings us is always nourished within us. Moreover, I believe, dearest Eudora, that half your wrongs are in your own imagination. I too am a foreigner; but I have been very happy within the walls of Athens."

"Because you have never been a slave," retorted her companion; "and you have shared privileges that strangers are seldom allowed to share. You have been one of the Canephoræ; you have walked in the grand procession of the

Panathenæa: and your statue in pure Pentelic marble, upholds the canopy over the sacred olive-tree. I know that your skilful fingers, and your surpassing beauty have deserved these honours; but you must pardon me, if I do not like the proud Athenians quite so well as you do."

"I gratefully acknowledge the part I have been allowed to take in the sacred service of Pallas," replied the maiden; "but I owe it neither to my beauty, nor my skill in embroidery. It was a tribute to that wise and good old man, my grandfather."

"And I," said Eudora, in a tone of deep melancholy, "have neither grandfather, parent, or brother to care for me."

"Who could have proved a better protector than Phidias has been?" inquired her gentle friend.

"Philothea, I cannot forget that I am his slave. What I said just now in anger, I repeat in sober sadness; it would be better for me to have a slave's mind with a slave's destiny."

"I have no doubt," replied Philothea, "that Phidias continues to be your master merely that he may retain lawful power to protect you, until you are the wife of Philæmon."

"Some slaves have been publicly registered as adopted children," said Eudora.

"But in order to do that," rejoined her friend, "it is necessary to swear to their parentage; and yours is unknown. If it were not for this circumstance, I believe Phidias would be most willing to adopt you."

"No, Philothea—Phidias would do no such thing. He is good and kind. I know that I have spoken of him as I ought not to have spoken. But he is a proud man. He would not adopt a nameless orphan, found with a poor goatherd of Phelle. Had I descended from any of the princes conquered by Grecian valour, or were I even remotely allied with any of the illustrious men that Athens has ostracised, then indeed I might be the adopted daughter of Phidias," After a short pause, she added, "If he enfranchised me without adoption, I think I should have no difficulty in finding a protector;" and again the maiden gave a triumphant glance at her mirror.

"I am aware that your marriage with Philæmon has only awaited the termination of these unfortunate law-suits," replied Philothea: "Though he is not rich, it cannot be very long before he is able to take you under his protection; and as soon as he has the power, he will have the disposition."

"Will he, indeed!" exclaimed Eudora; and she trotted her little foot impatiently.

"You are altogether mysterious to-night," said Philothea: "Has any disagreement arisen between you and Philæmon, during my absence?"

"He is proud, and jealous; and wishes me to be influenced by every whim of his," answered the offended beauty.

"The fetters of love are a flowery bondage," rejoined Philothea: "Blossoms do not more easily unfold themselves to the sunshine, than woman obeys the object of her affections. Don't you remember the little boy we found piping so sweetly, under the great plane-tree by the fountain of Callirhöe? When my grandfather asked him where he learned to play so well, he answered; with a look of wondering simplicity, that it 'piped itself.' Methinks this would be the reply of a loving woman, to one who inquired how her heart had learned submission. But what has Philæmon required, that you consider so unreasonable?"

"He dislikes to have me visit Aspasia; and was angry because I danced with Alcibiades."

"And did you tell him that you went to Aspasia's house, in conformity with the express directions of Phidias?" inquired Philothea.

"Why don't you say of my *master*?" interrupted Eudora, contemptuously.

Without noticing the peevishness of this remark, her friend continued: "Are you quite sure that you have not been more frequently than you would have been, if you had acted merely in reluctant obedience to the will of Phidias. I am not surprised that Philæmon is offended at your dancing with Alcibiades; assuredly a practice, so boldly at variance with the customs of the country, is somewhat unmaidenly."

"It is enough to be one man's slave," replied Eudora. "I will dance with whom I please. Alcibiades is the handsomest, and the most graceful, and the most agreeable man in Athens—at least every body says so. I don't know why I should offend him to please Philæmon."

"I thought there was a very satisfactory reason," observed Philothea, quietly: "Alcibiades is the husband of Hipparete, and you are the promised wife of Philæmon. I would not have believed the person who told me that Eudora seriously called Alcibiades the handsomest and most agreeable man in Athens."

"The sculptors think him pre-eminently beautiful," answered Eudora; "or they would not so often copy his statue in the sacred images of Hermes. Socrates applied Anacreon's eloquent praise of Bathyllus to him, and said he saw in his lips 'Persuasion sleeping upon roses.'"

"That must have been in the days of youthful innocence," replied Philothea: "Surely his countenance has now nothing divine in its expression; though I grant the colouring rich, and the features regular. He reminds me of the Alexandrian coin; outwardly pleasing to the eye but inwardly made of base metal. Urania alone confers the beauty-giving zone. The temple of Aphrodite in the Piræus is a fitting place for the portrait of Alcibiades; and no doubt he is well pleased that the people go there in throngs to see him represented leaning on the shoulder of the shameless Nemea."

"If Aristophon chose to paint him side by side with the beautiful Nemea, it is no fault of his," said Eudora.

"The artist would not have dared so to represent Plato, or Philæmon, or Paralus," rejoined Philothea; "nor would Alcibiades allow his picture thus to minister to the corruption of the Athenians, if he had any perception of what is really beautiful. I confess, Eudora, it pained me to see you listen to his idle flattery. He worships every handsome woman, who will allow herself to be polluted by his incense. Like Anacreon, his heart is a nest for wanton loves. He is never without a brood of them—some trying their wings, some in the egg, and some just breaking the shell."

With slight resentment in her manner, Eudora answered: "Anacreon is the most beautiful of poets; and I think you speak too harshly of the son of Clinias."

"I am sorry for you, if you can perceive the beautiful where the pure is wanting," rejoined Philothea; "You have changed, since my residence in the Acropolis. The cherub Innocence, that was once the ever-present deity in your soul, has already retired deeper within the shrine, and veils his face in presence of the vain thoughts you have introduced there. I fear Aspasia has made you believe that a passion for distinction is but another name for love of the good, the true, and the beautiful. Eudora, if this false man has flattered you, believe me, he is always ready to bestow the same upon others. He has told me that I was the loveliest of earthly objects; no doubt he has told you the same; but both cannot be true."

"You!" exclaimed her companion: "Where could he find opportunity to address such language to you?"

"Where a better man would have had better thoughts," replied Philothea: "It was during the sacred festival of the Panathenæa. A short time before midnight, it was my duty to receive the sacred basket from the hands of the priestess, and deposit it in the cave, beneath the Temple of Urania, in the gardens. Eucoline, the daughter of Agatho, attended me, carrying a lighted torch. Having entered the cave, I held the torch while she took up the other sacred basket, which was there in readiness to be conveyed to the Parthenon; and we again stepped forth into the gardens. A flood of light streamed from the Temple, so clear and strong, that I could distinctly see the sacred doves, among the multitude of fragrant roses—some sleeping in the shaded nooks, others fluttering from bush to bush, or wheeling round in giddy circles, frightened by the glare. Near a small lake in the centre of the gardens, stood Myron's statue of the heavenly Urania, guiding a dove to her temple by a garland of flowers. It had the pure and placid expression of the human soul, when it dwells in love and peace. In this holy atmosphere we paused for a moment in silent reverence. A smiling band of infant hours came clustering round my memory, and softly folded themselves about my heart. I thought of those early days, when, hand in hand with Paralus, I walked forth in the spring-time, welcoming the swallows to our shores, and gathering fragrant thyme to feed my bees. We did not then know that bees and young hearts need none to take thought for their joy, but best gather their own sweet nourishment in sunlight and freedom. I remembered the helpless kid that Paralus confided to my care. When we dressed the little creature in wreaths, we mourned that flowers would not *grow* in garlands; for it grieved our childish hearts to see them wither. Once we found, in the crevice of a moss-covered rock, a small nest with three eggs. Paralus took one of them in his hand; and when we had admired its beauty, he kissed it reverently, and returned it to its hiding-place. It was the natural outpouring of a heart brimful of love for all things pure and simple. Paralus ever lived in affectionate communion with the birds and the flowers. Firm in principle, but gentle in affection, he himself is like the rock, in whose bosom the loving bird found a sheltered nook, so motherly and safe, where she might brood over her young hopes in quiet joy."

The maiden's heart had unconsciously followed her own innocent recollections, like the dove led by a garland; and for a few moments she remained silent in thoughtful tenderness.

Eudora's changeful and perturbed spirit had been soothed by the serene influence of her friend; and she too was silent for awhile. But the giddy images that had of late been reeling their wild dance through her brain, soon came back in glittering fantasy.

"Philothea!" she exclaimed, abruptly, "you have not told me where you met Alcibiades?"

The maiden looked up suddenly, like an infant startled from sweet dreams by some rude noise. Recovering from her surprise, she smiled, and said, "Eudora, your question came upon me like his unexpected and unwelcome presence in the sacred gardens. I told you that we stood by that quiet lake in meek reverence; worshipping,—not the marble image before us,—but the Spirit of Beauty, that glides through the universe, breathing the invisible through visible forms, in such mysterious harmony. Suddenly Eucoline touched my arm with a quick and timid motion. I turned and saw a young man gazing earnestly upon us. Our veils, which had been thrown back while we looked at the statue, were instantly dropped, and we hastily retraced our steps. The stranger followed us, until we passed under the shade of the olive grove, within sight of the Propylæa. He then knelt, and attempting to hold me by the robe, poured forth the wildest protestations of love. I called aloud for protection; and my voice was heard by the priests, who were passing in and out of the Acropolis, in busy preparation for the festival. The young man suddenly disappeared; but he was one of the equestrians that shared in the solemnities of the night, and I again saw him as I took my place in the procession. I had then never seen Alcibiades; but when I met him to-night, I immediately recognized the stranger who spoke so rudely in the olive-grove."

"You must forgive me," said Eudora, "if I am not much disposed to blame mortal man for wishing to look upon your face a second time. Even Plato does homage to woman's beauty."

"True, Eudora; but there is reverence mingled with his homage. The very atmosphere around Alcibiades seemed unholy. I never before met such a glance; and the gods grant I may never meet such another. I should not have mentioned the occurrence, even to you, had I not wished to warn you how lightly this volatile Athenian can make love."

"I heard something of this before," rejoined Eudora; "but I did not know the particulars."

"How could you have heard of it?" inquired Philothea, with an accent of strong surprise.

"Alcibiades had a more eager curiosity than yourself," replied Eudora. "He soon ascertained the name of the lovely Canephoræ that he saw in the Gardens of Urania; and he has never ceased importuning Aspasia, until you were persuaded to visit her house."

The face, neck, and arms of the modest maiden were flushed with indignant crimson. "Was it for this purpose," she said, "that I was induced to yield my own sense of propriety to the solicitations of Pericles? It is ever thus, when we disobey the gods, to please mortals. How could I believe that any motive so harmless as idle curiosity induced that seductive and dangerous woman to urge me into her unhallowed presence?"

"I marvelled at your courage in talking to her as you did," said Eudora.

"Something within impelled me," replied Philothea, reverently;—"I did not speak from myself."

Eudora remained in serious silence for a moment; and then said, "Can you tell me, Philothea, what you meant by saying you once heard the stars sing? Or is that one of those things concerning which you do not love to have me inquire?"

The maiden replied: "As I sat at my grandfather's feet, near the statue of Phoebus in the portico, at early dawn, I heard music, of soft and various sounds, floating in the air; and I thought perchance it was the farewell hymn of the stars, or the harps of the Pleiades, mourning for their lost sister.—I had never spoken of it; but to-night I forgot the presence of all save Plato, when I heard him discourse so eloquently of music."

"And were you as unhappy as you expected to be during this visit?" inquired her friend.

"Some portions of the evening I enjoyed exceedingly," replied Philothea. "I could have listened to Plato and Tithonus, until I grew old in their presence. Their souls seem to move in glowing moonlight, as if surrounded by bright beings from a better world."

Eudora looked thoughtfully in her friend's face. "It is strange," she said, "how closely you associate all earthly objects with things divine. I have heard Anaxagoras say that when you were a little child, you chased the fleeting sunshine through the fields, and called it the glittering wings of Phoebus Apollo, as he flew over the verdant earth. And still, dearest Philothea, your heart speaks the same language. Wherever you look, you see the shining of god-like wings. Just so you talked of the moonlight, the other evening. To Hipparete, that solemn radiance would have suggested no thought except that lamp-light was more favourable to the complexion; and Hermippus would merely have rejoiced in it, because it saved him the expense of an attendant and a torch, as he reeled home from his midnight revels. I seldom think of sacred subjects, except when I am listening to you; but they then seem so bright, so golden, so divine, that I marvel they ever appear to me like cold, dim shadows."

"The flowers of the field are unlike, but each has a beauty of its own; and thus it is with human souls," replied Philothea.

For a brief space there was silence. But Eudora, true to the restless vivacity of her character, soon seized her lyre, and carelessly touching the strings, she hummed one of Sappho's ardent songs:

"More happy than the gods is he,
Who soft reclining sits by thee;
His ears thy pleasing talk beguiles,
His eyes thy sweetly dimpled smiles.
This, this, alas! alarmed my breast,
And robbed me of my golden rest."

Philothea interrupted her, by saying, "I should much rather hear something from the pure and tender-hearted Simonides."

But the giddy damsel, instead of heeding her request, abruptly exclaimed, "Did you observe the sandals of Artaphernes sparkle as he walked? How richly Tithonus was dressed! Was it not a magnificent costume?"

Philothea, smiling at her childish prattle, replied, "It was gorgeous, and well fancied; but I preferred Plato's simple robe, distinguished only by the fineness of its materials, and the tasteful adjustment of its folds."

"I never saw a philosopher that dressed so well as Plato," said Eudora.

"It is because he loves the beautiful, even in its minutest forms," rejoined Philothea; "in that respect he is unlike the great master he reverences so highly."

"Yes—men say it is a rare thing to meet either Socrates or his robe lately returned from the bath," observed Eudora; "yet, in those three beautiful statues, which Pericles has caused to be placed in the Propylæa, the philosopher has carved admirable drapery. He has clothed the Graces, though the Graces never clothed him. I wonder Aristophanes never thought of that jest. Notwithstanding his willingness to please the populace with the coarse wit current in the Agoras, I think it gratifies his equestrian pride to sneer at those who are too frugal to buy coloured robes, and fill the air with delicious perfumes as they pass. I know you seldom like the comic writers. What did you think of Hermippus?"

"His countenance and his voice troubled me, like the presence of evil," answered Philothea. "I rejoiced that my grandfather withdrew with us, as soon as the goblet of the Good Genius passed round, and before he began to dance the indecent cordax."

"He has a sarcastic, suspicious glance, that might sour the ripest grapes in Chios," rejoined Eudora. "The comic writers are over-jealous of Aspasia's preference to the tragic poets; and I suppose she permitted this visit to bribe his enmity; as ghosts are said to pacify Cerberus with a cake. But hark! I hear Geta unlocking the outer gate. Phidias has returned; and he likes to have no lamp burn later than his own. We must quickly prepare for rest; though I am as wakeful as the bird of Pallas."

She began to unclasp her girdle, as she spoke, and something dropped upon the floor.

Philothea was stooping to unlace her sandal, and she immediately picked it up.

It was a beautiful cameo of Alcibiades, with the quiver and bow of Eros.

Eudora took it with a deep blush, saying, "Aspasia gave it to me."

Her friend looked very earnestly in her face for a moment, and sighed as she turned away. It was the first time she had ever doubted Eudora's truth.

CHAPTER V.

"Two several gates
Transmit those airy phantoms. One of horn,
And of sawn ivory one. Such dreams as pass
The gate of ivory, prove empty sounds;
While others, through the polished horn effused,
Whose eye soe'er they visit, never fail."
                    HOMER.

The dwellings of Anaxagoras and Phidias were separated by a garden entirely sheltered from public observation. On three sides it was protected by the buildings, so as to form a hollow square; the remainder was screened by a high stone wall. This garden was adorned with statues and urns, among which bloomed many choice shrubs and flowers. The entire side of Anaxagoras' house was covered with a luxuriant grape-vine, which stretched itself out on the roof, as if enjoying the sunshine. The women's apartments communicated by a private avenue, which enabled the friends to see each other as conveniently as if they had formed one household.

The morning after the conversation we have mentioned, Philothea rose early, and returned to her own dwelling. As she passed through the avenue, she looked into the garden, and smiled to see, suspended by a small cord thrown over the wall, a garland, fastened with a delicately-carved arrow, bearing the inscription—"To Eudora, the most beautiful, most beloved."

Glad to assist in the work of reconciliation, she separated the wreath from the string, and carried it to her for whom it was intended. "Behold the offering of Philæmon!" she exclaimed, joyfully: "Dearest Eudora, beware how you estrange so true a heart."

The handsome maiden received her flowers with evident delight, not unmingled with confusion; for she suspected that they came from a greater flatterer than Philæmon.

Philothea returned to her usual avocations, with anxiety somewhat lessened by this trifling incident.

Living in almost complete seclusion, the simple-hearted maiden was quite unconscious that the new customs, introduced by Aspasia, had rendered industry and frugality mere vulgar virtues, But the restraint of public opinion was unnecessary to keep her within the privacy of domestic life; for it was her own chosen home. She loved to prepare her grandfather's frugal repast of bread and grapes, and wild honey; to take care of his garments; to copy his manuscripts; and to direct the operations of Milza, a little Arcadian peasant girl, who was her only attendant. These duties, performed with cheerful alacrity, gave a fresh charm to the music and embroidery with which she employed her leisure hours.

Anaxagoras was extremely attached to his lovely grandchild; and her great intellectual gifts, accompanied as they were by uncommon purity of character, had procured from him and his friends a degree of respect not usually bestowed upon women of that period. She was a most welcome auditor to the philosophers, poets, and artists, who were ever fond of gathering round the good old man; and when it was either necessary or proper to remain in her own apartment, there was the treasured wisdom of Thales, Pythagoras, Hesiod, Homer, Simonides, Ibycus, and Pindar. More than one of these precious volumes were transcribed entirely by her own hand.

In the midst of such communion, her spirit drank freely from the fountains of sublime knowledge; which, "like the purest waters of the earth, can be obtained only by digging deep,—but when they are found, they rise up to meet us."

The intense love of the beautiful, thus acquired, far from making the common occupations of life distasteful, threw over them a sort of poetic interest, as a richly painted window casts its own glowing colours on mere boards and stones. The higher regions of her mind were never obscured by the clouds of daily care; but thence descended perpetual sunshine, to gild the vapour.

On this day, however, Philothea's mind was less serene than usual. The unaccountable change in Eudora's character perplexed and troubled her. When she parted from her to go into the Acropolis, she had left her as innocent and contented as a little child; and so proud and satisfied in Philæmon's love, that she deemed herself the happiest of all happy beings: at the close of six short months, she found her transformed into a vain, restless, ambitious woman, wild for distinction, and impatient of restraint.

All this Philothea was disposed to pity and forgive; for she felt that frequent intercourse with Aspasia might have dazzled even a stronger mind, and changed a less susceptible heart. Her own diminished influence, she regarded as the inevitable result of her friend's present views and feelings; and she only regretted it because it lessened her power of doing good where she was most desirous to be useful.

Several times, in the course of the day, her heart yearned toward the favourite of her childhood; and she was strongly impelled to go to her and confess all her anxieties. But Eudora came not, as she had ever been wont to do, in the intervals of household occupation; and this obvious neglect drove Philothea's kind impulses back upon her heart.

Hylax, as he ran round the garden, barking and jumping at the birds in the air, instantly knew her voice, and came capering in, bounding up at her side, and licking her hand. The tears came to Philothea's eyes, as she stooped to caress the affectionate animal: "Poor Hylax," said she, "*you* have not changed." She gathered some flowers, and twined them round the dog's neck, thinking this simple artifice might bring a visit from her friend.

But the sun went down, and still she had not caught a glimpse of Eudora, even in the garden. Her affectionate anxiety was almost deepening into sadness, when Anaxagoras returned, accompanied by the Ethiopian boy.

"I bring an offering from the munificent Tithonus," said the philosopher: "He came with my disciples to-day, and we have had much discourse together. To-morrow he departs from Athens; and he bade me say that he hoped his farewell gift would not be unacceptable to her whose voice made even Pindar's strains more majestic and divine."

The boy uncovered an image he carried in his arms, and with low obeisance presented it to Philothea. It was a small statue of Urania, wrought in ivory and gold. The beautiful face was turned upward, as if regarding the heavens with quiet contemplation. A crown of golden planets encircled the head, and the scarf, enamelled with deep and vivid azure, likewise glowed with stars.

Philothea smiled, as she glanced round the apartment, and said, "It is a humble shrine for a Muse so heavenly."

"Honesty and innocence are fitter companions for the gods, than mere marble and gold," replied the philosopher.

As a small indication of respect and gratitude, the maiden sent Tithonus a roll of papyrus, on which she had neatly copied Pindar's Odes; and the boy, having received a few oboli for his trouble, returned charged with thanks and good wishes for his master.

Philothea, spontaneously yielding to the old habit of enjoying everything with her friend, took the statue in her arms, and went directly to her room. Eudora was kind and cheerful, but strangely fluttered. She praised the beautiful image in the excessive terms of one who feels little, and is therefore afraid of not saying enough. Her mind was evidently disturbed with thoughts quite foreign to the subject of her conversation; but, making an effort at self-possession, she said, "I too have had a present: Artaphernes sent it because my voice reminded him of one he loved in his youth." She unfolded a roll of perfumed papyrus, and displayed a Persian veil of gold and silver tissue. Philothea pronounced it fit for the toilette of a queen; but frankly confessed that it was too gorgeous to suit her taste.

At parting, she urged Eudora to share her apartment for the night. The maiden refused, under the pretext of illness; but when her friend offered to remain with her, she hastily replied that she should be much better alone.

As Philothea passed through the sheltered avenue, she saw Milza apparently assisting Geta in cleansing some marbles; and thinking Phidias would be pleased with the statue, she asked Geta to convey it to his room. He replied, "My master has gone to visit a friend at Salamis, and will not return until morning." The maiden was much surprised that her friend had made no allusion to this circumstance; but she forbore to return and ask an explanation.

Another subject attracted her attention and occupied some share of her thoughts. She had observed that Geta and Milza appeared much confused when she spoke to them. When she inquired what Geta had been saying, the pretty

Arcadian, with an averted face, replied, "He called me to see a marble dog, barking as if he had life in him; only he did not make any noise."

"Was that all Geta talked of?" said Philothea.

"He asked me if I liked white kids," answered the blushing peasant.

"And what did you tell him?" inquired the maiden.

With a bashful mixture of simplicity and archness, the young damsel answered, "I told him I liked white kids very much."

Philothea smiled, and asked no more questions. When she repeated this brief conversation to Anaxagoras, he heard it with affectionate interest in Milza's welfare, and promised to have a friendly talk with honest-hearted Geta.

The wakefulness and excitement of the preceding night had been quite at variance with the tranquil regularity of Philothea's habits; and the slight repose, which she usually enjoyed in the afternoon, had been disturbed by her grandfather, who came to say that Paralus was with him, and wished to see her a few moments, before they went out to the Piræus together. Being therefore unusually weary, both in body and mind, the maiden early retired to her couch; and with mingled thoughts of her lover and her friend, she soon fell into a profound sleep.

She dreamed of being with Paralus in an olive grove, over the deep verdure of which shining white blossoms were spread, like a silver veil. Her lover played upon his flute, while she leaned against a tree and listened. Soon, the air was filled with a multitude of doves, flocking from every side; and the flapping of their wings kept time to the music.

Then, suddenly, the scene changed to the garden of Phidias. The statues seemed to smile upon her, and the flowers looked up bright and cheerful, in an atmosphere more mild than the day, but warmer than the moon. Presently, one of the smiling statues became a living likeness of Eudora, and with delighted expression gazed earnestly on the ground. Philothea looked to see what excited her admiration—and lo! a large serpent, shining with green and gold, twisted itself among the flowers in manifold involutions; and wheresoever the beautiful viper glided, the blossoms became crisped and blackened, as if fire had passed over them. With a sudden spring the venomous creature coiled itself about Eudora's form, and its poisoned tongue seemed just ready to glance into her heart; yet still the maiden laughed merrily, heedless of her danger.

Philothea awoke with a thrill of anguish; but thankful to realize that it was all a dream, she murmured a brief prayer, turned upon her couch, and soon yielded to the influence of extreme drowsiness.

In her sleep, she seemed to be working at her embroidery; and Hylax came and tugged at her robe, until she followed him into the garden. There Eudora stood smiling, and the glittering serpent was again dancing before her.

Disturbed by the recurrence of this unpleasant dream, the maiden remained awake for a considerable time, listening to the voices of her grandfather and his guests, which still came up with a murmuring sound from the room below. Gradually her senses were lulled into slumber; and again the same dream recurred to distress and waken her.

Unable longer to resist the strength of her impressions, Philothea arose, and descending a few of the steps, which led to the lower part of the house, she looked into the garden, through one of the apertures that had been left in the wall for the admission of light. Behind a statue of Erato, she was sure that she saw coloured drapery floating in the moonlight. Moving on to the next aperture, she distinctly perceived Eudora standing by the statue; and instead of the graceful serpent, Alcibiades knelt before her. His attitude and gesture were impassioned; and though the expression of Eudora's countenance could not be seen, she was evidently giving him no ungracious audience.

Philothea put her hand to her heart, which throbbed violently with painful emotion. Her first thought was to end this interview at all hazards; but she was of a timid nature; and when she had folded her robe and veil about her, her courage failed. Again she looked through the aperture and saw that the arm of Alcibiades rested on the shoulder of her misguided friend.

Without taking time for a second thought, she sprang down the remaining steps, darted through the private avenue into the garden, and standing directly before the deluded girl, she exclaimed, in a tone of earnest expostulation, "Eudora!"

With a half-suppressed scream, the maiden disappeared. Alcibiades, with characteristic boldness, seized Philothea's robe, exclaiming, "What have we here? So help me Aphrodite! it is the lovely Canephora of the gardens! Now Eros forsake me if I lose this chance to look on her heavenly face again."

He attempted to raise the veil, which the terrified maiden grasped convulsively, as she tried to extricate herself from his hold.

At that instant, a stern voice sounded from the opposite wall; and Philothea, profiting by the sudden surprise into which Alcibiades was thrown, darted through the avenue, bolted the door, and in an instant after was within the sanctuary of her own chamber.

Here the tumult of mingled emotion subsided in a flood of tears. She mourned over the shameful infatuation of Eudora, and she acutely felt the degradation attached to her own accidental share in the scene. With these thoughts was mingled deep pity for the pure-minded and excellent Philæmon. She was sure that it was his voice she had heard from the wall; and she rightly conjectured that, after his prolonged interview with Anaxagoras, he had partly ascended the ladder leading to the house-top, and looked through the fluttering grape-leaves at the dwelling of his beloved.

The agitation of her mind prevented all thoughts of sleep. Again and again she looked out anxiously. All was hushed and motionless. The garden reposed in the moonbeams, like truths, which receive no warmth from the heart—seen only in the clear, cold light of reason. The plants were visible, but colourless; and the statues stood immovable in their silent, lifeless beauty.

CHAPTER VI.

Persuasive is the voice of Vice,
That spreads the insidious snare.
                ÆSCHYLUS.

Early the next morning, painful as the task was, Philothea went to Eudora's room; for she felt that if she ever hoped to save her, she must gain influence now.

The maiden had risen from her couch, and was leaning her head on her hand, in an attitude of deep thought. She raised her eyes as Philothea entered, and her face was instantly suffused with the crimson flush of shame. She made no reply to the usual salutations of the morning, but with evident agitation twisted and untwisted some shreds that had fallen from her embroidery.

For a moment her friend stood irresolute. She felt a strong impulse to put her arm around Eudora's neck and conjure her, even for her own sake, to be frank and confiding; but the scene in the garden returned to her memory, and she recoiled from her beloved companion, as from something polluted.

Still ignorant how far the deluded girl was involved, she felt that the manner in which she deported herself toward her, might perhaps fix her destiny for good or evil. With a kind, but trembling voice, she said, "Eudora, will you tell me whether the interview I witnessed last night was an appointed one?"

Eudora persevered in silence, but her agitation obviously increased.

Her friend looked earnestly in her excited countenance for a moment, and then said, "Eudora, I do entreat you to tell me the whole truth in this matter."

"I have not yet learned what right you have to inquire," replied the misguided maiden.

Philothea's eyes were filled with tears, as she said, "Does the love we have felt for each other from our earliest childhood, give me no claim to your confidence? Had we ever a cake, or a bunch of grapes, of which one did not reserve for the other the largest and best portion? I well remember the day when you broke the little marble kid Phidias had given you. You fairly sobbed yourself to sleep in my lap, while I smoothed back the silky curls all wet with your tears, and sung my childish songs to please you. You came to me with all your infant troubles—and in our maturer years, have we not shared all our thoughts? Oh, still trust to the affection that never deceived you. Believe me, dear Eudora, you would not wish to conceal your purposes and actions from your earliest and best friend, unless you had an inward consciousness of something wrong. Every human being has, like Socrates, an attendant spirit; and wise are they who obey its signals. If it does not always tell us what to do, it always cautions us what not to do. Have you not of late struggled against the warnings of this friendly spirit? Is it safe to contend with him, till his voice recedes, like music in the distance, and is heard no more?"

She looked earnestly in Eudora's face for a moment, and perceiving that her feelings were somewhat softened, she added, "I will not again ask whether the meeting of last night was an appointed one; for you surely would repel the suspicion, if you could do so with truth. It is too evident that this insinuating man has fascinated you, as he already has done hundreds of others; and for the sake of his transient flattery, you have thrown away Philæmon's pure and constant love. Yet the passing notice of Alcibiades is a distinction you will share with half the maidens of Athens. When another new face attracts his fancy, you will be forgotten; but you cannot so easily forget your own folly. The friends you cast from you can never be regained; tranquillity of mind will return no more; conscious innocence, which makes the human countenance a tablet for the gods to write upon, can never be restored. And for what will you lose all this? Think for a moment what is the destiny of those women, who, following the steps of Aspasia, seek happiness in the homage paid to triumphant beauty—youth wasted in restless excitement, and old age embittered by the consciousness of deserved contempt. For this, are you willing to relinquish the happiness that attends a quiet discharge of duty, and the cheerful intercourse of true affection?"

In a tone of offended pride, Eudora answered: "Philothea, if I were what you seem to believe me, your words would be appropriate; but I have never had any other thought than that of being the acknowledged wife of Alcibiades."

"Has he then made you believe that he would divorce Hipparete?"

"Yes—he has solemnly sworn it. Such a transaction would have nothing remarkable in it. Each revolving moon sees similar events occur in Athens. The wife of Pericles had a destiny like that of her namesake; of whom the poets write that she was beloved for awhile by Olympian Zeus, and afterward changed into a quail. Pericles promised Aspasia that he would divorce Asteria and marry her; and he has kept his word. Hipparete is not so very beautiful or gifted, as to make it improbable that Alcibiades might follow his example."

"It is a relief to my heart," said Philothea, "to find that you have been deluded with hopes, which, however deceitful, render you comparatively innocent. But believe me, Eudora, Alcibiades will never divorce Hipparete. If he should do so, the law would compel him to return her magnificent dowry. Her connections have wealth and influence; and her brother Callias has promised that she shall be his heir. The paternal fortune of Alcibiades has all been expended, except his estate near Erchia; and this he knows full well is quite insufficient to support his luxury and pride."

Eudora answered warmly, "If you knew Alcibiades, you would not suspect him of such sordid motives. He would throw money into the sea like dust, if it stood in the way of his affections."

"I am well aware of his pompous wastefulness, when he wishes to purchase popularity by lavish expenditure," replied Philothea. "But Alcibiades has found hearts a cheap commodity, and he will not buy with drachmæ, what he can so easily obtain by flattery. Your own heart, I believe, is not really touched. Your imagination is dazzled with his splendid chariots of ivory inlaid with silver; his unrivalled stud of Phasian horses; his harnesses of glittering brass; the golden armour which he loves to display at festivals; his richly-coloured garments, fresh from the looms of Sardis, and redolent with the perfumes of the East. You are proud of his notice, because you see that other maidens are flattered by it; because his statue stands among the Olympionicæ, in the sacred groves of Zeus, and because all Athens rings with the praises of his beauty, his gracefulness, his magnificence, and his generosity."

"I am not so weak as your words imply," rejoined Eudora. "I believe that I love Alcibiades better than I ever loved Philæmon; and if the consent of Phidias can be obtained, I cannot see why you should object to our marriage."

For a few moments, Philothea remained in hopeless silence; then, in a tone of tender expostulation, she continued: "Eudora, I would the power were given me to open your eyes before it is too late! If Hipparete be not beautiful, she certainly is not unpleasing; her connections have high rank and great wealth; she is virtuous and affectionate, and the mother of his children. If, with all these claims, she can be so lightly turned away for the sake of a lovelier face, what can you expect, when your beauty no longer has the charm of novelty? You, who have neither wealth nor powerful connections, to serve the purposes of that ambitious man? And think for yourself, Eudora, if Alcibiades means as he says, why does he seek stolen interviews at midnight, in the absence of Phidias?"

"It is because he knows that Phidias has an uncommon regard for Philæmon," replied Eudora; "but he thinks he can, in time, persuade him to consult our wishes. I know, better than you possibly can, what reasons I have to trust the strength of his affection. Aspasia says she has never seen him so deeply in love as he is now."

"It is as I feared," said Philothea; "the voice of that siren is luring you to destruction."

Eudora answered, in an angry tone, "I love Aspasia; and it offends me to hear her spoken of in this manner. If you are content to be a slave, like the other Grecian women, who bring water and grind corn for their masters, I have no objection. I have a spirit within me that demands a wider field of action, and I enjoy the freedom that reigns in Aspasia's house. Alcibiades says he does not blame women for not liking to be shut up within four walls all their life-time, ashamed to show their faces like other mortals."

Quietly, but sadly, Philothea replied: "Farewell, Eudora. May the powers that guide our destiny, preserve you from any real cause for shame. You are now living in Calypso's island; and divine beings alone can save you from the power of her enchantments."

Eudora made no response, and did not even raise her eyes, as her companion left the apartment.

As Philothea passed through the garden, she saw Milza standing in the shadow of the vines, feeding a kid with some flowers she held in her hand, while Geta was fastening a crimson cord about its neck. A glad influence passed from this innocent group into the maiden's heart, like the glance of a sunbeam over a dreary landscape.

"Is the kid yours, Milza?" she asked, with an affectionate smile.

The happy little peasant raised her eyes with an arch expression, but instantly lowered them again, covered with blushes. It was a look that told all the secrets of her young heart more eloquently than language.

Philothea had drank freely from those abundant fountains of joy in the human soul, which remain hidden till love reveals their existence, as secret springs are said to be discovered by a magic wand. With affectionate sympathy she placed her hand gently on Milza's head, and said, "Be good—and the gods will ever provide friends for you."

The humble lovers gazed after her with a blessing in their eyes; and in the consciousness of this, her meek spirit found a solace for the wounds Eudora had given.

CHAPTER VII.

O Zeus! why hast thou given us certain proof
To know adulterate gold, but stamped no mark,
Where it is needed most, on man's base metal?
                    EURIPIDES.

When Philothea returned to her grandfather's apartment, she found the good old man with an open tablet before him, and the remainder of a rich cluster of grapes lying on a shell by his side.

"I have wanted you, my child," said he, "Have you heard the news all Athens is talking of, that you sought your friend so early in the day? You are not wont to be so eager to carry tidings."

"I have not heard the rumours whereof you speak," replied Philothea. "What is it, my father?"

"Hipparete went from Aspasia's house to her brother Callias, instead of the dwelling of her husband," rejoined Anaxagoras: "by his advice she refused to return; and she yesterday appealed to the archons for a divorce from Alcibiades, on the plea of his notorious profligacy. Alcibiades, hearing of this, rushed into the assembly, with his usual boldness, seized his wife in his arms, carried her through the crowd, and locked her up in her own apartment. No man ventured to interfere with this lawful exercise of his authority. It is rumoured that Hipparete particularly accused him of promising marriage to Electra the Corinthian, and Eudora, of the household of Phidias."

For the first time in her life, Philothea turned away her face, to conceal its expression, while she inquired in a tremulous tone whether these facts had been told to Philæmon, the preceding evening.

"Some of the guests were speaking of it when he entered," replied Anaxagoras; "but no one alluded to it in his presence. Perhaps he had heard the rumour, for he seemed sad and disquieted, and joined little in the conversation."

Embarrassed by the questions which her grandfather was naturally disposed to ask, Philothea briefly confessed that a singular change had taken place in Eudora's character, and begged permission to silent on a subject so painful to her feelings. She felt strongly inclined to return immediately to her deluded friend; but the hopelessness induced by her recent conversation, combined with the necessity of superintending Milza in some of her household occupations, occasioned a few hours' delay.

As she attempted to cross the garden for that purpose, she saw Eudora enter hastily by the private gate, and pass to her own apartment. Philothea instantly followed her, and found that she had thrown herself on the couch, sobbing violently. She put her arms about her neck, and affectionately inquired the cause of her distress.

For a long time the poor girl resisted every soothing effort, and continued to weep bitterly. At last, in a voice stifled with sobs, she said, "I was indeed deceived; and you, Philothea, was my truest friend; as you have always been."

The tender-hearted maiden imprinted a kiss upon her hand, and asked whether it was Hipparete's appeal to the archons, that had so suddenly convinced her of the falsehood of Alcibiades.

"I have heard it all," replied Eudora, with a deep blush; "and I have heard my name coupled with epithets never to be repeated to your pure ears. I was so infatuated that, after you left me this morning, I sought the counsels of Aspasia, to strengthen me in the course I had determined to pursue. As I approached her apartment, the voice of Alcibiades met my ear. I stopped and listened. I heard him exult in his triumph over Hipparete; I heard my name joined with Electra, the wanton Corinthian. I heard him boast how easily our affections had been won; I heard—"

She paused for a few moments, with a look of intense shame, and the tears fell fast upon her robe.

In gentle tones Philothea said, "These are precious tears, Eudora. They will prove like spring-showers, bringing forth fragrant blossoms."

With sudden impulse, the contrite maiden threw her arms around her neck, saying, in a subdued voice, "You must not be so kind to me—it will break my heart."

By degrees the placid influence of her friend calmed her perturbed spirit. "Philothea," she said, "I promise with solemn earnestness to tell you every action of my life, and every thought of my soul; but never ask me to repeat all I heard at Aspasia's dwelling. The words went through my heart like poisoned arrows."

"Nay," replied Philothea, smiling; "they have healed, not poisoned."

Eudora sighed, as she added, "When I came away, in anger and in shame, I heard that false man singing in mockery:

"Count me on the summer trees
Every leaf that courts the breeze;
Count me on the foamy deep
Every wave that sinks to sleep;
Then when you have numbered these,
Billowy tides and leafy trees,
Count me all the flames I prove,
All the gentle nymphs I love."

Philothea, how could you, who are so pure yourself, see so much clearer than I did the treachery of that bad man?"

The maiden replied, "Mortals, without the aid of experience, would always be aware of the presence of evil, if they sought to put away the love of it in their own hearts, and in silent obedience listened to the voice of their guiding spirit. Flowers feel the approach of storms, and birds need none to teach them the enmity of serpents. This knowledge is given to them as perpetually as the sunshine; and they receive it fully, because their little lives are all obedience and love."

"Then, dearest Philothea, you may well know when evil approaches. By some mysterious power you have ever known my heart better than I myself have known it. I now perceive that you told me the truth when you said I was not blinded by love, but by foolish pride. If it were not so, my feelings could not so easily have turned to hatred. I have more than once tried to deceive you, but you will feel that I am not now speaking falsely. The interview you witnessed was the first and only one I ever granted to Alcibiades."

Philothea freely expressed her belief in this assertion, and her joy that the real character of the graceful hypocrite had so soon been made manifest. Her thoughts turned towards Philæmon; but certain recollections restrained the utterance of his name. They were both silent for a few moments; and Eudora's countenance was troubled. She looked up earnestly in her friend's face, but instantly turned away her eyes, and fixing them on the ground, said, in a low and timid voice, "Do you think Philæmon can ever love me again?"

Philothea felt painfully embarrassed; for when she recollected how deeply Philæmon was enamoured of purity in women, she dared not answer in the language of hope.

While she yet hesitated, Dione came to say that her master required the attendance of Eudora alone in his apartment.

Phidias had always exacted implicit obedience from his household, and Eudora's gratitude towards him had ever been mingled with fear. The consciousness of recent misconduct filled her with extreme dread. Her countenance became deadly pale, as she turned toward her friend, and said, "Oh, Philothea, go with me."

The firm-hearted maiden took her arm gently within her own, and whispered, "Speak the truth, and trust in the Divine Powers."

CHAPTER VIII.

Thus it is; I have made those
Averse to me whom nature formed my friends;
Those, who from me deserved no ill, to win
Thy grace, I gave just cause to be my foes;
And thou, most vile of men, thou hast betrayed me.
                    EURIPIDES.

Phidias was alone, with a large unfinished drawing before him, on a waxen tablet. Various groups of statues were about the room; among which was conspicuous the beautiful workmanship of Myron, representing a kneeling Paris offering the golden apple to Aphrodite; and by a mode of flattery common with Athenian artists, the graceful youth bore the features of Alcibiades. Near this group was Hera and Pallas, from the hand of Phidias; characterized by a severe majesty of expression, as they looked toward Paris and his voluptuous goddess in quiet scorn.

Stern displeasure was visible in the countenance of the great sculptor. As the maidens entered, with their faces covered, he looked up, and said coldly, "I bade that daughter of unknown parents come into my presence unattended."

Eudora keenly felt the reproach implied by the suppression of her name, which Phidias deemed she had dishonoured; and the tremulous motion of her veil betrayed her agitation.

Philothea spoke in a mild, but firm voice: "Son of Charmides, by the friendship of my father, I conjure you do not require me to forsake Eudora in this hour of great distress."

In a softened tone, Phidias replied: "The daughter of Alcimenes knows that for his sake, and for the sake of her own gentle nature, I can refuse her nothing."

"I give thee thanks," rejoined the maiden, "and relying on this assurance, I will venture to plead for this helpless orphan, whom the gods committed to thy charge. The counsels of Aspasia have led her into error; and is the son of Charmides blameless, for bringing one so young within the influence of that seductive woman?"

After a short pause, Phidias answered: "Philothea, it is true that my pride in her gift of sweet sounds first brought her into the presence of that bad and dangerous man; it was contrary to Philæmon's wishes, too; and in this I have erred. If that giddy damsel can tell me the meeting in the garden was not by her own consent, I will again restore her to my confidence. Eudora, can you with truth give me this assurance?"

Eudora made no reply; but she trembled so violently, that she would have sunk, had she not leaned on the arm of her friend.

Philothea, pitying her distress, said, "Son of Charmides, I do not believe Eudora can truly give the answer you wish to receive; but remember in her favour that she does not seek to excuse herself by falsehood. Alcibiades has had no other interview than that one, of which the divine Phoebus sent a messenger to warn me in my sleep. For that fault, the deluded maiden has already suffered a bitter portion of shame and grief."

After a short silence, Phidias spoke: "Eudora, when I called you hither, it was with the determination of sending you to the temple of Castor and Polydeuces, there to be offered for sale to your paramour, who has already tried, in a secret way, to purchase you, by the negociation of powerful friends; but Philothea has not pleaded for you in vain. I will not punish your fault so severely as Alcibiades ventured to hope. You shall remain under my protection. But from henceforth you must never leave your own apartment, without my express permission, which will not soon be granted. I dare not trust your sudden repentance; and shall therefore order a mastiff to be chained to your door. Dione will bring you bread and water only. If you fail in obedience, the fate I first intended will assuredly be yours, without time given for expostulation. Now go to the room that opens into the garden; and there remain, till I send Dione to conduct you to your own apartment."

Eudora was so completely humbled, that these harsh words aroused no feeling of offended pride. Her heart was too full for utterance; and her eyes so blinded with tears, that, as she turned to leave the apartment, she frequently stumbled over the scattered fragments of marble.

It was a day of severe trials for the poor maiden. They had remained but a short time waiting for Dione, when Philæmon entered, conducted by Phidias, who immediately left the apartment. Eudora instantly bowed her head upon the couch, and covered her face with her hands.

In a voice tremulous with emotion, the young man said, "Eudora, notwithstanding the bitter recollection of where I last saw you, I have earnestly wished to see you once more—to hear from your own lips whether the interview I witnessed in the garden was by your own appointment. Although many things in your late conduct have surprised and grieved me, I am slow to believe that you could have taken a step so unmaidenly; particularly at this time, when it has pleased the gods to load me with misfortunes. By the affection I once cherished, I entreat you to tell me whether that meeting was unexpected."

He waited in vain for any other answer than audible sobs. After a slight pause, he continued: "Eudora, I wait for a reply more positive than silence. Let me hear from your own lips the words that must decide my destiny. Perchance it is the last favour I shall ever ask."

The repentant maiden, without looking up, answered, in broken accents, "Philæmon, I will not add deceit to other wrongs, I must speak the truth, if my heart is broken. I did consent to that interview."

The young man bowed his head in silent anguish against one of the pillars— his breast heaved, and his lips quivered. After a hard struggle with himself, he said, "Farewell, Eudora. I shall never again intrude upon your presence. Many will flatter you; but none will love you as I have loved."

With a faint shriek, Eudora sprung forward, and threw herself at his feet. She would have clasped his knees, but he involuntarily recoiled from her touch, and gathered the folds of his robe about him.

Then the arrow entered deeply into her heart, She rested her burning forehead against the marble pillar, and said, in tones of agonized entreaty, "I never met him but once."

Philothea, who during this scene had wept like an infant, laid her hand beseechingly on his arm, and added, "Son of Chærilaüs, remember that was the only interview."

Philæmon shook his head mournfully, as he replied, "But I cannot forget that it was an appointed one.—We can never meet again."

He turned hastily to leave the room; but lingered on the threshold, and looked back upon Eudora with an expression of unutterable sadness.

Philothea perceived the countenance of her unhappy friend grow rigid beneath his gaze. She hastened to raise her from the ground whereon she knelt, and received her senseless in her arms.

CHAPTER IX.

Fare thee well, perfidious maid!
My soul,—its fondest hopes betrayed,
Betrayed, perfidious girl, by thee,—
Is now on wing for liberty.
I fly to seek a kindlier sphere,
Since thou hast ceased to love me here.
ANACREON.

Not long after the parting interview with Eudora, Philæmon, sad and solitary, slowly wended his way from Athens. As he passed along the banks of the Illyssus, he paused for a moment, and stood with folded arms, before the chaste and beautiful little temple of Agrotera, the huntress with the unerring bow.

The temple was shaded by lofty plane trees, and thickly intertwined willows, among which transparent rivulets glided in quiet beauty; while the marble nymphs, with which the grove was adorned, looked modestly down upon the sparkling waters, as if awe-stricken by the presence of their sylvan goddess.

A well-known voice said, "Enter Philæmon. It is a beautiful retreat. The soft verdant grass tempts to repose; a gentle breeze brings fragrance from the blossoms; and the grasshoppers are chirping with a summer-like and sonorous sound. Enter, my son."

"Thanks, Anaxagoras," replied Philæmon, as he moved forward to give and receive the cordial salutation of his friend: "I have scarcely travelled far enough to need repose; but the day is sultry, and this balmy air is indeed refreshing."

"Whither leads your path, my son?" inquired the good old man. "I perceive that no servant follows you with a seat whereon to rest, when you wish to enjoy the prospect, and your garments are girded about you, like one who travels afar."

"I seek Mount Hymettus, my father," replied Philæmon: "There I shall stop to-night, to take my last look of Athens. To-morrow, I join a company on their way to Persia; where they say Athenian learning is eagerly sought by the Great King and his nobles."

"And would you have left Athens without my blessing?" inquired Anaxagoras.

"In truth, my father, I wished to avoid the pain of parting," rejoined Philæmon. "Not even my beloved Paralus is aware that the homeless outcast of ungrateful Athens has left her walls forever."

The aged philosopher endeavoured to speak, but his voice was tremulous with emotion. After a short pause, he put his arm within Philæmon's, and said, "My son, we will journey together. I shall easily find my way back to Athens before the lamps of evening are lighted."

The young man spoke of the wearisome walk; and reminded him that Ibycus, the beloved of the gods, was murdered while returning to the city after twilight. But the philosopher replied, "My old limbs are used to fatigue, and everybody knows that the plain robe of Anaxagoras conceals no gold."

As they passed along through the smiling fields of Agra, the cheerfulness of the scene redoubled the despondency of the exile. Troops of laughing girls were returning from the vineyards with baskets full of grapes; women were grinding corn, singing merrily, as they toiled; groups of boys were throwing quoits, or seated on the grass eagerly playing at dice, and anon filling the air with their shouts; in one place was a rural procession in honour of Dionysus; in another, loads of pure Pentelic marble were on their way from the quarry, to increase the architectural glory of Athens.

"I could almost envy that senseless stone!" exclaimed Philæmon. "It goes where I have spent many a happy hour, and where I shall never enter more. It is destined for the Temple of the Muses, which Plato is causing to be built among the olive-groves of Academus. The model is more beautifully simple than anything I have ever seen."

"The grove of Academus is one of the few places now remaining where virtue is really taught and encouraged," rejoined Anaxagoras. "As for these new teachers, misnamed philosophers, they are rapidly hastening the decay of a state whose diseases produced them."

"A few days since, I heard one of the sophists talking to crowds of people in the old Agora," said Philæmon; "and truly his doctrines formed a strange contrast with the severe simplicity of virtue expressed in the countenances of Solon, Aristides, and the other god-like statues that stood around him. He told the populace that it was unquestionably a great blessing to commit an injury with impunity; but as there was more evil in suffering an injury than there was good in committing one, it was necessary to have the subject regulated by laws: that justice, correctly defined, meant nothing more than the interest of the strongest; that a just man always fared worse than the unjust, because he neglected to aggrandize himself by dishonest actions, and thus became unpopular among his acquaintances; while those who were less scrupulous, grew rich and were flattered. He said the weak very naturally considered justice as a common right; but he who had power, if he had likewise courage, would never submit to any such agreement: that they who praised virtue, did it because they had some object to gain from those who had less philosophy than themselves; and these pretended worthies, if they could act invisibly, would soon be found in the same path with the villain. He called rhetoric the noblest of the arts, because it enabled an ignorant man to appear to know as much as one who was thoroughly master of his subject. Some of the people demanded what he had to say of the gods, since he had spoken so ably of men. With an unpleasant mixture of derision and feigned humility, the sophist replied, that he left such vast subjects to be discussed by the immortal Socrates. He forthwith left the Agora, and many a loud laugh and profane jest followed his departure. When such doctrines can be uttered without exciting indignation, it is easy to foresee the destinies of the state."

"Thucydides speaks truly," rejoined Anaxagoras: "In the history he is writing, he says,—The Athenian people are beginning to be more fond of calling dishonest men able, than simple men honest; and that statesmen begin to be ashamed of the more worthy title, while they take pride in the other: thus sincerity, of which there is much in generous natures, will be laughed down; while wickedness and hypocrisy are everywhere triumphant."

"But evil grows weary of wearing a mask in reluctant homage to good," replied Philæmon; "she is ever seeking to push it aside, with the hope that men may become accustomed to her face, and find more beauty therein, than in the disguise she wears. The hidden thought at last struggles forth into expression, and cherished passions assume a form in action. One of the sophists has already given notice that he can teach any young man how to prove that right is wrong, or wrong is right. It is said that Xanthippus has sent his son to benefit by these instructions, with a request that he may learn the art thoroughly, but be taught to use it only in the right way."

"Your words are truth, my son," answered the philosopher; "and the blame should rest on those who taint the stream at its source, rather than with them who thoughtlessly drink of it in its wanderings. The great and the gifted of Athens, instead of yielding reverent obedience to the unchangeable principle of truth, have sought to make it the servant of their own purposes. Forgetful of its eternal nature, they strive to change it into arbitrary forms of their own creating; and then marvel because other minds present it in forms more gross and disgusting than their own. They do not ask what is just or unjust, true or untrue, but content themselves with recommending virtue, as far as it advances interest, or contributes to popularity; and when virtue ceases to be fashionable, the multitude can no longer find a satisfactory reason for adhering to it. But when the teachers of the populace hear their vulgar pupils boldly declare that vice is as good as virtue, provided a man can follow it with success, pride prevents them from seeing that this maxim is one of their own doctrines stripped of its equestrian robes, and shown in democratic plainness. They did not venture to deride the gods, or even to assert that they took no cognizance of human affairs; but they declared that offences against divine beings might be easily atoned for by a trifling portion of their own gifts—a sheep, a basket of fruit, or a few grains of salt, offered at stated seasons, with becoming decorum; and then when alone together, they smiled that such concessions were necessary to satisfy the superstitions of the vulgar. But disbelief in divine beings, and the eternal nature of truth, cannot long be concealed by pouring the usual libations, or maintaining a cautious reserve. The whispered opinions of false philosophers will soon be loudly echoed by the popular voice, which is less timid, because it is more honest. Even thus did Midas laboriously conceal the deformity of his head; but his barber, who saw him without disguise, whispered his secret in the earth, and when the winds arose, the voices of a thousand reeds proclaimed to the world, 'King Midas hath ass's ears.'"

"The secret has already been whispered to the ground," answered Philæmon, smiling: "If it were not so, the comic writers would not be able to give with impunity such grotesque and disgusting representations of the gods."

"And yet," rejoined the old man, "I hear that Hermippus, who has himself personified Hera on the stage, as an angry woman attempting to strike infuriated Zeus, is about to arraign me before the public tribunal, because I said the sun was merely a great ball of fire. This he construes into blasphemy against the life-giving Phoebus."

"The accusation may be thus worded," said Philæmon; "but your real crime is that you stay away from political assemblies, and are therefore suspected of being unfriendly to democratic institutions. Demos reluctantly admits that the right to hold such opinions is an inherent part of liberty. Soothe the vanity of the dicasts by humble acknowledgments, and gratify their avarice by a plentiful distribution of drachmæ; flatter the self-conceit of the Athenians, by assurances that they are the greatest, most glorious, and most consistent people upon earth; be careful that Cleon the tanner, and Thearion the baker, and Theophrastus the maker of lyres, are supplicated and praised in due form—and, take my word for it, the gods will be left to punish you for whatever offences you commit against them. They will receive no assistance from the violet-crowned city."

"And you, my son," replied the philosopher, "would never have been exiled from Athens, if you had debated in the porticos with young citizens, who love to exhibit their own skill in deciding whether the true cause of the Trojan war were Helen, or the ship that carried her away, or the man that built the ship, or the wood whereof it was made; if in your style you had imitated the swelling pomp of Isagoras, where one solitary idea is rolled over and over in an ocean of words, like a small pearl tossed about in the Ægean; if you had supped with Hyperbolus, or been seen in the agoras, walking arm in arm with Cleon. With such a man as you to head their party, Pericles could not always retain the ascendancy, by a more adroit use of their own weapons."

"As soon would I league myself with the Odomantians of Thrace!" exclaimed Philæmon, with an expression of strong disgust. "It is such men who destroy the innocence of a republic, and cause that sacred name to become a mockery among tyrants. The mean-souled wretches! Men who take from the poor daily interest for a drachma, and spend it in debauchery. Citizens who applauded Pericles because he gave them an obolus for a vote, and are now willing to see him superseded by any man that will give two oboli instead of one! No, my father—I could unite with none but an honest party—men who love the state and forget themselves; and such are not now found in Athens. The few that exist dare not form a barrier against the powerful current that would inevitably drive them to destruction."

"You speak truth, Philæmon," rejoined Anaxagoras: "Pallas Athenæ seems to have deserted her chosen people. The proud Spartans openly laugh at our approaching downfall, while the smooth Persians watch for a favourable moment to destroy the freedom already rendered so weak by its own insanity."

"The fault will be attributed to democratic principles," said Philæmon; "but the real difficulty exists in that love of power which hides itself beneath the mask of Democracy, until a corrupted public can endure its undisguised features without execration. No one can believe that Pericles lessened the power of the Areopagus from a sincere conviction that it was for the good of the people. It was done to obtain personal influence, by purchasing the favour of those who had sufficient reasons for desiring a less equitable tribunal. Nor could he have ever supposed that the interests of the republic would be advanced by men whom the gift of an obolus could induce to vote. The Athenians have been spoiled by ambitious demagogues, who now try to surfeit them with flattery, as nurses seek to pacify noisy children with sponges dipped in honey. They strive to drown the din of domestic discord in boasts of foreign conquests; and seek to hide corruption in a blaze of glory, as they concealed their frauds amid the flames of the treasury."

"Pericles no doubt owes his great popularity to skill in availing himself of existing circumstances," replied Anaxagoras; "and I am afraid that the same motives for corrupting, and the same willingness to be corrupted, will always be found in democratic institutions."

"It has always been matter of surprise to me," said Philæmon, "that one so humble and frugal as yourself, and so zealous for the equal rights of all men, even the meanest citizens, should yet be so little friendly to that popular idol which the Athenians call Demos."

The philosopher rejoined: "When I was young, I heard it said of Lycurgus, that being asked why he, who was such a friend to equality, did not bestow a democratic government upon Sparta, he answered: "Go and try a democracy in your own house." The reply pleased me; and a long residence in Athens has not yet taught me to believe that a man who is governed by ten thousand masters has more freedom than he who is governed by one."

"If kings had the same natural affection for their subjects that parents have for their children, the comparison of Lycurgus would be just," answered Philæmon.

"And what think you of the paternal kindness of this republican decree whereby five thousand citizens have been sold into slavery, because the unjust confiscation of their estates rendered them unable to pay their debts?" said Anaxagoras.

"Such an edict was passed because Athens is *not* a republic," replied Philæmon. "All things are under the control of Pericles; and Aspasia rules him. When she heard that I remonstrated against his shameful marriage, she said she would sooner or later bring a Trojan horse into my house. She has fulfilled her threat by the same means that enabled Pericles to destroy the political power of some of his most influential enemies."

"Pericles has indeed obtained unbounded influence," rejoined Anaxagoras; "but he did it by counterfeiting the very principle that needed to be checked; and this is so easily counterfeited, that democracy is always in danger of becoming tyranny in disguise. The Athenians are as servile to their popular idol, as the

Persians to their hereditary one; but the popular idol seeks to sustain his power by ministering to that love of change, which allows nothing to remain sacred and established. Hence, two opposite evils are combined in action—the reality of despotism with the form of democracy; the power of a tyrant with the irresponsibility of a multitude. But, in judging of Pericles, you, my son, should strive to guard against political enmity, as I do against personal affection. It cannot be denied that he has often made good use of his influence. When Cimon brought the remains of Theseus to Athens, and a temple was erected over them in obedience to the oracle, it was he who suggested to the people that a hero celebrated for relieving the oppressed could not be honoured more appropriately than by making his temple a refuge for abused slaves."

"Friendly as I am to a government truly republican," answered Philæmon, "it is indeed difficult to forgive the man who seduces a democracy to the commission of suicide, for his own advancement. His great abilities would receive my admiration, if they were not employed in the service of ambition. As for this new edict, it will prove a rebounding arrow, striking him who sent it. He will find ten enemies for one in the kindred of the banished."

"While we have been talking thus sadly," said the old philosopher, "the fragrant thyme and murmuring bees give cheerful notice that we are approaching Mount Hymettus. I see the worthy peasant, Tellus, from whom I have often received refreshment of bread and grapes; and if it please you we will share his bounty now."

The peasant respectfully returned their friendly greeting, and readily furnished clusters from his luxuriant vineyard. As the travellers seated themselves beneath the shelter of the vines, Tellus asked, "What news from Athens?"

"None of importance," replied Anaxagoras, "excepting rumours of approaching war, and this new edict, by which so many citizens are suddenly reduced to poverty."

"There are always those in Athens who are like the eel-catchers, that choose to have the waters troubled," observed the peasant. "When the lake is still, they lose their labour; but when the mud is well stirred, they take eels in plenty. My son says he gets twelve oboli for a conger-eel, in the Athenian markets; and that is a goodly price."

The travellers smiled, and contented themselves with praising his grapes, without further allusion to the politics of Athens. But Tellus resumed the discourse, by saying, "So, I hear my old neighbour, Philargus, has been tried for idleness."

"Even so," rejoined Anaxagoras; "and his condemnation has proved the best luck he ever had. The severe sentence of death was changed into a heavy fine; and Lysidas, the Spartan, immediately begged to be introduced to him, as the only gentleman he had seen or heard of in Athens. He has paid the fine for him, and invited him to Lacedæmon; that he may show his proud countrymen one Athenian who does not disgrace himself by industry."

"That comes of having the Helots among them," said Tellus. "My boy married a Spartan wife, and I can assure you she is a woman that looks lightning, and speaks mustard. When my son first told her to take the fish from his basket, she answered angrily, that she was no Helot."

"I heard this same Lysidas, the other day," said Philæmon, "boasting that the Spartans were the only real freemen; and Lacedæmon the only place where courage and virtue always found a sure reward. I asked him what reward the Helots had for bravery or virtue. 'They are not scourged; and that is sufficient reward for the base hounds,' was his contemptuous reply. He approves the law forbidding masters to bestow freedom on their slaves; and likes the custom which permits boys to whip them, merely to remind them of their bondage. He ridicules the idea that injustice will weaken the strength of Sparta, because the gods are enemies to injustice. He says the sun of liberty shines brighter with the dark atmosphere of slavery around it; as temperance seems more lovely to the Spartan youth, after they have seen the Helots made beastly drunk for their amusement. He seems to forget that the passions are the same in every human breast; and that it is never wise in any state to create natural enemies at her own doors. But the Lacedæmonians make it a rule never to speak of danger from their slaves. They remind me of the citizens of Amyclæ, who, having been called from their occupations by frequent rumours of war, passed a vote that no man should be allowed, under heavy penalties, to believe any report of intended invasion. When the enemy really came, no man dared to speak of their approach, and Amyclæ was easily conquered. Lysidas boasted of salutary cruelty; and in the same breath told me the Helots loved their masters."

"As the Spartan boys love Orthia, at whose altar they yearly receive a bloody whipping," said Tellus, laughing.

"There is one great mistake in Lacedæmonian institutions," observed Anaxagoras: "They seek to avoid the degrading love of money, by placing every citizen above the necessity of laborious occupation; but they forget that the love of tyranny may prove an evil still more dangerous to the state."

"You speak justly, my father," answered Philæmon: "The Athenian law, which condemns any man for speaking disrespectfully of his neighbour's trade, is most wise; and it augurs ill for Athens that some of her young equestrians begin to think it unbecoming to bring home provisions for their own dinner from the agoras."

"Alcibiades, for instance!" exclaimed the philosopher: "He would consider himself disgraced by any other burthen than his fighting quails, which he carries out to take the air."

Philæmon started up suddenly—for the name of Alcibiades stung him like a serpent. Immediately recovering his composure, he turned to recompense the hospitality of the honest peasant, and to bid him a friendly farewell.

But Tellus answered bluntly; "No, young Athenian; I like your sentiments, and will not touch your coin. The gods bless you."

The travellers having heartily returned his parting benediction, slowly ascended Mount Hymettus. When they paused to rest upon its summit, a glorious prospect lay stretched out before them. On the north, were Megara, Eleusis, and the cynosure of Marathon; in the south, numerous islands, like a flock of birds, reposed on the bright bosom of the Aegean; to the west, was the broad Piræus with its thousand ships, and Athens in all her magnificence of beauty; while the stately buildings of distant Corinth mingled with the cloudless sky. The declining sun threw his refulgent mantle over the lovely scene, and temples, towers, and villas glowed in the purple light.

The travellers stood for a few moments in perfect silence—Philæmon with folded arms, and Anaxagoras leaning on his staff. At length, in tones of deep emotion, the young man exclaimed, "Oh, Athens, how I have loved thee! Thy glorious existence has been a part of my own being! For thy prosperity how freely would I have poured out my blood! The gods bless thee, and save thee from thyself!"

"Who could look upon her and not bless her in his heart?" said the old philosopher: "There she stands, fair as the heaven-born Pallas, in all her virgin majesty! But alas for Athens, when every man boasts of his own freedom, and no man respects the freedom of his neighbour. Peaceful, she seems, in her glorious beauty; but the volcano is heaving within, and already begins to throw forth its showers of smoke and stones."

"Would that the gods had permitted me to share her dangers—to die and mingle with her beloved soil!" exclaimed Philæmon.

The venerable philosopher looked up, and saw intense wretchedness in the countenance of his youthful friend. He laid his hand kindly upon Philæmon's arm; "Nay, my son," said he; "You must not take this unjust decree so much to heart. Of Athens nothing can be so certainly predicted as change. Things as trifling as the turning of a shell may restore you to your rights. You can even now return, if you will submit to be a mere sojourner in Athens. After all, what vast privileges do you lose with your citizenship. You must indeed wrestle at Cynosarges, instead of the Lyceum or the Academia; but in this, the great Themistocles has given you honourable example. You will not be allowed to enter the theatre while the Athenians keep the second day of their festival Anthesteria; but to balance this privation, you are forbidden to vote, and are thus freed from all blame belonging to unjust and capricious laws."

"My father, playful words cannot cure the wound," replied the exile, seriously: "The cherished recollections of years cannot be so easily torn from the heart. Athens, with all her faults, is still my own, my beautiful, my beloved land. They might have killed me, if they would, if I had but died an Athenian citizen."

He spoke with a voice deeply agitated; but after a few moments of forced composure, he continued more cheerfully: "Let us speak of other subjects. We are standing here, on the self-same spot where Aristo and Perictione laid the infant Plato, while they sacrificed to the life-giving Phoebus. It was here the bees clustered about his infant mouth, and his mother hailed the omen of his future eloquence. Commend me to that admirable man, and tell him I shall vainly seek throughout the world to find another Plato.

"Commend me likewise to the Persian Artaphernes. To his bounty I am much indebted. Lest he should hope that I carry away feelings hostile to Athens, and favourable to her enemies, say to the kind old man, that Philæmon will never forget his country or his friends. I have left a long letter to Paralus, in which my full heart has but feebly expressed its long-cherished friendship. When you return, you will find a trifling token of remembrance for yourself and Philothea. May Pallas shower her richest blessings upon that pure and gifted maiden."

With some hesitation, Anaxagoras said, "You make no mention of Eudora; and I perceive that both you and Philothea are reserved when her name is mentioned. Do not believe every idle rumour, my son. The gayety of a light-hearted maiden is often unmixed with boldness, or crime. Do not cast her from you too lightly."

Philæmon averted his face for a moment, and struggled hard with his feelings. Then turning abruptly, he pressed the old man's hand, and said, "Bid Philothea, guide and cherish her deluded friend, for my sake. And now, farewell, Anaxagoras! Farewell, forever! my kind, my good old master. May the gods bless the wise counsels and virtuous example you have given me."

The venerable philosopher stretched forth his arms to embrace him. The young man threw himself upon that friendly bosom, and overcome by a variety of conflicting emotions, sobbed aloud.

As they parted, Anaxagoras again pressed Philæmon to his heart, and said, "May that God, whose numerous attributes the Grecians worship, forever bless thee, my dear son."

CHAPTER X.

Courage, Orestes! if the lots hit right,
If the black pebbles don't exceed the white,
You're safe.

EURIPIDES.

Pericles sought to please the populace by openly using his influence to diminish the power of the Areopagus; and a decree had been passed that those who denied the existence of the gods, or introduced new opinions about celestial things, should be tried by the people. This event proved fortunate for some of his personal friends; for Hermippus soon laid before the Thesmothetæ Archons an accusation of blasphemy against Anaxagoras, Phidias, and Aspasia. The case was tried before the fourth Assembly of the people; and the fame of the accused, together with the well-known friendship of Pericles, attracted an immense crowd; insomuch that the Prytaneum was crowded to overflowing. The prisoners came in, attended by the Phylarchi of their different wards. Anaxagoras retained his usual bland expression and meek dignity. Phidias walked with a haughtier tread, and carried his head more proudly. Aspasia was veiled; but as she glided along, gracefully as a swan on the bosom of still waters, loud murmurs of approbation were heard from the crowd. Pericles seated himself near them, with deep sadness on his brow. The moon had not completed its revolution since he had seen Phidias arraigned before the Second Assembly of the people, charged by Menon, one of his own pupils, with having defrauded the state of gold appropriated to the statue of Pallas. Fortunately, the sculptor had arranged the precious metal so that it could be taken off and weighed; and thus his innocence was easily made manifest. But the great statesman had seen, by many indications, that the blow was in part aimed at himself through his friends; and that his enemies were thus trying to ascertain how far the people could be induced to act in opposition to his well-known wishes. The cause had been hurried before the assembly, and he perceived that his opponents were there in great numbers. As soon as the Epistates began to read the accusation, Pericles leaned forward, and burying his face in his robe, remained motionless.

Anaxagoras was charged with not having offered victims to the gods; and with having blasphemed the divine Phoebus, by saying the sun was only a huge ball of fire. Being called upon to answer whether he were guilty of this offence, he replied: "Living victims I have never sacrificed to the gods; because, like the Pythagoreans, I object to the shedding of blood; but, like the disciples of their sublime philosopher, I have duly offered on their altars small goats and rams made of wax. I did say I believed the sun to be a great ball of fire; and deemed not that in so doing I had blasphemed the divine Phoebus."

When he had finished, it was proclaimed aloud that any Athenian, not disqualified by law, might speak. Cleon arose, and said it was well known to the disciples of Anaxagoras, that he taught the existence of but one God. Euripides, Pericles, and others who had been his pupils, were separately called to bear testimony; and all said he taught One Universal Mind, of which all other divinities were the attributes; even as Homer represented the inferior deities subordinate to Zeus.

When the philosopher was asked whether he believed in the gods, he answered, "I do: but I believe in them as the representatives of various attributes in One Universal Mind." He was then required to swear by all the gods, and by the dreaded Erinnys, that he had spoken truly.

The Prytanes informed the assembly that their vote must decide whether this avowed doctrine r endered Anaxagoras of Clazomenæ worthy of death. A brazen urn was carried round, in which every citizen deposited a pebble. When counted, the black pebbles predominated over the white, and Anaxagoras was condemned to die.

The old man heard it very calmly, and replied: "Nature pronounced that sentence upon me before I was born. Do what you will, Athenians, ye can only injure the outward case of Anaxagoras; the real, immortal Anaxagoras is beyond your power."

Phidias was next arraigned, and accused of blasphemy, in having carved the likeness of himself and Pericles on the shield of heaven-born Pallas; and of having said that he approved the worship of the gods, merely because he wished to have his own works adored. The sculptor proudly replied, "I never declared that my own likeness, or that of Pericles, was on the shield of heaven-born Pallas; nor can any Athenian prove that I ever intended to place them there. I am not answerable for offences which have their origin in the eyes of the multitude. If *their* quick discernment be the test, crimes may be found written even on the glowing embers of our household altars. I never said I approved the worship of the gods because I wished to have my own works adored; for I should have deemed it irreverent thus to speak of divine beings. Some learned and illustrious guests, who were at the symposium in Aspasia's house, discoursed concerning the worship of images, apart from the idea of any divine attributes, which they represented. I said I approved not of this; and playfully added, that if it were otherwise, I might perchance be excused for sanctioning the worship of mere images, since mortals were ever willing to have their own works adored." The testimony of Pericles, Alcibiades, and Plato, confirmed the truth of his words.

Cleon declared it was commonly believed that Phidias decoyed the maids and matrons of Athens to his house, under the pretence of seeing sculpture; but in reality to minister to the profligacy of Pericles. The sculptor denied the charge; and required that proof should be given of one Athenian woman, who had visited his house, unattended by her husband or her father. The enemies of Pericles could easily have procured such evidence with gold; but when Cleon sought again to speak, the Prytanes commanded silence; and briefly reminded the people that the Fourth Assembly had power to decide concerning religious matters only. Hermippus, in a speech of considerable length, urged that Phidias seldom sacrificed to the gods; and that he must have intended likenesses on the shield of Pallas, because even Athenian children recognized them.

The brazen urn was again passed round, and the black pebbles were more numerous than they had been when the fate of Anaxagoras was decided. When Phidias heard the sentence, he raised himself to his full stature, and waving his right arm over the crowd, said, in a loud voice: "Phidias can never die! Athens herself will live in the fame of Charmides' son." His majestic figure and haughty bearing awed the multitude; and some, repenting of the vote they had given, said, "Surely, invisible Phoebus is with him!"

Aspasia was next called to answer the charges brought against her. She had dressed herself, in deep mourning, as if appealing to the compassion of the citizens; and her veil was artfully arranged to display an arm and shoulder of exquisite whiteness and beauty, contrasted with glossy ringlets of dark hair, that carelessly rested on it. She was accused of saying that the sacred baskets of Demeter contained nothing of so much importance as the beautiful maidens who carried them; and that the temple of Poseidon was enriched with no offerings from those who had been wrecked, notwithstanding their supplications—thereby implying irreverent doubts of the power of Ocean's god. To this, Aspasia, in clear and musical tones, replied: "I said not that the sacred baskets of Demeter contained nothing of so much importance as the beautiful maidens who carried them. But, in playful allusion to the love of beauty, so conspicuous in Alcibiades, I said that *he*, who was initiated into the mysteries of Eleusis, might think, the baskets less attractive than the lovely maidens who carried them. Irreverence was not in my thoughts; but inasmuch as my careless words implied it, I have offered atoning sacrifices to the mother of Persephone, during which I abstained from all amusements. When I declared that the temple of Poseidon contained no offerings in commemoration of men that had been wrecked, I said it in reproof of those who fail to supplicate the gods for the manes of the departed. They who perish on the ocean, may have offended Poseidon, or the Virgin Sisters of the Deep; and on their altars should offerings be laid by surviving friends.

"No man can justly accuse me of disbelief in the gods; for it is well known that with every changing moon I offer on the altars of Aphrodite, doves and sparrows, with baskets of apples, roses and myrtles: and who in Athens has not seen the ivory car drawn by golden swans, which the grateful Aspasia placed in the temple of that love-inspiring deity?"

Phidias could scarcely restrain a smile, as he listened to this defence; and when the fair casuist swore by all the gods, and by the Erinnys, that she had spoken truly, Anaxagoras looked up involuntarily, with an expression of child-like astonishment. Alcibiades promptly corroborated her statement. Plato, being called to testify, gravely remarked that she had uttered those words, and she alone could explain her motives. The populace seemed impressed in her favour; and when it was put to vote whether sentence of death should be passed, an universal murmur arose, of "Exile! Exile!"

The Epistates requested that all who wished to consider it a question of exile, rather than of death, would signify the same by holding up their hands. With very few exceptions, the crowd were inclined to mercy. Hermippus gave tokens of displeasure, and hastily rose to accuse Aspasia of corrupting the youth of Athens, by the introduction of singing and dancing women, and by encouraging the matrons of Greece to appear unveiled.

A loud laugh followed his remarks; for the comic actor was himself far from aiding public morals by an immaculate example.

The Prytanes again reminded him that charges of this nature must be decided by the First Assembly of the people; and, whether true or untrue, ought to have no influence on religious questions brought before the Fourth Assembly.

Hermippus was perfectly aware of this; but he deemed that the vote might be affected by his artful suggestion.

The brazen urn was again carried round; and fifty-one pebbles only appeared in disapprobation of exile.

Then Pericles arose, and looked around him with calm dignity. He was seldom seen in public, even at entertainments; hence, something of sacredness was attached to his person, like the Salaminian galley reserved for great occasions. A murmur like the Distant ocean was heard, as men whispered to each other, "Lo, Pericles is about to speak!" When the tumult subsided, he said, in a loud voice, "If any here can accuse Pericles of having enriched himself at the expense of the state, let him hold up his right hand!"

Not a hand was raised—for his worst enemies could not deny that he was temperate and frugal.

After a slight pause, he again resumed: "If any man can show that Pericles ever asked a public favour for himself or his friends, let him speak!" No words were uttered; but a murmur of discontent was heard in the vicinity of Cleon and Hermippus.

The illustrious statesman folded his arms, and waited in quiet majesty for the murmur to assume a distinct form. When all was hushed, he continued: "If any man believes that Athens has declined in beauty, wealth, or power, since the administration of Pericles, let him give his opinion freely!"

National enthusiasm was kindled; and many voices exclaimed, "Hail Pericles! All hail to Athens in her glory!"

The statesman gracefully waved his hand toward the multitude, as he replied, "Thanks, friends and brother-citizens. Who among you is disposed to grant to Pericles one favour, not inconsistent with your laws, or in opposition to the decrees of this assembly?"

A thousand hands were instantly raised. Pericles again expressed his thanks, and said, "The favour I have to ask is, that the execution of these decrees be suspended, until the oracle of Amphiaraus can be consulted. If it please you, let a vote be taken who shall be the messenger."

The proposal was accepted; and Antiphon, a celebrated diviner, appointed to consult the oracle.

As the crowd dispersed, Cleon muttered to Hermippus, "By Circe! I believe he has given the Athenians philtres to make them love him. No wonder Archidamus of Sparta said, that when he threw Pericles in wrestling, he insisted he was never down, and persuaded the very spectators to believe him."

Anaxagoras and Phidias, being under sentence of death, were placed in prison, until the people should finally decide upon their fate. The old philosopher cheerfully employed his hours in attempts to square the circle. The sculptor carved a wooden image, with many hands and feet, and without a head; upon the pedestal of which he inscribed Demos, and secretly reserved it as a parting gift to the Athenian people.

Before another moon had waned, Antiphon returned from Oropus, whither he had been sent to consult the oracle. Being called before the people, he gave the following account of his mission: "I abstained from food until Phoebus had twice appeared above the hills, in his golden chariot; and for three days and three nights, I tasted no wine. When I had thus purified myself, I offered a white ram to Amphiaraus; and spreading the skin on the ground, I invoked the blessing of Phoebus and his prophetic son, and laid me down to sleep. Methought I walked in the streets of Athens. A lurid light shone on the walls of the Piræus, and spread into the city, until all the Acropolis seemed glowing beneath a fiery sky. I looked up—and lo! the heavens were in a blaze! Huge masses of flame were thrown backward and forward, as if Paridamator and the Cyclops were hurling their forges at each other's heads. Amazed, I turned to ask the meaning of these phenomena; and I saw that all the citizens were clothed in black; and wherever two were walking together, one fell dead by his side. Then I heard a mighty voice, that seemed to proceed from within the Parthenon. Three times it pronounced distinctly, 'Wo! wo! wo unto Athens!

"I awoke, and after a time slept again. I heard a rumbling noise, like thunder; and from the statue of Amphiaraus came a voice, saying, 'Life is given by the gods.'

"Then all was still. Presently I again heard a sound like the multitudinous waves of ocean, when it rises in a storm—and Amphiaraus said, slowly, 'Count the pebbles on the seashore—yea, count them twice.' Then I awoke; and having bathed in the fountain, I threw therein three pieces of gold and silver, and departed."

The people demanded of Antiphon the meaning of these visions. He replied: "The first portends calamity to Athens, either of war or pestilence. By the response of the oracle, I understand that the citizens are commanded to vote twice, before they take away life given by the gods."

The wish to gain time had chiefly induced Pericles to request that Amphiaraus might be consulted. In the interval, his emissaries had been busy in softening the minds of the people; and it became universally known that in case Aspasia's sentence were reversed, she intended to offer sacrifices to Aphrodite, Poseidon, and Demeter; during the continuance of which, the citizens would be publicly feasted at her expense.

In these exertions, Pericles was zealously assisted by Clinias, a noble and wealthy Athenian, the friend of Anaxagoras and Phidias, and a munificent patron of the arts. He openly promised, if the lives of his friends were spared, to evince his gratitude to the gods, by offering a golden lamp to Pallas Parthenia, and placing in each of the agoras any statue or painting the people thought fit to propose.

Still, Pericles, aware of the bitterness of his enemies, increased by the late severe edict against those of foreign parentage, felt exceedingly fearful of the result of a second vote. A petition, signed by Pericles, Clinias, Ephialtes, Euripides, Socrates, Plato, Alcibiades, Paralus, and many other distinguished citizens, was sent into the Second Assembly of the people, begging that the accused might have another trial; and this petition was granted.

When the Fourth Assembly again met, strong efforts were made to fill the Prytaneum at a very early hour with the friends of Pericles.

The great orator secluded himself for three preceding days, and refrained from wine. During this time, he poured plentiful libations of milk and honey to Hermes, god of Eloquence, and sacrificed the tongues of nightingales to Peitho, goddess of Persuasion.

When he entered the Prytaneum, it was remarked that he had never before been seen to look so pale; and this circumstance, trifling as it was, excited the ready sympathies of the people. When the Epistates read the accusation against Anaxagoras, and proclaimed that any Athenian, not disqualified by law, might speak, Pericles arose. For a moment he looked on the venerable countenance of the old philosopher, and seemed to struggle with his emotions. Then, with sudden impulse, he exclaimed, "Look on him, Athenians! and judge ye if he be one accursed of the gods!—He is charged with having said that the sun is a great ball of fire; and therein ye deem that the abstractions of philosophy have led him to profane the sacred name of Phoebus. We are told that Zeus assumed the form of an eagle, a serpent, and a golden shower; yet these forms do not affect our belief in the invisible god. If Phoebus appeared on earth in the disguise of a woman and a shepherd, is it unpardonable for a philosopher to suppose that the same deity may choose to reside within a ball of fire? In the garden of Anaxagoras, you will find a statue of Pallas, carved from an olive-tree. He brought it with him from Ionia; and those disciples who most frequent his house, can testify that sacrifices were ever duly offered upon her altar. Who among you ever received an injury from that kind old man? He was the descendant of princes,—yet gave up gold for philosophy, and forbore to govern mankind, that he might love them more perfectly. Ask the young noble, who has been to him as a father; and his response will be 'Anaxagoras.' Ask the poor fisherman at the gates, who has been to him as a brother; and he will answer 'Anaxagoras.' When the merry-hearted boys throng your doors to sing their welcome to Ornithæ, inquire from whom they receive the kindest word and the readiest gift; and they will tell you, 'Anaxagoras.' The Amphiaraus of Eschylus, says, 'I do not wish to *appear* to be a good man, but I wish to *be* one.' Ask any of the poets, what living man most resembles Amphiaraus in this sentiment; and his reply will surely be, 'It is Anaxagoras.'

"Again I say, Athenians, look upon his face; and judge ye if he be one accursed of the gods!"

The philosopher had leaned on his staff, and looked downward, while his illustrious pupil made this defence; and when he had concluded, a tear was seen slowly trickling down his aged cheek. His accusers again urged that he had taught the doctrine of one god, under the name of One Universal Mind; but the melodious voice and fluent tongue of Pericles had so wrought upon the citizens, that when the question was proposed, whether the old man were worthy of death, there arose a clamourous cry of "Exile! Exile!"

The successful orator did not venture to urge the plea of entire innocence; for he felt that he still had too much depending on the capricious favour of the populace.

The aged philosopher received his sentence with thanks; and calmly added, "Anaxagoras is not exiled from Athens; but Athens from Anaxagoras. Evil days are coming on this city; and those who are too distant to perceive the trophy at Salamis will deem themselves most blessed. Pythagoras said, 'When the tempest is rising,'tis wise to worship the echo.'"

After the accusation against Phidias had been read, Pericles again rose and said, "Athenians! I shall speak briefly; for I appeal to what every citizen values more than his fortune or his name. I plead for the glory of Athens. When strangers from Ethiopia, Egypt, Phoenicia, and distant Taprobane, come to witness the far-famed beauty of the violet-crowned city, they will stand in mute worship before the Parthenon; and when their wonder finds utterance, they will ask what the Athenians bestowed on an artist so divine. Who among you could look upon the image of Virgin Pallas, resplendent in her heavenly majesty, and not blush to tell the barbarian stranger that death was the boon you bestowed on Phidias?

"Go, gaze on the winged statue of Rhamnusia, where vengeance seems to breathe from the marble sent by Darius to erect his trophy on the plains of Marathon! Then turn and tell the proud Persian that the hand which wrought those fair proportions, lies cold and powerless, by vote of the Athenian people. No—ye could not say it: your hearts would choke your voices. Ye could not tell the barbarian that Athens thus destroyed one of the most gifted of her sons."

The crowd answered in a thunder of applause; mingled with the cry of "Exile! Exile!" A few voices shouted, "A fine! A fine!" Then Cleon arose and said: "Miltiades asked for an olive crown; and a citizen answered, 'When Miltiades conquers alone, let him be crowned alone.' When Phidias can show that he built the Parthenon without the assistance of Ictinus, Myron, Callicrates, and others, then let him have the whole credit of the Parthenon."

To this, Pericles replied, "We are certainly much indebted to those artists for many of the beautiful and graceful details of that sublime composition; but with regard to the majestic design of the Parthenon, Phidias conquered alone, and may therefore justly be crowned alone."

A vote was taken on the question of exile, and the black pebbles predominated. The sculptor heard his sentence with a proud gesture, not unmingled with scorn; and calmly replied, "They can banish Phidias from Athens, more easily than I can take from them the fame of Phidias."

When Pericles replied to the charges against Aspasia, his countenance became more pale, and his voice was agitated: "You all know," said he, "That Aspasia is of Miletus. That city which poets call the laughing daughter of Earth and Heaven: where even the river smiles, as it winds along in graceful wanderings, eager to kiss every new blossom, and court the dalliance of every breeze. Do ye not find it easy to forgive a woman, born under those joyful skies, where beauty rests on the earth in a robe of sunbeams, and inspires the gayety which pours itself forth in playful words? Can ye judge harshly of one, who from her very childhood has received willing homage, as the favourite of Aphrodite, Phoebus, and the Muses? If she spoke irreverently, it was done in thoughtless mirth; and she has sought to atone for it by sacrifices and tears.

"Athenians! I have never boasted; and if I seem to do it now, it is humbly,— as befits one who seeks a precious boon. In your service I have spent many toilsome days and sleepless nights. That I have not enriched myself by it, is proved by the well-known fact that my own son blames my frugality, and reproachfully calls me the slave of the Athenian people."

He paused for a moment, and held his hand over Aspasia's head, as he continued: "In the midst of perplexities and cares, here I have ever found a solace and a guide. Here are treasured up the affections of my heart. It is not for Aspasia, the gifted daughter of Axiochus, that I plead. It is for Aspasia, the beloved wife of Pericles."

Tears choked his utterance; but stifling his emotion, he exclaimed, "Athenians! if ye would know what it is that thus unmans a soul capable of meeting death with calmness, behold, and judge for yourselves!"

As he spoke, he raised Aspasia's veil. Her drapery had been studiously arranged to display her loveliness to the utmost advantage; and as she stood forth radiant in beauty, the building rung with the acclamations that were sent forth, peal after peal, by the multitude.

Pericles had not in vain calculated on the sympathies of a volatile and ardent people, passionately fond of the beautiful, in all its forms. Aspasia remained in Athens, triumphant over the laws of religion and morality.

Clinias desired leave to speak in behalf of Philothea, grandchild of Anaxagoras; and the populace, made good-humoured by their own clemency, expressed a wish to hear. He proceeded as follows: "Philothea,—whom you all know was, not long since, one of the Canephoræ, and embroidered the splendid peplus exhibited at the last Panathenæa—humbly begs of the Athenians, that Eudora, Dione, and Geta, slaves of Phidias, may remain under his protection, and not be confiscated with his household goods. A contribution would have been raised, to buy these individuals of the state, were it not deemed an insult to that proud and generous people, who fined a citizen for proposing marble as a cheaper material than ivory for the statue of Pallas Parthenia."

The request, thus aided by flattery, was almost unanimously granted. One black pebble alone appeared in the urn; and that was from the hand of Alcibiades.

Clinias expressed his thanks, and holding up the statue of Urania, he added: "In token of gratitude for this boon, and for the life of a beloved grandfather, Philothea consecrates to Pallas Athenæ this image of the star-worshipping muse; the gift of a munificent Ethiopian."

The populace, being in gracious mood, forthwith voted that the exiles had permission to carry with them any articles valued as the gift of friendship.

The Prytanes dismissed the assembly; and as they dispersed, Alcibiades scattered small coins among them. Aspasia immediately sent to the Prytaneum an ivory statue of Mnemosyne, smiling as she looked back on a group of Hours; a magnificent token that she would never forget the clemency of the Athenian people.

Hermippus took an early opportunity to proclaim the exhibition of a new comedy called Hercules and Omphale; and the volatile citizens thronged the theatre, to laugh at that infatuated tenderness, which in the Prytaneum had well nigh moved them to tears. The actor openly ridiculed them for having been so much influenced by their orator's least-successful attempt at eloquence; but in the course of the same play, Cratinus raised a laugh at his expense, by saying facetiously: "Lo! Hermippus would speak like Pericles! Hear him, Athenians! Is he not as successful as Salmoneus, when he rolled his chariot over a brazen bridge, and hurled torches to imitate the thunder and lightning of Zeus?"

When the day of trial had passed, Pericles slept soundly; for his heart was relieved from a heavy pressure. But personal enemies and envious artists were still active; and it was soon buzzed abroad that the people repented of the vote they had given. The exiles had been allowed ten days to sacrifice to the gods, bid farewell to friends, and prepare for departure; but on the third day, at evening twilight, Pericles entered the dwelling of his revered old master. "My father," said he, "I am troubled in spirit. I have just now returned from the Piræus, where I sought an interview with Clinias, who daily visits the Deigma, and has a better opportunity than I can have to hear the news of Athens. I found him crowned with garlands; for he had been offering sacrifices in the hall. He told me he had thus sought to allay the anxiety of his mind with regard to yourself and Phidias. He fears the capricious Athenians will reverse their decree."

"Alas, Pericles," replied the old man, "what can you expect of a people, when statesmen condescend to buy justice at their hands, by promised feasts, and scattered coin?"

"Nay, blame me not, Anaxagoras," rejoined Pericles; "I cannot govern as I would. I found the people corrupted; and I must humour their disease. Your life must be saved; even if you reprove me for the means. At midnight, a boat will be in readiness to conduct you to Salamis, where lies a galley bound for Ionia. I hasten to warn Phidias to depart speedily for Elis."

The parting interview between Philothea and her repentant friend was almost too painful for endurance. Poor Eudora felt that she was indeed called to drink the cup of affliction, to its last bitter drop. Her heart yearned to follow the household of Anaxagoras; but Philothea strengthened her own conviction that duty and gratitude both demanded she should remain with Phidias.

Geta and Milza likewise had their sorrows—the harder to endure, because they were the first they had ever encountered. The little peasant was so young, and her lover so poor, that their friends thought a union had better be deferred. But Milza was free: and Anaxagoras told her it depended on her own choice, to go with them, or follow Geta. The grateful Arcadian dropped on one knee, and kissing Philothea's hand, while the tears flowed down her cheeks, said: "She has been a mother to orphan Milza, and I will not leave her now. Geta says it would be wrong to leave her when she is in affliction."

Philothea, with a gentle smile, put back the ringlets from her tearful eyes, and told her not to weep for her sake; for she should be resigned and cheerful, wheresover the gods might place her; but Milza saw that her smiles were sad.

At midnight, Pericles came, to accompany Anaxagoras to Salamis. Paralus and Philothea had been conversing much, and singing their favourite songs together, for the last time. The brow of the ambitious statesman became clouded, when he observed that his son had been in tears; he begged that preparations for departure might be hastened. The young man followed them to the Piræus; but Pericles requested him to go no further. The restraint of his presence prevented any parting less formal than that of friendship. But he stood watching the boat that conveyed them over the waters; and when the last ripple left in its wake had disappeared, he slowly returned to Athens.

The beautiful city stoood before him, mantled in moonlight's silvery veil. Yet all seemed cheerless; for the heart of Paralus was desolate. He looked toward the beloved mansion near the gate Diocharis; drew from his bosom a long lock of golden hair; and leaning against the statue of Hermes, bowed down his head and wept.

CHAPTER XI.

"How I love the mellow sage,
Smiling through the veil of age!
Age is on his temples hung,
But his heart—his heart is young!"
                    ANACREON

A few years passed away, and saw Anaxagoras the contented resident of a small village near Lampsacus, in Ionia. That he still fondly cherished Athens in his heart was betrayed only by the frequent walks he took to a neighbouring eminence, where he loved to sit and look toward the Ægean; but the feebleness of age gradually increased, until he could no longer take his customary exercise. Philothea watched over him with renewed tenderness; and the bright tranquillity he received from the world he was fast approaching, shone with reflected light upon her innocent soul. At times, the maiden was so conscious of this holy influence, that all the earthly objects around her seemed like dreams of some strange foreign land.

One morning, after they had partaken their frugal repast, she said, in a cheerful tone, "Dear grandfather, I had last night a pleasant dream; and Milza says it is prophetic, because she had filled my pillow with fresh laurel leaves. I dreamed that a galley, with three banks of oars, and adorned with fillets, came to carry us back to Athens."

With a faint smile, Anaxagoras replied, "Alas for unhappy Athens! If half we hear be true, her exiled children can hardly wish to be restored to her bosom. Atropos has decreed that I at least shall never again enter her walls. I am not disposed to murmur. Yet the voice of Plato would be pleasant to my ears, as music on the waters in the night-time. I pray you bring forth the writings of Pythagoras, and read me something that sublime philosopher has said concerning the nature of the soul, and the eternal principle of life. As my frail body approaches the Place of Sleep, I feel less and less inclined to study the outward images of things, the forms whereof perish; and my spirit thirsteth more and more to know its origin and its destiny. I have thought much of Plato's mysterious ideas of light. Those ideas were doubtless brought from the East; for as that is the quarter where the sun rises, so we have thence derived many vital truths, which have kept a spark of life within the beautiful pageantry of Grecian mythology."

"Paralus often said that the Persian Magii, the Egyptian priests, and the Pythagoreans imbibed their reverence for light from one common source," rejoined Philothea.

Anaxagoras was about to speak, when a deep but gentle voice, from some invisible person near them, said:

"The unchangeable principles of Truth act upon the soul like the sun upon the eye, when it turneth to him. But the *one* principle, better than intellect, from which all things flow, and to which all things tend, is Good. As the sun not only makes objects visible, but is the cause of their generation, nourishment, and increase, so the Good, through Truth, imparts being, and the power of being known, to every object of knowledge. For this cause, the Pythagoreans greet the sun with music and with reverence."

The listeners looked at each other in surprise, and Philothea was the first to say, "It is the voice of Plato!"

"Even so, my friends," replied the philosopher, smiling, as he stood before them.

The old man, in the sudden joy of his heart, attempted to rise and embrace him; but weakness prevented. The tears started to his eyes, as he said, "Welcome, most welcome, son of Aristo. You see that I am fast going where we hope the spirit is to learn its own mysteries."

Plato, affected at the obvious change in his aged friend, silently grasped his hand, and turned to answer the salutation of Philothea. She too had changed; but she had never been more lovely. The colour on her cheek, which had always been delicate as the reflected hue of a rose, had become paler by frequent watchings; but her large dark eyes were more soft and serious, and her whole countenance beamed with the bright stillness of a spirit receiving the gift of prophecy.

The skies were serene; the music of reeds came upon the ear, softened by distance; while the snowy fleece of sheep and lambs formed a beautiful contrast with the rich verdure of the landscape.

"All things around you are tranquil," said Plato; "and thus I ever found it, even in corrupted Athens. Not the stillness of souls that sleep, but the quiet of life drawn from deep fountains."

"How did you find our peaceful retreat?" inquired Philothea. "Did none guide you?"

"Euago of Lampsacus told me what course to pursue," he replied; "and not far distant I again asked of a shepherd boy—well knowing that all the children would find out Anaxagoras as readily as bees are guided to the flowers. As I approached nearer I saw at every step new tokens of my friends. The clepsydra, in the little brook, dropping its pebbles to mark the hours; the arytæna placed on the rock for thirsty travellers; the door loaded with garlands, placed there by glad-hearted boys; the tablet covered with mathematical lines, lying on the wooden bench, sheltered by grape-vines trained in the Athenian fashion, with a distaff among the foliage; all these spoke to me of souls that unite the wisdom of age with the innocence of childhood."

"Though we live in indolent Ionia, we still believe Hesiod's maxim, that industry is the guardian of virtue," rejoined Anaxagoras. "Philothea plies her distaff as busily as Lachesis spinning the thread of mortal life." He looked upon his beautiful grandchild, with an expression full of tenderness, as he added, "And she does indeed spin the thread of the old man's life; for her diligent fingers gain my bread. But what news bring you from unhappy Athens? Is Pericles yet alive?"

"She is indeed unhappy Athens," answered Plato. "The pestilence is still raging; a manifested form of that inward corruption, which, finding a home in the will of man, clothed itself in thought, and now completes its circle in his corporeal nature. The dream at the cave of Amphiaraus is literally fulfilled. Men fall down senseless in the street, and the Piræus has been heaped with unburied dead. All the children of Clinias are in the Place of Sleep. Hipparete is dead, with two of her little ones. Pericles himself was one of the first sufferers; but he was recovered by the skill of Hippocrates, the learned physician from Cos. His former wife is dead, and so is Xanthippus his son. You know that that proud young man and his extravagant wife could never forgive the frugality of Pericles. Even in his dying moments he refused to call him father, and made no answer to his affectionate inquiries. Pericles has borne all his misfortunes with the dignity of an immortal. No one has seen him shed a tear, of heard him utter a complaint. The ungrateful people blame him for all their troubles, as if he had omnipotent power to avert evils. Cleon and Tolmides are triumphant. Pericles is deprived of office, and fined fifty drachmæ."

He looked at Philothea, and seeing her eyes fixed earnestly upon him, her lips parted, and an eager flush spread over her whole countenance, he said, in a tone of tender solemnity, "Daughter of Alcimenes, your heart reproaches me, that I forbear to speak of Paralus. That I have done so has not been from forgetfulness, but because I have, with vain and self-defeating prudence, sought for cheerful words to convey sad thoughts. Paralus breathes and moves, but is apparently unconscious of existence in this world. He is silent and abstracted, like one just returned from the cave of Trophonius. Yet, beautiful forms are ever with him, in infinite variety; for his quiescent soul has now undisturbed recollection of the divine archetypes in the ideal world, of which all earthly beauty is the shadow."

"He is happy, then, though living in the midst of death," answered Philothea: "But does his memory retain no traces of his friends?"

"One—and one only," he replied. "The name of Philothea was too deeply engraven to be washed away by the waters of oblivion. He seldom speaks; but when he does, you are ever in his visions. The sound of a female voice accompanying the lyre is the only thing that makes him smile; and nothing moves him to tears save the farewell song of Orpheus to Eurydice. In his drawings there is more of majesty and beauty than Phidias or Myron ever conceived; and one figure is always there—the Pythia, the Muse, the Grace, or something combining all these, more spiritual than either."

As the maiden listened, tears started from fountains long sealed, and rested like dew-drops on her dark eyelashes.

Farewell to Eurydice! Oh, how many thoughts were wakened by those words! They were the last she heard sung by Paralus, the night Anaxagoras departed from Athens. Often had the shepherds of Ionia heard the melancholy notes float on the evening breeze; and as the sounds died away, they spoke to each other in whispers, and said, "They come from the dwelling of the divinely-inspired one!"

Plato perceived that the contemplative maiden was busy with memories of the past. In a tone of gentle reverence, he added, "What I have told you proves that your souls were one, before it wandered from the divine home; and it gives hope that they will be re-united, when they return thither after their weary exile in the world of shadows."

"And has this strange pestilence produced such an effect on Paralus only?" inquired Anaxagoras.

"Many in Athens have recovered health without any memory of the images of things," replied Plato; "but I have known no other instance where recollections of the ideal world remained more bright and unimpaired, than they possibly can be while disturbed by the presence of the visible. Tithonus formerly told me of similar cases that occurred when the plague raged in Ethiopia and Egypt; and Artaphernes says he has seen a learned Magus, residing among the mountains that overlook Taoces, who recovered from the plague with a perpetual oblivion of all outward forms, while he often had knowledge of the thoughts passing in the minds of those around him. If an unknown scroll were placed before him, he would read it, though a brazen shield were interposed between him and the parchment; and if figures were drawn on the water, he at once recognized the forms, of which no visible trace remained."

"Marvellous, indeed, is the mystery of our being," exclaimed Anaxagoras.

"It involves the highest of all mysteries," rejoined Plato; "for if man did not contain within himself a type of all that is,—from the highest to the lowest plane of existence,—he could not enter the human form. At times, I have thought glimpses of these eternal truths were revealed to me; but I lost them almost as soon as they were perceived, because my soul dwelt so much with the images of things. Thus have I stood before the thick veil which conceals the shrine of Isis, while the narrow streak of brilliant light around its edges gave indication of unrevealed glories, and inspired the eager but fruitless hope that the massive folds would float away, like a cloud before the sun. There are indeed times when I lose the light entirely, and cannot even perceive the veil that hides it from me. This is because my soul, like Psyche bending over the sleeping Eros, is too curious to examine, by its own feeble taper, the lineaments of the divinity whereby it hath been blessed."

"How is Pericles affected by this visitation of the gods upon the best beloved of his children?" inquired Anaxagoras.

"It has softened and subdued his ambitious soul," answered Plato; "and has probably helped him to endure the loss of political honours with composure. I have often observed that affliction renders the heart of man like the heart of a little child; and of this I was reminded when I parted from Pericles at Salamis, whence the galley sailed for Ionia. You doubtless remember the little mound, called Cynos-sema? There lies the faithful dog, that died in consequence of swimming after the ship which carried the father of Pericles, when the Athenians were all leaving their beloved city by advice of Themistocles. The illustrious statesman has not been known to shed a tear amid the universal wreck of his popularity, his family, and his friends; but standing by this little mound, the recollections of childhood came over him, and he wept as an infant weeps for its lost mother."

There was a tremulous motion about the lips of the old man, as he replied, "Perchance he was comparing the constancy of that affectionate animal with the friendship of men, and the happy unconsciousness of his boyhood with the anxious cares that wait on greatness. Pericles had a soft heart in his youth; and none knew this better than the forgotten old man, whom he once called his friend."

Plato perceived his emotion, and answered, in a soothing voice, "He has since been wedded to political ambition, which never brought any man nearer to his divine home; but Anaxagoras is not forgotten. Pericles has of late often visited the shades of Academus, where he has talked much of you and Philothea, and expressed earnest hopes that the gods would again restore you to Athens, to bless him with your wise counsels."

The aged philosopher shook his head, as he replied, "They who would have a lamp should take care to supply it with oil. Had Philothea's affection been like that of Pericles, this old frame would have perished for want of food."

"Nay, Anaxagoras," rejoined Plato, "you must not forget that this Peloponessian war, the noisy feuds in Athens, and afflictions in his own family, have involved him in continual distractions. He who gives his mind to politics, sails on a stormy sea, with a giddy pilot. Pericles has now sent you substantial proofs of his gratitude; and if his power equalled his wishes, I have no doubt he would make use of the alarmed state of public feeling to procure your recall."

"You have as yet given us no tidings of Phidias and his household," said Philothea.

"The form of Phidias sleeps," replied Plato: "His soul has returned to those sacred mysteries, once familiar to him; the recollection of which enabled him while on earth to mould magnificent images of supernal forms—images that awakened in all who gazed upon them some slumbering memory of ideal worlds; though few knew whence it came, or why their souls were stirred. The best of his works is the Olympian Zeus, made at Elis after his exile. It is far more sublime than the Pallas Parthenia. The Eleans consider the possession of it as a great triumph over ungrateful Athens."

"Under whose protection is Eudora placed?" inquired Philothea.

"I have heard that she remains at the house where Phidias died," rejoined Plato. "The Eleans have given her the yearly revenues of a farm, in consideration of the affectionate care bestowed on her illustrious benefactor.—Report says that Phidias wished to see her united to his nephew Pandænus; but I have never heard of the marriage. Philæmon is supposed to be in Persia, instructing the sons of the wealthy satrap Megabyzus."

"And where is the faithful Geta?" inquired Anaxagoras.

"Geta is at Lampsacus; and I doubt not will hasten hither, as soon as he has taken care of certain small articles of merchandize that he brought with him. Phidias gave him his freedom the day they left Athens; and after his death, the people of Elis bestowed upon him fifty drachmæ. He has established himself at

Phalerum, where he tells me he has doubled this sum by the sale of anchovies. He was eager to attend upon me for the sake, as he said, of once more seeing his good old master Anaxagoras, and that maiden with mild eyes, who always spoke kind words to the poor; but I soon discovered there was a stronger reason for his desire to visit Lampsacus. From what we had heard, we expected to find you in the city. Geta looked very sorrowful, when told that you were fifty stadia farther from the sea."

"When we first landed on the Ionian shore,"replied Anaxagoras, "I took up my abode two stadia from Lampsacus, and sometimes went thither to lecture in the porticos. But when I did this, I seemed to breathe an impure air; and idle young men so often followed me home, that the maidens were deprived of the innocent freedom I wished them to enjoy. Here I feel, more than I have ever felt, the immediate presence of divinity."

"I know not whether it be good or bad," said Plato; "but philosophy has wrought in me a dislike of conversing with many persons. I do not imitate the Pythagoreans, who close their gates; for I perceive that truth never ought to be a sealed fountain; but I cannot go into the Prytanæum, the agoras, and the workshops, and jest, like Socrates, to captivate the attention of young men. When I thus seek to impart hidden treasures, I lose without receiving; and few perceive the value of what is offered. I feel the breath of life taken away from me by the multitude. Their praises cause me to fear, lest, according to Ibycus, I should offend the gods, but acquire glory among men. For these reasons, I have resolved never to abide in cities."

"The name of Socrates recalls Alcibiades to my mind," rejoined Anaxagoras. "Is he still popular with the Athenians?"

"He is; and will remain so," replied Plato, "so long as he feasts them at his own expense, and drinks three cotylæ of wine at a draught. I know not of what materials he is made; unless it be of Carpasian flax, which above all things burns and consumes not."

"Has this fearful pestilence no power to restrain the appetites and passions of the people?" inquired the old man.

"It has but given them more unbridled license," rejoined Plato. "Even when the unburied dead lay heaped in piles, and the best of our equestrians were gasping in the streets, robbers took possession of their dwellings, drinking wine from their golden vessels, and singing impure songs in the presence of their household gods. Men seek to obtain oblivion of danger by reducing themselves to the condition of beasts, which have no perception above the immediate wants of the senses. All pursuits that serve to connect the soul with the world whence it came are rejected. The Odeum is shut; there is no more lecturing in the porticos; the temples are entirely forsaken, and even the Diasia are no longer observed. Some of the better sort of citizens, weary of fruitless prayers and sacrifices to Phoebus, Phoebe, Pallas, and the Erinnys. have erected an altar to the Unknown God; and this altar only is heaped with garlands, and branches of olive twined with wool."

"A short time ago, he who had dared to propose the erection of such an altar would have been put to death," said Anaxagoras. "The pestilence has not been sent in vain, if the faith in images is shaken, and the Athenians have been led to reverence One great Principle of Order, even though they call it unknown."

"It is fear, unmingled with reverence, in the minds of many," replied the philosopher of Academus. "As for the multitude, they consider all principles of right and wrong as things that may exist, or not exist, according to the vote of the Athenian people. Of ideas eternal in their nature, and therefore incapable of being created or changed by the will of a majority, they cannot conceive. When health is restored, they will return to the old worship of forms, as readily as they changed from Pericles to Cleon, and will again change from him to Pericles."

The aged philosopher shook his head and smiled, as he said: "Ah, Plato! Plato! where will you find materials for your ideal republic?"

"In an ideal Atlantis," replied the Athenian, smiling in return; "or perchance in the fabled groves of Argive Hera, where the wild beasts are tamed—the deer and the wolf lie down together—and the weak animal finds refuge from his powerful pursuer. But the principle of a republic is none the less true, because mortals make themselves unworthy to receive it. The best doctrines become the worst, when they are used for evil purposes. Where a love of power is the ruling object, the tendency is corruption; and the only difference between Persia and Athens is, that in one place power is received by birth, in the other obtained by cunning.

"Thus it will ever be; while men grope in the darkness of their outward nature; which receives no light from the inward, because they will not open the doors of the temple, where a shrine is placed, from which it ever beams forth with occult and venerable splendour.

"Philosophers would do well if they ceased to disturb themselves with the meaning of mythologic fables, and considered whether they have not within themselves a serpent possessing more folds than Typhon, and far more raging and fierce. When the wild beasts within the soul are destroyed, men will no longer have to contend against their visible forms."

"But tell me, O admirable Plato!" said Anaxagoras, "what connection can there be between the inward allegorical serpent, and the created form thereof?"

"One could not exist without the other," answered Plato, "because where there is no ideal, there can be no image. There are doubtless men in other parts of the universe better than we are, because they stand on a higher plane of existence, and approach nearer to the *idea* of man. The celestial lion is intellectual, but the sublunary irrational; for the former is nearer the *idea* of a lion. The lower planes of existence receive the influences of the higher, according to the purity and stillness of the will. If this be restless and turbid, the waters from a pure fountain become corrupted, and the corruption flows down to lower planes of existence, until it at last manifests itself in corporeal forms. The sympathy thus produced between things earthly and celestial is the origin of imagination; by which men have power to trace the images of supernal forms, invisible to mortal eyes. Every man can be elevated to a higher plane by quiescence of the will; and thus may become a prophet. But none are perfect ones; because all have a tendency to look downward to the opinions of men in the same existence with themselves: and this brings them upon a lower plane, where the prophetic light glimmers and dies. The Pythia at Delphi, and the priestess in Dodona, have been the cause of very trifling benefits, when in a cautious, prudent state; but when agitated by a divine mania, they have produced many advantages, both public and private, to the Greeks."

The conversation was interrupted by the merry shouts of children; and presently a troop of boys and girls appeared, leading two lambs decked with garlands. They were twin lambs of a ewe that had died; and they had been trained to suck from a pipe placed in a vessel of milk. This day, for the first time, the young ram had placed his budding horns under the throat of his sister lamb, and pushed away her head that he might take possession of the pipe himself. The children were greatly delighted with this exploit, and hastened to exhibit it before their old friend Anaxagoras, who always entered into their sports with a cheerful heart. Philothea replenished the vessel of milk; and the gambols of the young lambs, with the joyful laughter of the children, diffused a universal spirit of gladness. One little girl filled the hands of the old philosopher with tender leaves, that the beautiful animals might come and eat; while another climbed his knees, and put her little fingers on his venerable head, saying, "Your hair is as white as the lamb's; will Philothea spin it, father?"

The maiden, who had been gazing at the little group with looks full of tenderness, timidly raised her eyes to Plato, and said, "Son of Aristo, these have not wandered so far from their divine home as we have!"

The philosopher had before observed the peculiar radiance of Philothea's expression, when she raised her downcast eyes; but it never before appeared to him so much like light suddenly revealed from the inner shrine of a temple.

With a feeling approaching to worship, he replied, "Maiden, your own spirit has always remained near its early glories."

When the glad troop of children departed, Plato followed them to see their father's flocks, and play quoits with the larger boys. Anaxagoras looked after him with a pleased expression, as he said, "He will delight their minds, as he has elevated ours. Assuredly, his soul is like the Homeric, chain of gold, one end of which rests on earth, and the other terminates in Heaven."

Milza was daily employed in fields not far distant, to tend a neighbour's goats, and Philothea, wishing to impart the welcome tidings, took up the shell with which she was accustomed to summon her to her evening labours. She was about to apply the shell to her lips, when she perceived the young Arcadian standing in the vine-covered arbour, with Geta, who had seized her by each cheek and was kissing her after the fashion of the Grecian peasantry. With a smile and a blush, the maiden turned away hastily, lest the humble lovers should perceive they were discovered.

The frugal supper waited long on the table before Plato returned. As he entered, Anaxagoras pointed to the board, which rested on rude sticks cut from the trees, and said, "Son of Aristo, all I have to offer you are dried grapes, bread, wild honey, and water from the brook."

"More I should not taste if I were at the table of Alcibiades," replied the philosopher of Athens. "When I see men bestow much thought on eating and drinking, I marvel that they will labour so diligently in building their own prisons. Here, at least, we can restore the Age of Innocence, when no life was taken to gratify the appetite of man, and the altars of the gods were unstained with blood."

Philothea, contrary to the usual custom of Grecian women, remained with her grandfather and his guest during their simple repast, and soon after retired to her own apartment.

When they were alone, Plato informed his aged friend that his visit to Lampsacus was at the request of Pericles. Hippocrates had expressed a hope that the presence of Philothea might, at least in some degree, restore the health of Paralus; and the heart-stricken father had sent to intreat her consent to a union with his son.

"Philothea would not leave me, even if I urged it with tears," replied Anaxagoras; "and I am forbidden to return to Athens."

"Pericles has provided an asylum for you, on the borders of Attica," answered Plato; "and the young people would soon join you, after their marriage. He did not suppose that his former proud opposition to their loves would be forgotten; but he said hearts like yours would forgive it all, the more readily because he was now a man deprived of power, and his son suffering under a visitation of the gods. Alcibiades laughed aloud when he heard of this proposition; and said his uncle would never think of making it to any but a maiden who sees the zephyrs run and hears the stars sing. He spoke truth in his profane merriment. Pericles knows that she who obediently listens to the inward voice will be most likely to seek the happiness of others, forgetful of her own wrongs."

"I do not believe the tender-hearted maiden ever cherished resentment against any living thing," replied Anaxagoras. "She often reminds me of Hesiod's description of Leto:

'Placid to men and to immortal gods;
Mild from the first beginning of her days;
Gentlest of all in Heaven.'

"She has indeed been a precious gift to my old age. Simple and loving as she is, there are times when her looks and words fill me with awe, as if I stood in the presence of divinity."

"It is a most lovely union when the Muses and the Charities inhabit the same temple," said Plato. "I think she learned of you to be a constant worshipper of the innocent and graceful nymphs, who preside over kind and gentle actions. But tell me, Anaxagoras, if this marriage is declined, who will protect the daughter of Alcimenes when you are gone?"

The philosopher replied, "I have a sister Heliodora, the youngest of my father's flock; who is Priestess of the Sun, at Ephesus. Of all my family, she has least despised me for preferring philosophy to gold; and report bespeaks her wise and virtuous. I have asked and obtained from her a promise to protect Philothea when I am gone; but I will tell my child the wishes of Pericles, and leave her to the guidance of her own heart. If she enters the home of Paralus, she will be to him, as she has been to me, a blessing like the sunshine."

CHAPTER XII.

Adieu, thou sun, and fields of golden light;
For the last time I drink thy radiance bright,
And sink to sleep.
                              ARISTOPHANES.

The galley that brought Plato from Athens was sent on a secret political mission, and was not expected to revisit Lampsacus until the return of another moon. Anaxagoras, always mindful of the happiness of those around him, proposed that the constancy of faithful Geta should be rewarded by an union with Milza. The tidings were hailed with joy; not only by the young couple, but by all the villagers. The superstition of the little damsel did indeed suggest numerous obstacles. The sixteenth of the month must on no account be chosen; one day was unlucky for a wedding, because as she returned from the fields, an old woman busy at the distaff had directly crossed her path; and another was equally so, because she had seen a weasel, without remembering to throw three stones as it passed. But at last there came a day against which no objections could be raised. The sky was cloudless, and the moon at its full; both deemed propitious omens. A white kid had been sacrificed to Artemis, and baskets of fruit and poppies been duly placed upon her altar. The long white veil woven by Milza and laid by for this occasion, was taken out to be bleached in the sunshine and dew. Philothea presented a zone, embroidered by her own skilful hands; Anaxagoras bestowed a pair of sandals laced with crimson; and Geta purchased a bridal robe of flaming colours.

Plato promised to supply the feast with almonds and figs. The peasant, whose goats Milza had tended, sent six large vases of milk, borne by boys crowned with garlands. And the matrons of the village, with whom the kind little Arcadian had ever been a favourite, presented a huge cake, carried aloft on a bed of flowers, by twelve girls clothed in white. The humble residence of the old philosopher was almost covered with the abundant blossoms brought by joyful children. The door posts were crowned with garlands anointed with oil, and bound with fillets of wool. The bride and bridegroom were carried in procession, on a litter made of the boughs of trees, plentifully adorned with garlands and flags of various colours; preceded by young men playing on reeds and flutes, and followed by maidens bearing a pestle and sieve. The priest performed the customary sacrifices at the altar of Hera; the omens were propitious; libations were poured; and Milza returned to her happy home, the wife of her faithful Geta. Feasting continued till late in the evening, and the voice of music was not hushed until past the hour of midnight.

The old philosopher joined in the festivity, and in the cheerfulness of his heart exerted himself beyond his strength. Each succeeding day found him more feeble; and Philothea soon perceived that the staff on which she had leaned from her childhood was about to be removed forever. On the twelfth day after

Milza's wedding, he asked to be led into the open portico, that he might enjoy the genial warmth. He gazed on the bright landscape, as if it had been the countenance of a friend. Then looking upward, with a placid smile, he said to Plato, "You tell me that Truth acts upon the soul, like the Sun upon the eye, when it turneth to him. Would that I could be as easily and certainly placed in the light of truth, as I have been in this blessed sunshine! But in vain I seek to comprehend the mystery of my being. All my thoughts on this subject are dim and shadowy, as the ghosts seen by Odysseus on the Stygian shore."

Plato answered: "Thus it must ever be, while the outward world lies so near us, and the images of things crowd perpetually on the mind. An obolus held close to the eye may prevent our seeing the moon and the stars; and thus does the ever-present earth exclude the glories of Heaven. But in the midst of uncertainty and fears, one feeling alone remains; and that is hope, strong as belief, that virtue can never die. In pity to the cravings of the soul, something will surely be given in future time more bright and fixed than the glimmering truths preserved in poetic fable; even as radiant stars arose from the ashes of Orion's daughters, to shine in the heavens an eternal crown."

The old man replied, "I have, as you well know, been afraid to indulge in your speculations concerning the soul, lest I should spend my life in unsatisfied attempts to embrace beautiful shadows."

"To me likewise they have sometimes appeared doctrines too high and solemn to be taught," rejoined Plato: "Often when I have attempted to clothe them in language, the airy forms have glided from me, mocking me with their distant beauty. We are told of Tantalus surrounded by water that flows away when he attempts to taste it, and with delicious fruits above his head, carried off by a sudden wind whenever he tries to seize them. It was his crime that, being admitted to the assemblies of Olympus, he brought away the nectar and ambrosia of the gods, and gave them unto mortals. Sometimes, when I have been led to discourse of ideal beauty, with those who perceive only the images of things, the remembrance of that unhappy son of Zeus has awed me into silence."

While they were yet speaking, the noise of approaching wheels was heard, and presently a splendid chariot, with four white horses, stopped before the humble dwelling.

A stranger, in purple robes, descended from the chariot, followed by servants carrying a seat of ivory inlaid with silver, a tuft of peacock feathers to brush away the insects, and a golden box filled with perfumes. It was Chrysippus, prince of Clazomenæ, the nephew of Anaxagoras. He had neglected and despised the old man in his poverty, but had now come to congratulate him on the rumour of Philothea's approaching marriage with the son of Pericles. The aged philosopher received him with friendly greeting, and made him known to Plato. Chrysippus gave a glance at the rude furniture of the portico, and gathered his perfumed robes carefully about him.

"Son of Basileon, it is the dwelling of cleanliness, though it be the abode of poverty," said the old man, in a tone of mild reproof.

Geta had officiously brought a wooden bench for the high-born guest; but he waited till his attendants had opened the ivory seat, and covered it with crimson cloth, before he seated himself, and replied:

"Truly, I had not expected to find the son of Hegesibulus in so mean a habitation. No man would conjecture that you were the descendant of princes."

With a quiet smile, the old man answered,—"Princes have not wished to proclaim kindred with Anaxagoras; and why should he desire to perpetuate the remembrance of what they have forgotten?"

Chrysippus looked toward Plato, and with some degree of embarrassment sought to excuse himself, by saying, "My father often told me that it was your own choice to withdraw from your family; and if they have not since offered to share their wealth with you, it is because you have ever been improvident of your estates."

"What! Do you not take charge of them?" inquired Anaxagoras. "I gave my estates to your father, from the conviction that he would take better care of them than I could do; and in this I deemed myself most provident."

"But you went to Athens, and took no care for your country," rejoined the prince.

The venerable philosopher pointed to the heavens, that smiled serenely above them,—and said, "Nay, young man, my greatest care has ever been for my country."

In a more respectful tone, Chrysippus rejoined: "Anaxagoras, all men speak of your wisdom; but does this fame so far satisfy you, that you never regret you sacrificed riches to philosophy?"

"I am satisfied with the pursuit of wisdom, not with the fame of it," replied the sage. "In my youth, I greatly preferred wisdom to gold; and as I approach the Stygian shore, gold has less and less value in my eyes. Charon will charge my disembodied spirit but a single obolus for crossing his dark ferry. Living mortals only need a golden bough to enter the regions of the dead."

The prince seemed thoughtful for a moment, as he gazed on the benevolent countenance of his aged relative.

"If it be as you have said, Anaxagoras is indeed happier than princes," he replied. "But I came to speak of the daughter of Alcimenes. I have heard that she is beautiful, and the destined wife of Paralus of Athens."

"It is even so," said the philosopher; "and it would gladden my heart, if I might be permitted to see her placed under the protection of Pericles, before I die."

"Has a sufficient dowry been provided?" inquired Chrysippus. "No one of our kindred must enter the family of Pericles as a slave."

A slight colour mantled in the old man's cheeks, as he answered, "I have friends in Athens, who will not see my precious child suffer shame for want of a few drachmæ."

"I have brought with me a gift, which I deemed in some degree suited to the dignity of our ancestors," rejoined the prince; "and I indulged the hope of giving it into the hands of the maiden."

As he spoke, he made a signal to his attendants, who straightway brought from the chariot a silver tripod lined with gold, and a bag containing a hundred golden staters. At the same moment, Milza entered, and in a low voice informed Anaxagoras that Philothea deemed this prolonged interview with the stranger dangerous to his feeble health; and begged that he would suffer himself to be placed on the couch. The invalid replied by a message desiring her presence. As she entered, he said to her, "Philothea, behold your kinsman Chrysippus, son of Basileon."

The illustrious guest was received with the same modest and friendly greeting, that would have been bestowed on the son of a worthy peasant. The prince felt slightly offended that his splendid dress and magnificent equipage produced so little effect on the family of the philosopher; but as the fame of Philothea's beauty had largely mingled with other inducements to make the visit, he endeavoured to conceal his pride, and as he offered the rich gifts, said in a respectful tone, "Daughter of Alcimenes, the tripod is from Heliodora, Priestess at Ephesus. The golden coin is from my own coffers. Accept them for a dowry; and allow me to claim one privilege in return. As I cannot be at the marriage feast, to share the pleasures of other kinsmen, permit the son of Basileon to see you now one moment without your veil."

He waved his hand for his attendants to withdraw; but the maiden hesitated, until Anaxagoras said mildly, "Chrysippus is of your father's kindred; and it is discreet that his request be granted."

Philothea timidly removed her veil, and a modest blush suffused her lovely countenance, as she said, "Thanks, Prince of Clazomenæ, for these munificent gifts. May the gods long preserve you a blessing to your family and people."

"The gifts are all unworthy of her who receives them," replied Chrysippus, gazing so intently that the maiden, with rosy confusion, replaced her veil.

Anaxagoras invited his royal guest to share a philosopher's repast, to which he promised should be added a goblet of wine, lately sent from Lampsacus. The prince courteously accepted his invitation; and the kind old man, wearied with the exertions he had made, was borne to his couch in an inner apartment. When Plato had assisted Philothea and Milza in arranging his pillows, and folding the robe about his feet, he returned to the portico. Philothea supposed the stranger was about to follow him; and without raising her head, as she bent over her grandfather's couch, she said: "He is feeble, and needs repose. In the days of his, strength, he would not have thus left you to the courtesy of our Athenian guest."

"Would to the gods that I had sought him sooner!" rejoined Chrysippus. "While I have gathered foreign jewels, I have been ignorant of the gems in my own family."

Then stooping down, he took Anaxagoras by the hand, and said affectionately, "Have you nothing to ask of your brother's son?"

"Nothing but your prayers for us, and a gentle government for your people," answered the old man. "I thank you for your kindness to this precious orphan. For myself, I am fast going where I shall need less than ever the gifts of princes."

"Would you not like to be buried with regal honour, in your native Clazomenæ?" inquired the prince.

The philosopher again pointed upward as he replied, "Nay. The road to heaven would be no shorter from Clazomenæ."

"And what monument would you have reared to mark the spot where Anaxagoras sleeps?" said Chrysippus.

"I wish to be buried after the ancient manner, with the least possible trouble and expense," rejoined the invalid. "The money you would expend for a monument may be given to some captive sighing in bondage. Let an almond tree be planted near my grave, that the boys may love to come there, as to a pleasant home."

"The citizens of Lampsacus, hearing of your illness, requested me to ask what they should do in honour of your memory, when it pleased the gods to call you hence. What response do you give to this message?" inquired the prince.

The philosopher answered, "Say to them that I desire all the children may have a holiday on the anniversary of my death."

Chrysippus remained silent for a few moments; and then continued: "Anaxagoras, I perceive that you are strangely unlike other mortals; and I know not how you will receive the proposal I am about to make. Philothea has glided from the apartment, as if afraid to remain in my presence. That graceful maiden is too lovely for any destiny meaner than a royal marriage. As a kinsman, I have the best claim to her; and if it be your will, I will divorce my Phoenician Astarte, and make Philothea princess of Clazomenæ."

"Thanks, son of Basileon," replied the old man; "but I love the innocent orphan too well to bestow upon her the burden and the dangers of royalty."

"None could dispute your own right to exchange power and wealth for philosophy and poverty," said Chrysippus; "but though you are the lawful guardian of this maiden, I deem it unjust to reject a splendid alliance without her knowledge."

"Philothea gave her affections to Paralus, even in the days of their childhood," replied Anaxagoras; "and she is of a nature too divine to place much value on the splendour that passes away."

The prince seemed disturbed and chagrined by this imperturbable spirit of philosophy; and after a few brief remarks retreated to the portico.

Here he entered into conversation with Plato; and after some general discourse, spoke of his wishes with regard to Philothea. "Anaxagoras rejects the alliance," said he, smiling; "but take my word for it, the maiden would not dismiss the matter thus lightly. I have never yet seen a woman who preferred philosophy to princes."

"Kings are less fortunate than philosophers," responded Plato; "I have known several women, who preferred wisdom to gold. Could Chrysippus look into those divine eyes, and yet believe that Philothea's soul would rejoice in the pomp of princes?"

The wealthy son of Basileon still remained incredulous of any exceptions to woman's vanity; and finally obtained a promise from Plato, that he would use his influence with his friend to have the matter left entirely to Philothea's decision.

When the maiden was asked by her grandfather, whether she would be the wife of Paralus, smitten by the hand of disease, or princess of Clazomenæ, surrounded by more grandeur than Penelope could boast in her proudest days— her innocent countenance expressed surprise, not unmingled with fear, that the mind of Anaxagoras was wandering. But when assured that Chrysippus seriously proposed to divorce his wife and marry her, a feeling of humiliation came over her, that a man, ignorant of the qualities of her soul, should be thus captivated by her outward beauty, and regard it as a thing to be bought with gold. But the crimson tint soon subsided from her transparent cheek, and she quietly replied, "Tell the prince of Clazomenæ that I have never learned to value riches; nor could I do so, without danger of being exiled far from my divine home."

When these words were repeated to Chrysippus, he exclaimed impatiently, "Curse on the folly which philosophers dignify with the name of wisdom!"

After this, nothing could restore the courtesy he had previously assumed. He scarcely tasted the offered fruit and wine; bade a cold farewell, and soon rolled away in his splendid chariot, followed by his train of attendants.

This unexpected interview produced a singular excitement in the mind of Anaxagoras. All the occurrences of his youth passed vividly before him; and things forgotten for years were remembered like events of the past hour. Plato sat by his side till the evening twilight deepened, listening as he recounted scenes long since witnessed in Athens. When they entreated him to seek repose, he reluctantly assented, and said to his friend, with a gentle pressure of the hand, "Farewell, son of Aristo. Pray for me before you retire to your couch."

Plato parted the silver hairs, and imprinted a kiss on his forehead; then crowning himself with a garland, he knelt before an altar that stood in the apartment, and prayed aloud: "O thou, who art King of Heaven, life and death are in thy hand! Grant what is good for us, whether we ask it, or ask it not; and refuse that which would be hurtful, even when we ask it most earnestly."

"That contains the spirit of all prayer," said the old philosopher. "And now, Plato, go to thy rest; and I will go to mine. Very pleasant have thy words been to me. Even like the murmuring of fountains in a parched and sandy desert." When left alone with his grandchild and Milza, the invalid still seemed unusually excited, and his eyes shone with unwonted brightness. Again he recurred to his early years, and talked fondly of his wife and children. He dwelt on the childhood of Philothea with peculiar pleasure. "Often, very often," said he, "thy infant smiles and artless speech led my soul to divine things; when, without thee, the link would have been broken, and the communication lost."

He held her hand affectionately in his, and often drew her toward him, that he might kiss her cheek. Late in the night, sleep began to steal over him with gentle influence; and Philothea was afraid to move, lest she should disturb his slumbers.

Milza reposed on a couch close by her side, ready to obey the slightest summons; the small earthen lamp that stood on the floor, shaded by an open tablet, burned dim; and the footsteps of Plato were faintly heard in the stillness of the night, as he softly paced to and fro in the open portico.

Philothea leaned her head upon the couch, and gradually yielded to the drowsy influence.

When she awoke, various objects in the apartment were indistinctly revealed by the dawning light. All was deeply quiet. She remained kneeling by her grandfather's side, and her hand was still clasped in his; but it was chilled beneath his touch. She arose, gently placed his arm on the couch, and looked upon his face. A placid smile rested on his features; and she saw that his spirit had passed in peace.

She awoke Milza, and desired that the household might be summoned. As they stood around the couch of that venerable man, Geta and Milza wept bitterly; but Philothea calmly kissed his cold cheek; and Plato looked on him with serene affection, as he said, "So sleep the good."

A lock of grey hair suspended on the door, and a large vase of water at the threshold, early announced to the villagers that the soul of Anaxagoras had passed from its earthly tenement. The boys came with garlands to decorate the funeral couch of the beloved old man; and no tribute of respect was wanting; for all that knew him blessed his memory.

He was buried, as he had desired, near the clepsydra in the little brook; a young almond tree was planted on his grave; and for years after, all the children commemorated the anniversary of his death, by a festival called Anaxagoreia.

Pericles had sent two discreet matrons, and four more youthful attendants, to accompany Philothea to Athens, in case she consented to become the wife of Paralus. The morning after the decease of Anaxagoras, Plato sent a messenger to Lampsacus, desiring the presence of these women, accompanied by Euago and his household. As soon as the funeral rites were passed, he entreated Philothea to accept the offered protection of Euago, the friend of his youth, and connected by marriage with the house of Pericles. "I urge it the more earnestly," said he, "because I think you have reason to fear the power and resentment of Chrysippus. Princes do not willingly relinquish a pursuit; and his train could easily seize you and your attendants, without resistance from these simple villagers."

Aglaonice, wife of Euago, likewise urged the orphan, in the most affectionate manner, to return with them to Lampsacus, and there await the departure of the galley. Philothea acknowledged the propriety of removal, and felt deeply thankful for the protecting influence of her friends. The simple household furniture was given to Milza; her own wardrobe, with many little things that had become dear to her, were deposited in the chariot of Euago; the weeping villagers had taken an affectionate farewell; and sacrifices to the gods had been offered on the altar in front of the dwelling.

Still Philothea lingered and gazed on the beautiful scenes where she had passed so many tranquil hours. Tears mingled with her smiles, as she said, "O, how hard it is to believe the spirit of Anaxagoras will be as near me in Athens, as it is here, where his bones lie buried!"

CHAPTER XIII.

One day, the muses twined the hands
Of infant love with flowery bands,
And gave the smiling captive boy
To be Celestial Beauty's joy.
            ANACREON.

While Philothea remained at Lampsacus, awaiting the arrival of the galley, news came that Chrysippus, with a company of horsemen, had been to her former residence, under the pretext of paying funeral rites to his deceased relative. At the same time, several robes, mantles, and veils, were brought from Heliodora at Ephesus; with the request that they, as well as the silver tripod, should be considered, not as a dowry, but as gifts to be disposed of as she pleased. The priestess mentioned feeble health as a reason for not coming in person to bid the orphan farewell; and promised that sacrifices and prayers for her happines should be duly offered at the shrine of radiant Phoebus.

Philothea smiled to remember how long she had lived in Ionia without attracting the notice of her princely relatives, until her name became connected with the illustrious house of Pericles; but she meekly returned thanks and friendly wishes, together with the writings of Simonides, beautifully copied by her own hand.

The day of departure at length arrived. All along the shore might be seen smoke rising from the altars of Poseidon, Æolus, Castor and Polydeuces, and the sea-green Sisters of the Deep. To the usual danger of winds and storms was added the fear of encountering hostile fleets; and every power that presided over the destinies of sailors was invoked by the anxious mariners. But their course seemed more like an excursion in a pleasure barge, than a voyage on the ocean. They rowed along beneath a calm and sunny sky, keeping close to the verdant shores where, ever and anon, temples, altars, and statues, peeped forth amid groves of cypress and cedar; under the shadow of which many a festive train hailed the soft approach of spring, with pipe, and song, and choral dance.

The tenth day saw the good ship Halcyone safely moored in the harbour of Phalerum, chosen in preference to the more crowded and diseased port of the Piræus. The galley having been perceived at a distance, Pericles and Clinias were waiting, with chariots, in readiness to convey Philothea and her attendants. The first inquiries of Pericles were concerning the health of Anaxagoras; and he seemed deeply affected, when informed that he would behold his face no more. Philothea's heart was touched by the tender solemnity of his manner when he bade her welcome to Athens. Plato anticipated the anxious question that trembled on her tongue; and a brief answer indicated that no important change had taken place in Paralus. Clinias kindly urged the claims of himself and wife to be considered the parents of the orphan; and they all accompanied her to his house, attended by boys burning incense, as a protection against the pestilential atmosphere of the marshy grounds.

When they alighted, Philothea timidly, but earnestly, asked to see Paralus without delay. Their long-cherished affection, the full communion of soul they had enjoyed together, and the peculiar visitation which now rested on him, all combined to make her forgetful of ceremony.

Pericles went to seek his son, and found him reclining on the couch where he had left him. The invalid seemed to be in a state of deep abstraction, and offered no resistance as they led him to the chariot. When they entered the house of Clinias, he looked around with a painful expression of weariness, until they tenderly placed him on a couch. He was evidently disturbed by the presence of those about him, but unmindful of any familiar faces, until Philothea suddenly knelt by his side, and throwing back her veil, said, "Paralus! dear Paralus! Do you not know me?" Then his whole face kindled with an expression of joy, so intense that Pericles for a moment thought the faculties of his soul were completely restored.

But the first words he uttered showed a total unconsciousness of past events. "Oh, Philothea!" he exclaimed, "I have not heard your voice since last night, when you came to me and sung that beautiful welcome to the swallows, which all the little children like so well."

On the preceding evening, Philothea, being urged by her maidens to sing, had actually warbled that little song; thinking all the while of the days of childhood, when she and Paralus used to sing it, to please their young companions. When she heard this mysterious allusion to the music, she looked at Plato with an expression of surprise; while Milza and the other attendants seemed afraid in the presence of one thus visited by the gods.

With looks full of beaming affection, the invalid continued: "And now, Philothea, we will again walk to that pleasant place, where we went when you finished the song."

In low and soothing tones, the maiden inquired, "Where did we go, Paralus?"

"Have you forgotten?" he replied. "We went hand in hand up a high mountain. A path wound round it in spiral flexures, ever ascending, and communicating with all above and all below. A stream of water, pure as crystal, flowed along the path, from the summit to the base. Where we stood to rest awhile, the skies were of transparent blue; but higher up, the light was purple and the trees full of doves. We saw little children leading lambs to drink at the stream, and they raised their voices in glad shouts, to see the bright waters go glancing and glittering down the sides of the mountain."

He remained silent and motionless for several minutes; and then continued: "But this path is dreary. I do not like this wide marsh, and these ruined temples. Who spoke then and told me it was Athens? But now I see the groves of Academus. There is a green meadow in the midst, on which rests a broad belt of sunshine. Above it, are floating little children with wings; and they throw down garlands to little children without wings, who are looking upward with joyful faces. Oh, how beautiful they are! Come, Philothea, let us join them."

The philosopher smiled, and inwardly hailed the words as an omen auspicious to his doctrines. All who listened were deeply impressed by language so mysterious.

The silence remained unbroken, until Paralus asked for music. A cithara being brought, Philothea played one of his favourite songs, accompanied by her voice. The well-remembered sounds seemed to fill him with joy beyond his power to express; and again his anxious parent cherished the hope that reason would be fully restored.

He put his hand affectionately on Philothea's head, as he said, "Your presence evidently has a blessed influence; but oh, my daughter, what a sacrifice you are making—young and beautiful as you are!"

"Nay, Pericles," she replied, "I deem it a privilege once more to hear the sound of his voice; though it speaks a strange, unearthly language."

When they attempted to lead the invalid from the apartment, and Philothea, with a tremulous voice, said, "Farewell, Paralus,"—an expression of intense gloom came over his countenance, suddenly as a sunny field is obscured by passing clouds. "Not farewell to Eurydice!" he said: "It is sad music—sad music."

The tender-hearted maiden was affected even to tears, and found it hard to submit to a temporary separation. But Pericles assured her that his son would probably soon fall asleep, and awake without any recollection of recent events. Before she retired to her couch, a messenger was sent to inform her that Paralus was in deep repose.

Clinias having removed from the unhealthy Piræus, in search of purer atmosphere, Philothea found him in the house once occupied by Phidias; and the hope that scenes of past happiness might prove salutary to the mind of Paralus, induced Pericles to prepare the former dwelling of Anaxagoras for his bridal home. The friends and relations of the invalid were extremely desirous to have Philothea's soothing influence continually exerted upon him; and the disinterested maiden earnestly wished to devote every moment of her life to the restoration of his precious health. Under these circumstances, it was deemed best that the marriage should take place immediately.

The mother of Paralus had died; and Aspasia, with cautious delicacy, declined being present at the ceremony, under the pretext of ill health; but Phoenarete, the wife of Clinias, gladly consented to act as mother of the orphan bride.

Propitiatory sacrifices were duly offered to Artemis, Hera, Pallas, Aphrodite, the Fates, and the Graces. On the appointed day, Philothea appeared in bridal garments, prepared by Phoenarete. The robe of fine Milesian texture, was saffron-coloured, with a purple edge. Over this, was a short tunic of brilliant crimson, confined at the waist by an embroidered zone, fastened with a broad clasp of gold. Glossy braids of hair were intertwined with the folds of her rose-coloured veil; and both bride and bridegroom were crowned with garlands of roses and myrtle. The chariot, in which they were seated, was followed by musicians, and a long train of friends and relatives. Arrived at the temple of Hera, the priest presented a branch, which they held between them as a symbol of the ties about to unite them. Victims were sacrificed, and the omens declared not unpropitious. When the gall had been cast behind the altar, Clinias placed Philothea's hand within the hand of Paralus; the bride dedicated a ringlet of her hair to Hera; the customary vows were pronounced by the priest; and the young couple were presented with golden cups of wine, from which they poured libations. The invalid was apparently happy; but so unconscious of the scene he was acting, that his father was obliged to raise his hand and pour forth the wine.

The ceremonies being finished, the priest reminded Philothea that when a good wife died, Persephone formed a procession of the best women to scatter flowers in her path, and lead her spirit to Elysium. As he spoke, two doves alighted on the altar; but one immediately rose, and floated above the other, with a tender cooing sound. Its mate looked upward for a moment; and then both of them rose high in the air, and disappeared. The spectators hailed this as an auspicious omen; but Philothea pondered it in her heart, and thought she perceived a deeper meaning than was visible to them.

As the company returned, with the joyful sound of music, many a friendly hand threw garlands from the housetops, and many voices pronounced a blessing.

In consideration of the health of Paralus, the customary evening procession was dispensed with. An abundant feast was prepared at the house of Clinias. The gentle and serious bride joined with her female friends in the apartments of the women; but no bridegroom appeared at the banquet of the men.

As the guests seated themselves at table, a boy came in covered with thorn-boughs and acorns, bearing a golden basket filled with bread, and singing, "I have left the worse and found the better." As he passed through the rooms, musicians began to play on various instruments, and troops of young dancers moved in airy circles to the sound.

At an early hour, Philothea went to the apartment prepared for her in the home of her childhood. Phoenarete preceded her with a lighted torch, and her female attendants followed, accompanied by young Pericles, bearing on his head a vase of water from the Fountain of Callirhöe, with which custom required that the bride's feet should be bathed. Music was heard until a late hour, and epithalamia were again resumed with the morning light.

The next day, a procession of women brought the bridal gifts of friends and relatives, preceded by a boy clothed in white, carrying a torch in one hand, and a basket of flowers in the other. Philothea, desirous to please the father of her husband, had particularly requested that this office might be performed by the youthful Pericles—a beautiful boy, the only son of Aspasia. The gifts were numerous; consisting of embroidered sandals, perfume boxes of ivory inlaid with gold, and various other articles, for use or ornament. Pericles sent a small ivory statue of Persephone gathering flowers in the vale of Enna; and Aspasia a clasp, representing the Naiades floating with the infant Eros, bound in garlands.

The figures were intaglio, in a gem of transparent cerulean hue, and delicately painted. When viewed from the opposite side, the effect was extremely beautiful; for the graceful nymphs seemed actually moving in their native element Alcibiades presented a Sidonian veil, of roseate hue and glossy texture. Phoenarete bestowed a ring, on which was carved a dancing Oread; and Plato a cameo clasp, representing the infant Eros crowning a lamb with a garland of lilies.

On the third day, custom allowed every relative to see the bride with her face unveiled; and the fame of her surpassing beauty induced the remotest connections of the family to avail themselves of the privilege. Philothea meekly complied with these troublesome requisitions; but her heart was weary for quiet hours, that she might hold free communion with Paralus, in that beautiful spirit-land, where his soul was wandering before its time.

Music, and the sound of Philothea's voice, seemed the only links that connected him with a world of shadows; but his visions were so blissful, and his repose so full of peace, that restless and ambitious men might well have envied a state thus singularly combining the innocence of childhood with the rich imagination of maturer years.

Many weeks passed away in bright tranquillity; and the watchful wife thought she at times perceived faint indication of returning health. Geta and Milza, in compliance with their own urgent entreaties, were her constant assistants in nursing the invalid; and more than once she imagined that he looked at them with an earnest expression, as if his soul were returning to the recollections of former years.

Spring ripened into summer. The olive-garlands twined with wool, suspended on the doors during the festival of Thargelia, had withered and fallen; and all men talked of the approaching commemoration of the Olympic games.

Hippocrates had been informed that Tithonus, the Ethiopian, possessed the singular power of leading the soul from the body, and again restoring it to its functions, by means of a soul-directing wand; and the idea arose in his mind, that this process might produce a salutary effect on Paralus.

The hopes of the anxious father were easily kindled; and he at once became desirous that his son should be conveyed to Olympia; for it was reported that Tithonus would be present at the games.

Philothea sighed deeply, as she listened to the proposition; for she had faith only in the healing power of perfect quiet, and the free communion of congenial souls. She yielded to the opinion of Pericles with characteristic humility; but the despondency of her tones did not pass unobserved.

"It is partly for your sake that I wish it, my poor child," said he. "If it may be avoided, I will not see the whole of your youth consumed in anxious watchings."

The young wife looked up with a serene and bright expression, as she replied, "Nay, my father, you have never seen me anxious, or troubled. I have known most perfect contentment since my union with your son."

Pericles answered affectionately, "I believe it, my daughter; and I have marvelled at your cheerfulness. Assuredly, with more than Helen's beauty, you have inherited the magical Egyptian powder, whereby she drove away all care and melancholy."

CHAPTER XIV.

Iphegenia—Absent so long, with joy I look on thee.
Agamemnon—And I on thee; so this is mutual joy.
EURIPIDES.

In accordance with the advice of Hippocrates, the journey to Olympia was undertaken. Some time before the commencement of the games, a party, consisting of Pericles, Plato, Paralus, Philothea, and their attendants, made preparations for departure.

Having kissed the earth of Athens, and sacrificed to Hermes and Hecate, the protectors of travellers, they left the city at the Dipylon Gate, and entered the road leading to Eleusis. The country presented a cheerless aspect; for fields and vineyards once fruitful were desolated by ferocious war. But religious veneration had protected the altars, and their chaste simplicity breathed the spirit of peace; while the beautiful little rustic temples of Demeter, in commemoration of her wanderings in search of the lost Persephone, spoke an ideal language, soothing to the heart amid the visible traces of man's destructive passions.

During the solemnization of the Olympic Games, the bitterest animosities were laid aside. The inhabitants of states carrying on a deadly war with each other, met in peace and friendship. Even Megara, with all her hatred to Athens, gave the travellers a cordial welcome. In every house they entered, bread, wine, and salt, were offered to Zeus Xinias, the patron of hospitality.

A pleasant grove of cypress trees announced the vicinity of Corinth, famed for its magnificence and beauty. A foot-path from the grove led to a secluded spot, where water was spouted forth by a marble dolphin, at the foot of a brazen statue of Poseidon.

The travellers descended from their chariots to rest under the shadow of the lofty plane trees, and refresh themselves with a draught from the fountain. The public road was thronged with people on their way to Olympia. Most of them drove with renewed eagerness to enter Corinth before the evening twilight; for nearly all travellers made it a point to visit the remarkable scenes in this splendid and voluptuous city, the Paris of the ancient world. A few were attracted by the cool murmuring of the waters, and turned aside to the fountain of Poseidon. Among these was Artaphernes the Persian, who greeted Pericles, and made known his friend Orsames, lately arrived from Ecbatana. The stranger said he had with him a parcel for Anaxagoras; and inquired whether any tidings of that philosopher had been lately received in Athens. Pericles informed them of the death of the good old man, and mentioned that his grand-daughter, accompanied by her husband and attendants, was then in a retired part of the grove. The Persian took from his chariot a roll of parchment and a small box, and placed them in the hands of Geta, to be conveyed to Philothea. The tears came to her eyes, when she discovered that it was a friendly epistle from Philæmon to his beloved old master. It appeared to have been written soon after he heard of his exile, and was accompanied by a gift of four minæ. His own situation was described as happy as it could be in a foreign land. His time was principally employed in instructing the sons of the wealthy satrap, Megabyzus; a situation which he owed to the friendly recommendation of Artaphernes. At the close, after many remarks concerning the politics of Athens, he expressed a wish to be informed of Eudora's fate, and an earnest hope that she was not beyond the reach of Philothea's influence.

This letter awakened busy thoughts. The happy past and a cheerful future were opened to her mind, in all the distinctness of memory and the brightness of hope. At such moments, her heart yearned for the ready sympathy she had been wont to receive from Paralus. As she drew aside the curtains of the litter, and looked upon him in tranquil slumber, she thought of the wonderful gift of Tithonus, with an intense anxiety, to which her quiet spirit was usually a stranger. Affectionate recollections of Eudora, and the anticipated joy of meeting, mingled with this deeper tide of feeling, and increased her desire to arrive at the end of their journey. Pericles shared her anxiety, and admitted no delays but such as were necessary for the health of the invalid.

From Corinth they passed into the pleasant valleys of Arcadia, encircled with verdant hills. Here nature reigned in simple beauty, unadorned by the magnificence of art. The rustic temples were generally composed of intertwined trees, in the recesses of which were placed wooden images of Pan, "the simple shepherd's awe-inspiring god." Here and there an aged man reposed in the shadow of some venerable oak; and the shepherds, as they tended their flocks, welcomed this brief interval of peace with the mingled music of reeds and flutes.

Thence the travellers passed into the broad and goodly plains of Elis; protected from the spoiler by its sacred character, as the seat of the Olympic Games. In some places, troops of women might be seen in the distance, washing garments in the river Alpheus, and spreading them out to whiten in the sun. Fertility rewarded the labours of the husbandmen, and the smiling fields yielded pasturage to numerous horses, which Phoebus himself might have prized for strength, fleetness, and majestic beauty.

Paralus passed through all these scenes entirely unconscious whether they were sad or cheerful. When he spoke, it was of things unrecognized by those of earthly mould; yet those who heard him found therein a strange and marvellous beauty, that seemed not altogether new to the soul, but was seen in a dim and pleasing light, like the recollections of infant years.

The travellers stopped at a small town in the neighbourhood of Olympia, where Paralus, Philothea, and their attendants were to remain during the solemnization of the games. The place chosen for their retreat was the residence of Proclus and his wife Melissa; worthy, simple-hearted people, at whose house Phidias had died, and under whose protection he had placed Eudora.

As the chariots approached the house, the loud barking of Hylax attracted the attention of Zoila, the merry little daughter of Proclus, who was playing in the fields with her brother Pterilaüs. The moment the children espied a sight so unusual in that secluded place, they ran with all speed to carry tidings to the household. Eudora was busy at the loom; but she went out to look upon the strangers, saying, as she did so, that they were doubtless travellers, who, in passing to the Olympic Games, had missed their way.

Her heart beat tumultuously when she saw Hylax capering and fawning about a man who bore a strong resemblance to Geta. The next moment, she recognized Pericles and Plato speaking with a tall, majestic looking woman, closely veiled. She darted forward a few paces, in the eagerness of her joy; but checked herself when she perceived that the stranger lingered; for she said, in her heart, "If it were Philothea, she could not be so slow in coming to meet me."

Thus she reasoned, not knowing that Philothea was the wife of Paralus, and that his enfeebled health required watchful care. In a few moments her doubts were dispelled, and the friends were locked in each others' arms.

Proclus gave the travellers a hospitable reception, and cheerfully consented that Paralus and his attendants should remain with them. Pericles, having made all necessary arrangements for the beloved invalid, bade an early farewell, and proceeded with Plato to Olympia.

When Geta and Milza had received a cordial welcome; and Hylax had somewhat abated his boisterous joy; and old Dione, with the tears in her eyes, had brought forward treasures of grapes and wine—Eudora eagerly sought a private interview with the friend of her childhood.

"Dearest Philothea!" she exclaimed, "I thought you were still in Ionia; and I never expected to see you again; and now you have come, my heart is *so* full"——

Unable to finish the sentence, she threw herself on that bosom where she had ever found sympathy in all her trials, and sobbed like a child.

"My beloved Eudora," said Philothea, "you still carry with you a heart easily kindled; affections that heave and blaze like a volcano."

The maiden looked up affectionately, and smiled through her tears, as she said, "The love you kindled in infancy has burned none the less strongly because there was no one to cherish it. If the volcano now blazes, it only proves how faithfully it has carried the hidden fire in its bosom."

She paused, and spoke more sadly, as she added, "There was, indeed, one brief period, when it was well-nigh smothered. Would to the gods, *that* might pass into oblivion! But it will not. After Phidias came to Elis, he made for Plato a small statue of Mnemosyne, that turned and looked upward to Heaven, while she held a half-opened scroll toward the earth. It was beautiful beyond description; but there was bitterness in my heart when I looked upon it; I thought Memory should be represented armed with the scourge of the Furies."

"And did you not perceive," said Philothea, "that yourself had armed the benignant goddess with a scourge? Thus do the best gifts from the Divine Fountain become changed by the will of those who receive them. But, dearest Eudora, though your heart retains its fire, a change has passed over your countenance. The cares of this world have driven away the spirit of gladness, that came with you from your divine home. That smiling twin of Innocence is ever present and visible while we are unconscious of its existence; but when in darkness and sorrow the soul asks where it has gone, a hollow voice, like the sound of autumn winds, echoes, 'Gone!'"

Eudora sighed, as she answered, "It is even so. But I know not where you could have learned it; for you have ever seemed to live in a region above darkness and storms. Earth has left no shadow on your countenance. It expresses the same transparent innocence, the same mild love. A light not of this world is gleaming there; and it has grown brighter and clearer since we parted. I could almost believe that you accompany Hera to the Fountain of Canathus, where it is said she every year bathes to restore her infant purity."

Philothea smiled, as she playfully laid her hand on Eudora's mouth, and said, "Nay, Eudora, you forget that flattery produces effects very unlike the Fountain of Canathus. We have been gazing in each other's faces, as if we fondly hoped there to read the record of all that has passed since we were separated. Yet, very little of all that we have known and felt—of all that has gradually become a portion of our life—is inscribed there. Perhaps you already know that Anaxagoras fell asleep in Ionia. The good old man died in peace, as he had lived in love. If I mistake not, while I talked with Pericles, Milza informed you that I was the wife of Paralus?"

"Yes, dearest Philothea; but not till she had first told me of her own marriage with Geta."

Philothea smiled, as she replied, "I believe it is the only case in which that affectionate creature thinks of herself, before she thinks of me; but Geta is to her an object of more importance than all the world beside. When we were in Ionia, I often found her whispering magical words, while she turned the sieve and shears, to ascertain whether her lover were faithful to his vows. I could not find it in my heart to reprove her fond credulity;—for I believe this proneness to wander beyond the narrow limits of the visible world is a glimmering reminiscence of parentage divine; and though in Milza's untutored mind the mysterious impulse takes an inglorious form, I dare not deride what the wisest soul can neither banish nor comprehend."

As she finished speaking, she glanced toward the curtain, which separated them from the room where Paralus reposed, watched by the faithful Geta. There was a tender solemnity in the expression of her countenance, whereby Eudora conjectured the nature of her thoughts. Speaking in a subdued voice, she asked whether Paralus would inquire for her, when he awoke.

"He will look for me, and seem bewildered, as if something were lost," replied Philothea. "Since I perceived this, I have been careful not to excite painful sensations by my absence. Geta will give me notice when slumber seems to be passing away."

"And do you think Tithonus can restore him?" inquired Eudora.

Philothea answered, "Fear is stronger than hope. I thought I perceived a healing influence in the perfect quiet and watchful love that surrounded him in Athens; and to these I would fain have trusted, had it been the will of Pericles. But, dearest Eudora, let us not speak on this subject. It seems to me like the sacred groves, into which nothing unconsecrated may enter."

After a short pause, Eudora said. "Then I will tell you my own history. After we came to Elis, Phidias treated me with more tenderness and confidence than he had ever done. Perhaps he observed that my proud, impetuous character was chastened and subdued by affliction and repentance. Though we were in the habit of talking unreservedly, he never alluded to the foolish conduct that offended him so seriously. I felt grateful for this generous forbearance; and by degress I learned to fear him less and love him deeply."

"We received some tidings of him when Plato came into Ionia," rejoined Philothea; "and we rejoiced to learn that he found in Elis a rich recompense for the shameful ingratitude of Athens."

"It was a rich recompense, indeed," replied Eudora. "The people reverenced him as if he were something more than mortal. His statue stands in the sacred grove at Olympia, bearing the simple inscription; 'Phidias, Son of Charmides, sculptor of the Gods.' At his death, the Elians bestowed gifts on all his servants; endowed me with the yearly revenues of a farm; and appointed his nephew Pandænus to the honourable office of preserving the statue of Olympian Zeus."

"Did Phidias express no anxiety concerning your unprotected situation?" inquired Philothea.

"It was his wish that I should marry Pandænus," answered Eudora; "but he urged the subject no farther, when he found that I regarded the marriage with aversion. On his death-bed he charged his nephew to protect and cherish me as a sister. He left me under the guardianship of Proclus, with strict injunctions that I should have perfect freedom in the choice of a husband. He felt no anxiety concerning my maintenance; for the Elians had promised that all persons connected with him should be liberally provided at the public expense; and I was universally considered as the adopted daughter of Phidias."

"And what did Pandænus say to the wishes of his uncle?" asked Philothea.

Eudora blushed slightly as she answered, "He tried to convince me that we should all be happier, if I would consent to the arrangement. I could not believe this; and Pandænus was too proud to repeat his solicitations to a reluctant listener. I seldom see him; but when there is opportunity to do me service, he is very kind."

Her friend looked earnestly upon her, as if seeking to read her heart; and inquired, "Has no other one gained your affections? I had some fears that I should find you married."

"And why did you fear?" said Eudora: "Other friends would consider it a joyful occasion."

"But I feared, because I have ever cherished the hope that you would be the wife of Philæmon," rejoined her companion.

The sensitive maiden sighed deeply, and turned away her head, as she said, with a tremulous voice, "I have little doubt that Philæmon has taken a Persian wife, before this time."

Philothea made no reply; but searched for the epistle she had received at Corinth, and placed it in the hands of her friend. Eudora started, when she saw the well-known writing of Philæmon. But when she read the sentence wherein he expressed affectionate solicitude for her welfare, she threw her arms convulsively about Philothea's neck, exclaiming, "Oh, my beloved friend, what a blessed messenger you have ever been to this poor heart!"

For some moments, her agitation was extreme; but that gentle influence, which had so often soothed her, gradually calmed her perturbed feelings; and they talked freely of the possibility of regaining Philæmon's love.

As Eudora stood leaning on her shoulder, Philothea, struck with the contrast in their figures, said: "When you were in Athens, we called you the Zephyr; and surely you are thinner now than you were then. I fear your health suffers from the anxiety of your mind. "See!" continued she, turning towards the mirror—"See what a contrast there is between us!"

"There should be a contrast," rejoined Eudora, smiling: "The pillars of agoras are always of lighter and less majestic proportions than the pillars of temples."

As she spoke, Geta lifted the curtain, and Philothea instantly obeyed the signal. For a few moments after her departure, Eudora heard the low murmuring of voices, and then the sound of a cithara, whose tones she well remembered. The tune was familiar to her in happier days, and she listened to it with tears.

Her meditations were suddenly disturbed by little Zoila, who came in with a jump and a bound, to show a robe full of flowers she had gathered for the beautiful Athenian lady. When she perceived that tears had fallen on the blossoms, she suddenly changed her merry tones, and with artless affection inquired, "What makes Dora cry?"

"I wept for the husband of that beautiful Athenian lady, because he is very ill," replied the maiden.

"See the flowers!" exclaimed Zoila. "It looks as if the dew was on it; but the tears will not make it grow again—will they?"

Eudora involuntarily shuddered at the omen conveyed in her childish words; but gave permission to carry her offering to the Athenian lady, if she would promise to step very softly, and speak in whispers. Philothea received the flowers thankfully, and placed them in vases near her husband's couch; for she still fondly hoped to win back the wandering soul by the presence of things peaceful, pure, and beautiful. She caressed the innocent little one, and tried to induce her to remain a few minutes; but the child seemed uneasy, as if in the presence of something that inspired fear. She returned to Eudora with a very thoughtful countenance; and though she often gathered flowers for "the tall infant," as she called Paralus, she could never after be persuaded to enter his apartment.

CHAPTER XV.

> They in me breathed a voice
> Divine; that I might know, with listening ears,
> Things past and future; and enjoined me praise
> The race of blessed ones, that live for aye.
>
> HESIOD

PHILOTHEA to PHILÆMON, greeting:

The body of Anaxagoras has gone to the Place of Sleep. If it were not so, his hand would have written in reply to thy kind epistle. I was with him when he died, but knew not the hour he departed, for he sunk to rest like an infant.

We lived in peaceful poverty in Ionia; sometimes straitened for the means whereby this poor existence is preserved, but ever cheerful in spirit.

I drank daily from the ivory cup thou didst leave for me, with thy farewell to Athens; and the last lines traced by my grandfather's hand still remain on the tablet thou didst give him. They are preserved for thee, to be sent in to Persia, if thou dost not return to Greece, as I hope thou wilt.

I am now the wife of Paralus; and Pericles has brought us into the neighbourhood of Olympia, seeking medical aid for my husband, not yet recovered from the effects of the plague. Pure and blameless, Paralus has ever been—with a mind richly endowed by the gods; and all this thou well knowest. Yet he is as one that dies while he lives; though not altogether as one unbeloved by divine beings. Wonderful are the accounts he brings of that far-off world, where his spirit wanders. Sometimes I listen with fear, till all philosophy seems dim, and I shrink from the mystery of our being. When they do not disturb him with earthly medicines, he is quiet and happy. Waking, he speaks of things clothed in heavenly splendour; and in his sleep, he smiles like a child whose dreams are pleasant. I think this blessing comes from the Divine, by reason of the innocence of his life.

We abide at the house of Proclus, a kind, truth-telling man, whose wife, Melissa, is at once diligent and quiet—a rare combination of goodly virtues. These worthy people have been guardians of Eudora, since the death of Phidias; and with much affection, they speak of her gentleness, patience, and modest retirement. Melissa told me Aspasia had urgently invited her to Athens, but she refused, without even asking the advice of her guardian. Thou knowest her great gifts would have been worshipped by the Athenians, and that Eudora herself could not be ignorant of this.

Sometimes a stream is polluted in the fountain, and its waters are tainted through all its wanderings; and sometimes the traveller throws into a pure rivulet some unclean thing, which floats awhile, and is then rejected from its bosom. Eudora is the pure rivulet. A foreign stain floated on the surface, but never mingled with its waters.

Phidias wished her to marry his nephew; and Pandænus would fain have persuaded her to consent; but they forebore to urge it, when they saw it gave her pain. She is deeply thankful to her benefactor for allowing her a degree of freedom so seldom granted to Grecian maidens.

The Elians, proud of their magnificent statue of Olympian Zeus, have paid extraordinary honours to the memory of the great sculptor, and provided amply for every member of his household. Eudora is industrious from choice, and gives liberally to the poor; particularly to orphans, who, like herself, have been brought into bondage by the violence of wicked men, or the chances of war. For some time past, she has felt all alone in the world;—a condition that marvellously helps to bring us into meekness and tenderness of spirit. When she read what thou didst write of her in thy epistle, she fell upon my neck and wept.

I return to thee the four minæ. He to whose necessities thou wouldst have kindly administered, hath gone where gold and silver avail not. Many believe that they who die sleep forever; but this they could not, if they had listened to words I have heard from Paralus.

Son of Chærilaüs, farewell. May blessings be around thee, wheresoever thou goest, and no evil shadow cross thy threshold.

Written in Elis, this thirteenth day of the increasing moon, in the month Hecatombæon, and the close of the eighty-seventh Olympiad."

Without naming her intention to Eudora, Philothea laid aside the scroll she had prepared, resolved to place it in the hands of Pericles, to be entrusted to the care of some Persian present at the games, which were to commence on the morrow.

Before the hour of noon, Hylax gave notice of approaching strangers, who proved to be Pericles and Plato, attended by Tithonus. The young wife received them courteously, though a sudden sensation of dread ran through her veins with icy coldness. It was agreed that none but herself, Pericles, and Plato, should be present with Tithonus; and that profound silence should be observed. Preparation was made by offering solemn sacrifices to Phoebus, Hermes, Hecate, and Persephone; and Philothea inwardly prayed to that Divine Principle, revealed to her only by the monitions of his spirit in the stillness of her will.

Tithonus stood behind the invalid, and remained perfectly quiet for many minutes. He then gently touched the back part of his head with a small wand, and leaning over him, whispered in his ear. An unpleasant change immediately passed over the countenance of Paralus; he endeavoured to place his hand on his head, and a cold shivering seized him. Philothea shuddered, and Pericles grew pale, as they watched these symptoms; but the silence remained unbroken. A second and a third time the Ethiopian touched him with his wand, and spoke in whispers. The expression of pain deepened; insomuch that his friends could not look upon him without anguish of heart. Finally his limbs straightened, and became perfectly rigid and motionless.

Tithonus, perceiving the terror he had excited, said soothingly, "Oh, Athenians, be not afraid. I have never seen the soul withdrawn without a struggle with the body. Believe me, it will return. The words I whispered, were those I once heard from the lips of Plato: 'The human soul is guided by two horses; one white, with a flowing mane, earnest eyes, and wings like a swan, whereby he seeks to fly; but the other is black, heavy and sleepy-eyed—ever prone to lie down upon the earth.'

"The second time, I whispered, 'Lo, the soul seeketh to ascend!' And the third time I said, 'Behold the winged separates from that which hath no wings.' When life returns, Paralus will have remembrance of these words."

"Oh, restore him! Restore him!" exclaimed Philothea, in tones of agonized entreaty.

Tithonus answered with respectful tenderness, and again stood in profound silence several minutes, before he raised the wand. At the first touch, a feeble shivering gave indication of returning life. As it was repeated a second and a third time, with a brief interval between each movement, the countenance of the sufferer grew more dark and troubled, until it became fearful to look upon. But the heavy shadow gradually passed away, and a dreamy smile returned, like a gleam of sunshine after storms. The moment Philothea perceived an expression familiar to her heart, she knelt by the couch, seized the hand of Paralus, and bathed it with her tears.

When the first gush of emotion had subsided, she said, in a soft, low voice, "Where have you been, dear Paralus?" The invalid answered: "A thick vapour enveloped me, as with a dark cloud; and a stunning noise pained my head with its violence. A voice said to me, 'The human soul is guided by two horses; one white, with a flowing mane, earnest eyes, and wings like a swan, whereby he seeks to fly; but the other is black, heavy, and sleepy-eyed—ever prone to lie down upon the earth.' Then the darkness began to clear away. But there was strange confusion. All things seemed rapidly to interchange their colours and their forms—the sound of a storm was in mine ears—the elements and the stars seemed to crowd upon me—and my breath was taken away. Then I heard a voice, saying, 'Lo, the soul seeketh to ascend!' And I looked and saw the chariot and horses, of which the voice had spoken. The beautiful white horse gazed upward, and tossed his mane, and spread his wings impatiently; but the black horse slept upon the ground. The voice again said, 'Behold the winged separates from that which hath no wings!' And suddenly the chariot ascended, and I saw the white horse on light fleecy clouds, in a far blue sky. Then I heard a pleasing, silent sound—as if dew-drops made music as they fell. I breathed freely, and my form seemed to expand itself with buoyant life. All at once, I was floating in the air, above a quiet lake, where reposed seven beautiful islands, full of the sound of harps; and Philothea slept at my side, with a garland on her head. I asked, 'Is this the divine home, whence I departed into the body?' And a voice above my head answered 'It is the divine home. Man never leaves it. He ceases to perceive.' Afterward, I looked downward, and saw my dead body lying on a couch. Then again there came strange confusion—and a painful clashing of sounds—and all things rushing together. But Philothea took my hand, and spoke to me in gentle tones, and the discord ceased."

Plato had listened with intense interest. He stood apart with Tithonus, and they spoke together in low tones, for several minutes before they left the apartment. The philosopher was too deeply impressed to return to the festivities of Olympia. He hired an apartment at the dwelling of a poor shepherd, and during the following day remained in complete seclusion, without partaking of food.

While Paralus revealed his vision, his father's soul was filled with reverence and fear, and he breathed with a continual consciousness of supernatural presence. When his feelings became somewhat composed, he leaned over the couch, and spoke a few affectionate words to his son; but the invalid turned away his head, as if disturbed by the presence of a stranger. The spirit of the strong man was moved, and he trembled like a leaf shaken by the wind. Unable to endure this disappointment of his excited hopes, he turned away hastily, and sought to conceal his grief in solitude.

During the whole of the ensuing day, Paralus continued in a deep sleep. This was followed by silent cheerfulness, which, flowing as it did from a hidden source, had something solemn and impressive in its character. It was sad, yet pleasant, to see his look of utter desolation whenever he lost sight of Philothea; and the sudden gleam of joy that illumined his whole face the moment she re-appeared.

The young wife sat by his side, hour after hour, with patient love; often cheering him with her soft, rich voice, or playing upon the lyre he had fashioned for her in happier days. She found a sweet reward in the assurance given by all his friends, that her presence had a healing power they had elsewhere sought in vain. She endeavoured to pour balm into the wounded heart of Pericles, and could she have seen him willing to wait the event with perfect resignation, her contentment would have been not unmingled with joy.

She wept in secret when she heard him express a wish to have Paralus carried to the games, to try the effect of a sudden excitement; for there seemed to her something of cruelty in thus disturbing the tranquillity of one so gentle and so helpless. But the idea had been suggested by a learned physician of Chios, and Pericles seemed reluctant to return to Athens without trying this experiment also. Philothea found it more difficult to consent to the required sacrifice, because the laws of the country made it impossible to accompany her beloved husband to Olympia; but she suppressed her feelings; and the painfulness of the struggle was never fully confessed, even to Eudora.

While the invalid slept, he was carefully conveyed in a litter, and placed in the vicinity of the Hippodrome. He awoke in the midst of a gorgeous spectacle. Long lines of splendid chariots were ranged on either side of the barrier; the horses proudly pawed the ground, and neighed impatiently; the bright sun glanced on glittering armour; and the shouts of the charioteers were heard high above the busy hum of that vast multitude.

Paralus instantly closed his eyes, as if dazzled by the glare; and an expression of painful bewilderment rested on his countenance.

In the midst of the barrier stood an altar, on the top of which was a brazen eagle. When the lists were in readiness, the majestic bird arose and spread its wings, with a whirring noise, as a signal for the racers to begin. Then was heard the clattering of hoofs, and the rushing of wheels, as when armies meet in battle. A young Messenian was, for a time, foremost in the race; but his horse took fright at the altar of Taraxippus—his chariot was overthrown—and Alcibiades gained the prize. The vanquished youth uttered a loud and piercing shriek, as the horses passed over him; and Paralus fell senseless in his father's arms.

It was never known whether this effect was produced by the presence of a multitude, by shrill and discordant sounds, or by returning recollection, too powerful for his enfeebled frame. He was tenderly carried from the crowd, and restoratives having been applied, in vain, the melancholy burden was slowly and carefully conveyed to her who so anxiously awaited his arrival.

During his absence, Philothea had earnestly prayed for the preservation of a life so precious to her; and as the time of return drew near, she walked in the fields, accompanied by Eudora and Milza, eager to catch the first glimpse of his father's chariot. She read sad tidings in the gloomy countenance of Pericles, before she beheld the lifeless form of her husband.

Cautiously and tenderly as the truth was revealed to her, she became dizzy and pale, with the suddenness of the shock. Pericles endeavoured to soothe her with all the sympathy of a parental love, mingled with deep feelings of contrition, that his restless anxiety had thus brought ruin into her paradise of peace: and Plato spoke gentle words of consolation; reminding her that every soul, which philosophized sincerely and loved beautiful forms, was restored to the full vigour of its wings, and soared to the blest condition from which it fell.

They laid Paralus upon a couch, with the belief that he slept to wake no more. But as Philothea bent over him, she perceived a faint pulsation of the heart. Her pale features were flushed with joy, as she exclaimed, "He lives! He will speak to me again! Oh, I could die in peace,—if I might once more hear his voice, as I heard it in former years."

She bathed his head with cool perfumed waters, and watched him with love that knew no weariness.

Proclus and Telissa deemed he had fallen by the dart of Phoebus Apollo; and fearing the god was angry for some unknown cause, they suspended branches of rhamn and laurel on the doors, to keep off evil demons.

For three days and three nights, Paralus remained in complete oblivion. On the morning of the fourth, a pleasant change was observed in his countenance; and he sometimes smiled so sweetly, and so rationally, that his friends still dared to hope his health might be fully restored.

At noon, he awoke; and looking at his wife with an expression full of tenderness, said: "Dearest Philothea, you are with me. I saw you no more, after the gate had closed. I believe it must have been a dream; but it was very distinct." He glanced around the room, as if his recollections were confused; but his eyes no longer retained the fixed and awful expression of one who walked in his sleep.

Speaking slowly and thoughtfully, he continued: "It could not be a dream. I was in the temple of the most ancient god. The roof was of heaven's pure gold, which seemed to have a ligat within it, like the splendour of the sun. All around the temple were gardens full of bloom. I heard soft, mumuring sounds, like the cooing of doves; and I saw the immortal Oreades and the Naiades pouring water from golden urns. Anaxagoras stood beside me; and he said we were living in the age of innocence, when mortals could gaze on divine beings unveiled, and yet preserve their reason. They spoke another language than the Greeks; but we had no need to learn it; we seemed to breathe it in the air. The Oreades had music written on scrolls, in all the colours of the rainbow. When I asked the meaning of this, they showed me a triangle. At the top was crimson, at the right hand blue, and at the left hand yellow. And they said, 'Know ye not that all life is three-fold!' It was a dark saying; but I then thought I faintly comprehended what Pythagoras has written concerning the mysterious signification of One and Three. Many other things I saw and heard, but was forbidden to relate. The gate of the temple was an arch, supported by two figures with heavy drapery, eyes closed, and arms folded. They told me these were Sleep and Death. Over the gate was written in large letters, 'The Entrance of Mortals.' Beyond it, I saw you standing with outstretched arms, as if you sought to come to me, but could not. The air was filled with voices, that sung:

Come! join thy kindred spirit, come!
Hail to the mystic two in one!
When Sleep hath passed, thy dreams remain—
What he hath brought, Death brings again.
Come hither, kindred spirits, come!
Hail to the mystic two in one!

I tried to meet you; but as I passed through the gate, a cold air blew upon me, and all beyond was in the glimmering darkness of twilight. I would have returned, but the gate had closed; and I heard behind me the sound of harps and of voices, singing:
Come hither, kindred spirits, come!
Hail to the mystic two in one!"

Philothea kissed his hand, and her face beamed with joy. She had earnestly desired some promise of their future union; and now she felt the prayer was answered.

"Could it be a dream?" said Paralus: "Methinks I hear the music now."

Philothea smiled affectionately, as she replied: "When sleep hath passed, thy dreams remain."

As she gazed upon him, she observed that the supernatural expression of his eyes had changed; and that his countenance now wore its familiar, household smile. Still she feared to cherish the hope springing in her heart, until he looked toward the place where her attendant sat, motionless and silent, and said, "Milza, will you bring me the lyre?"

The affectionate peasant looked earnestly at Philothea, and wept as she placed it in his hand.

Making an effort to rise, he seemed surprised at his own weakness. They gently raised him, bolstered him with pillows, and told him he had long been ill.

"I have not known it," he replied. "It seems to me I have returned from a far country."

He touched the lyre, and easily recalled the tune which he said he had learned in the Land of Dreams. It was a wild, unearthly strain, with sounds of solemn gladness, that deeply affected Philothea's soul.

Pericles had not visited his son since his return to perfect consciousness. When he came, Paralus looked upon him with a smile of recognition, and said, "My father!"

Milza had been sent to call the heart-stricken parent, and prepare him for some favourable change; but when he heard those welcome words, he dropped suddenly upon his knees, buried his face in the drapery of the couch, and his whole frame shook with emotion.

The invalid continued: "They tell me I have been very ill, dear father; but it appears to me that I have only travelled. I have seen Anaxagoras often—Plato sometimes—and Philothea almost constantly; but I have never seen you, since I thought you were dying of the plague at Athens."

Pericles replied, "You have indeed been ill, my son. You are to me as the dead restored to life. But you must be quiet now, and seek repose."

For some time after the interview with his father, Paralus remained very wakeful. His eyes sparkled, and a feverish flush was on his cheek. Philothea took her cithara, and played his favourite tunes. This seemed to tranquilize him; and as the music grew more slow and plaintive, he became drowsy, and at length sunk into a gentle slumber.

After more than two hours of deep repose, he was awakened by the merry shouts of little Zoila, who had run out to meet Plato, as he came from Olympia. Philothea feared, lest the shrill noise had given him pain; but he smiled; and said, "The voice of childhood is pleasant."

He expressed a wish to see his favourite philosopher; and their kindred souls held long and sweet communion together. When Plato retired from the couch, he said to Philothea, "I have learned more from this dear wanderer, than philosophers or poets have ever written. I am confirmed in my belief that no impelling truth is ever learned in this world; but that all is received directly from the Divine Ideal, flowing into the soul of man when his reason is obedient and still."

A basket of grapes, tastefully ornamented with flowers, was presented to the invalid; and in answer to his inquiries, he was informed that they were prepared by Eudora. He immediately desired that she might be called; and when she came, he received her with the most cordial affection. He alluded to past events with great clearness of memory, and asked his father several questions concerning the condition of Athens. When Philothea arranged his pillows and bathed his head, he pressed her hand affectionately, and said, "It almost seems as if you were my wife."

Pericles, deeply affected, replied, "My dear son, she is your wife. She forgot all my pride, and consented to marry you, that she might become your nurse, when we all feared that you would be restored to us no more."

Paralus looked up with a bright expression of gratitude, and said, "I thank you, father. This was very kind. Now you will be her father, when I am gone."

Perceiving that Pericles and Eudora wept, he added: "Do not mourn because I am soon to depart. Why would ye detain my soul in this world? Its best pleasures are like the shallow gardens of Adonis, fresh and fair in the morning, and perishing at noon."

He then repeated his last vision, and asked for the lyre, that they might hear the music he had learned from immortal voices.

There was melancholy beauty in the sight of one so pale and thin, touching the lyre with an inspired countenance, and thus revealing to mortal ears the melodies of Heaven.

One by one his friends withdrew; being tenderly solicitous that he should not become exhausted by interviews prolonged beyond his strength. He was left alone with Philothea; and many precious words were spoken, that sunk deep into her heart, never to be forgotten.

But sleep departed from his eyes; and it soon became evident that the soul, in returning to its union with the body, brought with it a consciousness of corporeal suffering. This became more and more intense; and though he uttered no complaint, he said to those who asked him, that bodily pain seemed at times too powerful for endurance.

Pericles had for several days remained under the same roof, to watch the progress of recovery; but at midnight, he was called to witness convulsive struggles, that indicated approaching death.

During intervals of comparative ease, Paralus recognized his afflicted parent, and conjured him to think less of the fleeting honours of this world, which often eluded the grasp, and were always worthless in the possession.

He held Philothea's hand continually, and often spoke to her in words of consolation. Immediately after an acute spasm of pain had subsided, he asked to be turned upon his right side, that he might see her face more distinctly. As she leaned over him, he smiled faintly, and imprinted a kiss upon her lips. He remained tranquil, with his eyes fixed upon hers; and a voice within impelled her to sing:

Come hither, kindred spirits, come!
Hail to the mystic two in one!

He looked upward with a radiant expression, and feebly pressed her hand. Not long after, his eyelids closed, and sleep seemed to cover his features with her heavy veil.

Suddenly his countenance shone with a strange and impressive beauty. The soul had departed to return to earth no more.

In all his troubles, Pericles had never shed a tear; but now he rent the air with his groans, and sobbed, like a mother bereft of her child.

Philothea, though deeply bowed down in spirit, was more composed: for she heard angelic voices singing:

When sleep hath passed, thy dreams remain—
What he hath brought, Death brings again.
Come hither, kindred spirits, come!
Hail to the mystic two in one!

CHAPTER XVI.

Thus a poor father, helpless and undone,
Mourns o'er the ashes of an only son;
Takes a sad pleasure the last bones to burn,
And pour in tears, ere yet they close the urn.

HOMER

Of the immense concourse collected together at Olympia, each one pursued his pleasure, or his interest, in the way best suited to his taste. Alcibiades was proud of giving a feast corresponding in magnificence to the chariots he had brought into the course. Crowds of parasites flattered him and the other victors, to receive invitations in return; while a generous few sympathized with the vanquished. Merchants were busy forming plans for profitable negociation, and statesmen were eagerly watching every symptom of jealousy between rival states and contending parties.

One, amid that mass of human hearts, felt so little interest in all the world could offer, that she seemed already removed beyond its influence. Philothea had herself closed the eyes of her husband, and imprinted her last kiss upon his lips. Bathed in pure water, and perfumed with ointment, the lifeless form of Paralus lay wrapped in the robe he had been accustomed to wear. A wreath of parsley encircled his head, and flowers were strewn around him in profusion.

In one hand was placed an obolus, to pay the ferryman that rowed him across the river of death; and in the other, a cake made of honey and flour, to appease the triple-headed dog, which guarded the entrance to the world of souls.

The bereaved wife sat by his side, and occasionally renewed the garlands, with a quiet and serene expression, as if she still found happiness in being occupied for him who had given her his heart in the innocence and freshness of its childhood.

The food prepared by Milza's active kindness was scarcely tasted; except when she observed the tears of her faithful attendant, and sought to soothe her feelings with characterestic tenderness.

The event soon became universally known; for the hair of the deceased, consecrated to Persephone, and a vase of water at the threshold, proclaimed tidings of death within the dwelling.

Many of the assembled multitude chose to remain until the funeral solemnities were past; some from personal affection for Paralus, others from respect to the son of Pericles.

Plato sent two large vases, filled with wine and honey; Eudora provided ointments and perfumes; Alcibiades presented a white cloak, richly embroidered with silver; and the young men of Athens, present at the games, gave a silver urn, on which were sculptured weeping genii, with their torches turned downward.

Enveloped in his glittering mantle, and covered with flowers, the form of Paralus remained until the third day. The procession, which was to attend the body to the funeral pile, formed at morning twilight; for such was the custom with regard to those who died in their youth. Philothea followed the bier, dressed in white, with a wreath of roses and myrtle around her head, and a garland about the waist. She chose this beautiful manner to express her joy that his pure spirit had passed into Elysium.

At the door of the house, the nearest relatives addressed the inanimate form, so soon to be removed from the sight of mortals. In tones of anguish, almost amounting to despair, Pericles exclaimed: "Oh, my son! my son! Why didst thou leave us? Why wast thou, so richly gifted of the gods, to be taken from us in thy youth? Oh, my son, why was I left to mourn for thee?"

Instead of the usual shrieks and lamentations of Grecian women, Philothea said, in sad, heart-moving accents: "Paralus, farewell! Husband of my youth, beloved of my heart, farewell!"

Then the dead was carried out; and the procession moved forward, to the sound of many voices and many instruments, mingled in a loud and solemn dirge. The body of Paralus was reverently laid upon the funeral pile, with the garments he had been accustomed to wear; his lyre and Phrygian flute; and vases filled with oil and perfumes.

Plentiful libations of wine, honey, and milk were poured upon the ground, and the mourners smote the earth with their feet, while they uttered supplications to Hermes, Hecate, and Pluto. Pericles applied the torch to the pile, first invoking the aid of Boreas and Zephyrus, that it might consume quickly. As the flames rose, the procession walked slowly three times around the pile, moving toward the left hand. The solemn dirge was resumed, and continued until the last flickering tongue of fire was extinguished with wine. Then those who had borne the silver urn in front of the hearse, approached. Pericles, with tender reverence, gathered the whitened bones, sprinkled them with wine and perfumes, placed them within the urn, and covered it with a purple pall, inwrought with gold; which Philothea's prophetic love had prepared for the occasion.

The procession again moved forward, with torches turned downward; and the remains of Paralus were deposited in the Temple of Persephone, until his friends returned to Athens.

In token of gratitude for kind attentions bestowed by the household of Proclus, Pericles invited his family to visit the far-famed wonders of the violet-crowned city; and the eager solicitations of young Pterilaüs induced the father to accept this invitation for himself and son. As an inhabitant of consecrated Elis, without wealth, and unknown to fame, it was deemed that he might return in safety, even after hostilities were renewed between the Peloponessian states. Eudora likewise obtained permission to accompany her friend; and her sad farewell was cheered by an indefinite hope that future times would restore her to that quiet home. The virtuous Melissa parted from them with many blessings and tears. Zoila was in an agony of childish sorrow; but she wiped her eyes with the corner of her robe, and listened, well pleased, to Eudora's parting promise of sending her a flock of marble sheep, with a painted wooden shepherd.

The women travelled together in a chariot, in front of which reposed the silver urn, covered with its purple pall. Thus sadly did Philothea return through the same scenes she had lately traversed with hopes, which, in the light of memory, now seemed like positive enjoyment. Pericles indeed treated her with truly parental tenderness; and no soothing attention, that respect or affection could suggest, was omitted by her friends. But he, of whose mysterious existence her own seemed a necessary portion, had gone to return no more; and had it not been for the presence of Eudora, she would have felt that every bond of sympathy with this world of forms had ceased forever.

At Corinth, the travellers again turned aside to the Fountain of Poseidon, that the curiosity of Pterilaüs might be satisfied with a view of the statues by which it was surrounded.

"When we are in Athens, I will show you something more beautiful than these," said Pericles. "You shall see the Pallas Athenæ, carved by Phidias."

"Men say it is not so grand as the statue of Zeus, that we have at Olympia," replied the boy.

"Had you rather witness the sports of the gymnasia than the works of artists?" inquired Plato.

The youth answered very promptly, "Ah, no indeed. I would rather gain one prize from the Choragus, than ten from the Gymnasiarch. Anniceris, the Cyrenæan, proudly displayed his skill in chariot-driving, by riding several times around the Academia, each time preserving the exact orbit of his wheels. The spectators applauded loudly; but Plato said, 'He who has bestowed such diligence to acquire trifling and useless things, must have neglected those that are truly admirable.' Of all sights in Athens, I most wish to see the philosophers; and none so much as Plato."

The company smiled, and the philosopher answered, "I am Plato."

"You told us that your name was Aristocles," returned Pterilaüs; "and we always called you so. Once I heard that Athenian lady call you Plato; and I could not understand why she did so."

"I was named Aristocles for my grandfather," answered the philosopher; "and when I grew older, men called me Plato."

"But you cannot be the Plato that I mean," said Pterilaüs; "for you carried my little sister Zoila on your shoulders—and played peep with her among the vines; and when I chased you through the fields, you ran so fast that I could not catch you." The philosopher smiled, as he replied, "Nevertheless, I am Plato; and they call me by that name, because my shoulders are broad enough to carry little children."

The boy still insisted that he alluded to another Plato. "I mean the philosopher, who teaches in the groves of Academus," continued he. "I knew a freedman of his, who said he never allowed himself to be angry, or to speak in a loud voice. He never but once raised his hand to strike him; and that was because he had mischievously upset a poor old woman's basket of figs; feeling that he was in a passion, he suddenly checked himself, and stood perfectly still. A friend coming in asked him what he was doing; and the philosopher replied, 'I am punishing an angry man.'

"Speusippus, his sister's son, was such a careless, indecent, and boisterous youth, that his parents could not control him. They sent him to his uncle Plato, who received him in a friendly manner, and forbore to reproach him. Only in his own example he was always modest and placid. This so excited the admiration of Speusippus, that a love of philosophy was kindled within him. Some of his relatives blamed Plato, because he did not chastise the impertinent youth; but he replied, 'There is no reproof so severe as to show him, by the manner of my own life, the contrast between virtue and baseness.'—That is the Plato I want you to show me, when we are in Athens."

Proclus, perceiving a universal smile, modestly added, by way of explanation: "My son means him whom men call the divine Plato. He greatly desires to see that philosopher, of whom it is said Socrates dreamed, when he first received him as his pupil. In his dream he saw a swan without wings, that came and sat upon his bosom; and soon after, its wings grew, and it flew high up in the air, with melodious notes, alluring all who heard it."

Pericles laid his hand on the philosopher's shoulder, and smiling, answered, "My unbelieving friend, this is the teacher of Academus; this is the divine Plato; this is the soaring swan, whose melodious notes allure all that hear him."

Proclus was covered with confusion, but still seemed half incredulous. "What would Melissa say," exclaimed he, "if she knew that her frolicsome little plaything, Zoila, had been rude enough to throw flowers at the divine Plato."

"Nay, my friend," replied the disciple of Socrates,—what better could a philosopher desire, than to be pelted with roses by childhood?"

Eudora looked up with an arch expression; and Philothea smiled as she said, "This is a new version of unknown Phoebus tending the flocks of Admetus."

Pterilaüs seemed utterly confounded by a discovery so unexpected. It was long before he regained his usual freedom; and from time to time he was observed to fix a scrutinizing gaze on the countenance of Plato, as if seeking to read the mystery of his hidden greatness.

As the travellers approached Athens, they were met by a numerous procession of magistrates, citizens, and young men bearing garlands, which they heaped on the urn in such profusion that it resembled a pyramid of flowers. They passed the chariots with their arms and ensigns of office all reversed; then turned and followed to the abode of Pericles, singing dirges as they went, and filling the air with the melancholy music of the Mysian flute.

The amiable character of the deceased, his genius, the peculiar circumstances attending his death, and the accumulated afflictions of his illustrious parent, all combined to render it an impressive scene. Even the gay selfishness of Alcibiades was subdued into reverence, as he carefully took the urn from the chariot, and gave it to attendants, who placed it beside the household altar.

Early the next morning, a procession again formed to convey the ashes of Paralus to the sepulchre of his fathers; called, in the beautiful language of the Greeks, a Place of Sleep.

When the urn was again brought forth, Philothea's long golden hair covered it, like a mantle of sunbeams. During his life-time, these shining tresses had been peculiarly dear to him; and in token of her love, she placed them on his grave. Her white robe was changed for coarse black garments; and instead of flowery wreaths, a long black veil covered the beautiful head, from which its richest ornament had just been severed. She had rejoiced for his happy spirit, and now she mourned her own widowed lot.

At the sepulchre, Pericles pronounced a funeral oration on the most gifted, and best-beloved of his children. In the evening, kindred and friends met at his house to partake a feast prepared for the occasion; and every guest had something to relate concerning the genius and the virtues of him who slept.

A similar feast was prepared in the apartments of the women, where Philothea remained silent and composed; a circumstance that excited no small degree of wonder and remark, among those who measured affection by the vehemence of grief.

As soon as all ceremonies were completed, she obtained leave to return to her early home, endeared by many happy scenes; and there, in the stillness of her own heart, she held communion with the dear departed.

CHAPTER XVII.

There await me till I die; prepare
A mansion for me, as again with me
To dwell; for in thy tomb will I be laid,
In the same cedar, by thy side composed:
For e'en in death I will not be disjoined.
                    EURIPIDES

It soon became evident that a great change had taken place in Philothea's health. Some attributed it to the atmosphere of Athens, still infected with the plague; others supposed it had its origin in the death of Paralus. The widowed one, far from cherishing her grief, made a strong effort to be cheerful; but her gentle smile, like moonlight in a painting, retained its sweetness when the life was gone. There was something in this perfect stillness of resignation more affecting than the utmost agony of sorrow. She complained of no illness, but grew thinner and thinner, like a cloud gradually floating away, and retaining its transparent beauty to the last. Eudora lavished the most affectionate attentions upon her friend, conscious that she was merely strewing flowers in her pathway to the tomb.

A few weeks after their return to Athens, she said, "Dearest Eudora, do you remember the story of the nymph Erato, who implored the assistance of Areas, when the swelling torrent threatened to carry away the tree over which she presided, and on whose preservation her life depended?"

"I remember it well," replied Eudora: "Dione told it to me when I was quite a child; and I could never after see a tree torn by the lightning, or carried away by the flood, or felled by the woodman, without a shrinking and shivering feeling, lest some gentle, fair-haired Dryad had perished with it."

Philothea answered, "Thus was I affected, when my grandfather first read to me Hesiod's account of the Muses:

'Far round, the dusky earth
Rings with their hymning voices; and beneath
Their many-rustling feet a pleasant sound
Ariseth, as they take their onward way
To their own father's presence.'

"I never after could hear the quivering of summer leaves, or the busy hum of insects, without thinking it was the echoed voices of those
'Thrice three sacred maids, whose minds are knit
In harmony; whose only thought is song.'

"There is a deep and hidden reason why the heart loves to invest every hill, and stream, and tree, with a mysterious principle of life. All earthly forms are but the clothing of some divine ideal; and this truth we *feel*, though we *know* it not.

But when I spoke of Arcus and the Wood Nymph, I was thinking that Paralus
had been the tree, on whose existence my own depended; and that now he was
removed, I should not long remain."

Eudora burst into a passionate flood of tears. "Oh, dearest Philothea, do not
speak thus," she said. "I shall indeed be left alone in the world. Who will guide
me, who will protect me, who will love me when you are gone?"

Her friend endeavoured to calm these agitated feelings, by every soothing art
her kindness could suggest.

"I would rather suffer much in silence, than to give you unnecessary pain,"
she replied, affectionately: "but I ought not to conceal from you that I am about
to follow my beloved husband. In a short time, I shall not have sufficient
strength to impart all I have to say. You will find my clothing and jewels done
up in parcels, bearing the names of those for whom they are intended. My dowry
returns to Chrysippus, who gave it; but Pericles has kindly given permission that
everything else should be disposed of according to my own wishes. Several of
my grandfather's manuscripts, and a copy of Herodotus, which I transcribed
while I was in Ionia, are my farewell gifts to him. When the silver tripod, which
Paralus gained as a prize for the best tragedy exhibited during the Dionysia, is
returned to his father's house, let them be placed within it. The statue of
Persephone, (that ominous bridal gift,) and the ivory lyre bestowed by Aspasia,
are placed in his trust for the youthful Pericles; together with all the books and
garments that belonged to his departed brother. In token of gratitude for the
parental care of Clinias and his wife, I have bestowed on them the rich tripod
received from Heliodora. In addition to the trifling memorials I have already
sent to Melissa, and her artless little Zoila, you will find others prepared for you
to deliver, when restored to your peaceful home in Elis. To my faithful Milza I
have given all the garments and household goods suited to her condition. My
grandfather's books have been divided, as he requested, between Plato and
Philæmon; the silver harp and the ivory tablet are likewise designed for them.
Everything else belongs to you, dearest Eudora. Among many tokens of my
affection, you will not value least the ivory cup lined with silver, which
Philæmon gave me when he departed from Athens. The clasp, representing the
Naiades binding Eros in garlands, will, I trust, be worn at your marriage with
Philæmon."

With tearful eyes, Eudora answered, "Oh, Philothea! in the days of my pride
and gayety, I little knew what a treasure I threw from me, when I lost
Philæmon's love. Had it not been for my own perverse folly, I should at this
moment be his happy, honoured wife. The hope of his forgiveness is now the
only gleam of sunshine in a world of gloom; but I hardly dare to cherish it."

Philothea kissed her affectionately, and said, "Believe me, you will yet be
united. Of this, there is an impression on my mind too strong to admit of doubt.
If at times you are tempted to despond, remember these words were uttered by
your friend, when she drew near the confines of another world: you will be
united to Philæmon."

As she spoke, Milza, who was occupied in the next apartment, sneezed aloud. The sound was at Eudora's right hand, and she received the auspicious omen with a sudden thrill of joy.

Philothea observed her emotion with a gentle smile, and added: "When we were at Elis, I wrote an epistle to Philæmon, in which I spoke of you as my heart dictated; and Artaphernes found opportunity to send it directly into Persia."

The maiden blushed deeply and painfully, as she replied, "Nay, my dearest friend—you know that I must appear contemptible in his eyes; and I would not have insulted him with the offer of a heart, which he has reason to believe is so capricious and ungrateful."

"Trust me, I said nothing whereby your modesty might be wounded," answered Philothea: "I wrote as I was moved; and I felt strong assurance that my words would waken a response in Philæmon's heart. But there is one subject, on which my mind is filled with foreboding. I hope you will leave Athens as soon as it is safe to return to Elis."

"Do you then fear that I would again dance over a pit, because it was artfully covered with garlands?" said Eudora. "Believe me, I have been tried with too many sorrows, and too long been bowed under a load of shame, to be again endangered by such treacherous snares."

Philothea looked upon her affectionately, as she replied: "You are good and pure; but you have ever been like a loving and graceful vine, ready to cling to its nearest support."

"'Tis you have made me so," rejoined Eudora, kissing her pale cheek: "To you I have always applied for advice and instruction; and when you gave it, I felt confident and happy, as if led by the gods."

"Then so much the more need that I should caution the weakness I have produced," responded Philothea. "Should Aspasia gain access to you, when I am gone, she will try to convince you that happiness consists not in the duties we perform, but in the distinction we acquire; that my hopes of Elysium are all founded on fable; that my beloved Paralus has returned to the elements of which he was composed; that he nourishes the plants, and forms some of the innumerable particles of the atmosphere. I have seen him in my dreams, as distinctly, as I ever saw him; and I believe the same power that enabled me to see him when these poor eyes were veiled in slumber, will restore him to my vision when they are closed in eternal sleep. Aspasia will tell you I have been a beautiful but idle dreamer all my life. If you listen to her syren tongue, the secret guiding voice will be heard no more. She will make evil appear good, and good evil, until your soul will walk in perpetual twilight, unable to perceive the real size and character of any object."

"Never," exclaimed Eudora. "Never could she induce me to believe you an idle dreamer. Moreover, she will never again have opportunity to exert influence over me. The conversation I heard between her and Alcibiades is too well impressed upon my memory; and while that remains unforgotten, I shall shun them both, as I would shun a pestilence."

Philothea answered: "I do indeed believe that no blandishments will now make you a willing victim. But I have a secret dread of the character and power of Alcibiades. It is his boast that he never relinquishes a pursuit. I have often heard Pericles speak of his childish obstinacy and perseverance. He was one day playing at dice with other boys, when a loaded wagon came near. In a commanding tone, he ordered the driver to stop; and finding his injunctions disregarded, he laid down before the horses' feet, and told him to go on if he dared. The same character remains with him now. He will incur any hazard for the triumph of his own will. From his youth, he has been a popular idol; a circumstance which has doubtless increased the requirements of his passions, without diminishing the stubbornness of his temper. Milza tells me he has already inquired of her concerning your present residence and future intentions. Obstacles will only increase his eagerness and multiply his artifices.

"I have asked Clinias, whose dwelling is so closely connected with our own, to supply the place of your distant guardian, while you remain in Athens. In Pericles you might likewise trust, if he were not so fatally under the influence of Aspasia. Men think so lightly of these matters, I sometimes fear they might both regard the persecutions of Alcibiades too trivial for their interference. For these reasons I wish you to return to Elis as soon as possible when I am gone."

Eudora's countenance kindled with indignation, as she listened to what Milza had told. In broken and contrite tones, she answered; "Philothea, whatever trials I may suffer, my former folly deserves them all. But rest assured, whenever it pleases the gods to remove your counsel and protection, I will not abide in Athens a single hour after it is possible to leave with safety."

"I find consolation in that assurance," replied Philothea; "and I have strong belief that a divine shield will guard you from impending evil. And now I will go to my couch; for I am weary, and would fain be lulled with music."

Eudora tenderly arranged the pillows, and played a succession of sweet and plaintive tunes, familiar to their childhood. Her friend listened with an expression of tranquil pleasure, slowly keeping time by the motion of her fingers, until she sunk into a peaceful sleep.

After long and sweet repose, she awoke suddenly, and looking up with a beaming glance, exclaimed, "I shall follow him soon!"

Eudora leaned over the couch, to inquire why she had spoken in such delighted accents.

Philothea answered: "I dreamed that I sat upon a bank of violets, with Paralus by my side; and he wove a garland and placed it on my head. Suddenly, golden sounds seemed floating in the air, melting into each other with liquid melody. It was such a scene as Paralus often described, when his soul lived apart from the body, and only returned at intervals, to bring strange tidings of its wanderings. I turned to tell him so; and I saw that we were both clothed in garments that shone like woven sunbeams. Then voices above us began to sing:
'Come hither, kindred spirits, come!
Hail to the mystic two in one!'

"Even after I awoke, I seemed to hear the chorus distinctly. It sounded like the voice of Paralus in his youth, when we used to sing together, to please my grandfather, as he sat by the side of that little sheltered brook, over whose bright waters the trees embrace each other in silent love. Dearest Eudora, I shall soon follow him."

The maiden turned away to conceal her tears; for resignation to this bereavement seemed too hard a lesson for her suffering heart.

For several weeks, there was no apparent change in Philothea's health or spirits. The same sad serenity remained—perpetually exciting the compassion it never seemed to ask. Each day the children of the neighbourhood brought their simple offering of flowers, with which she wove fresh garlands for the tomb of Paralus. When no longer able to visit the sepulchre herself, she intrusted them to the youthful Pericles, who reverently placed them on his brother's urn.

The elder Pericles seemed to find peculiar solace in the conversation of his widowed daughter. Scarcely a day passed without an interview between them, and renewed indications of his affectionate solicitude.

He came one day, attended by his son, on whom his desolated heart now bestowed a double portion of paternal love. They remained a long time, in earnest discourse; and when they departed, the boy was in tears.

Philothea, with feeble steps, followed them to the portico, and gazed after them, as long as she could see a fold of their garments. As she turned to lean on Eudora's arm, she said, "It is the last time I shall ever see them. It is the last. I have felt a sister's love for that dear boy. His heart is young and innocent."

For a few hours after, she continued to talk with unusual animation, and her eyes beamed with an expression of inspired earnestness. At her request, Geta and Milza were called; and the faithful servants listened with mournful gratitude to her parting words of advice and consolation.

At evening twilight, Eudora gave her a bunch of flowers, sent by the youthful Pericles. She took them with a smile, and said, "How fragrant is their breath, and how beautiful their colours! I have heard that the Persians write their music in colours; and Paralus spoke the same concerning music in the spirit-world. Perchance there was heavenly melody written on this fair earth in the age of innocence; but mortals have now forgotten its language." Perceiving Eudora's thoughtful countenance, she said: "Is my gentle friend disturbed, lest infant nymphs closed their brief existence when these stems were broken?"

"Nay;" replied Eudora: "My heart is sad; but not for the perished genii of the flowers."

Philothea understood the import of her words; and pressing her hand affectionately, said, "Your love has been as balm to my lonely heart; and let that remembrance comfort you, when I go hence. Listen in stillness to the whispered warnings of your attendant spirit, and he will never leave you. I am weary; and would fain repose on your affectionate bosom."

Eudora gently placed her head as she desired; and carefully supporting the precious burden, she began to sing, in low and soothing tones.

After some time, the quiet and regular respiration of the breath announced that the invalid had fallen into tranquil slumber. Milza came, to ask if the lamps were wanted; but receiving a silent signal from Eudora, she crept noiselessly away.

For more than an hour, there was perfect stillness, as the shades of evening deepened. All at once, the room was filled with soft, clear light! Eudora turned her head quickly, to discover whence it came; but could perceive no apparent cause for the sudden radiance.

With an undefined feeling of awe, she looked in the countenance of her friend. It was motionless as marble; but never had she seen anything so beautiful, and so unearthly.

As she gazed, doubting whether this could indeed be death, there was a sound of music in the air—distinct, yet blended, like the warbling of birds in the spring-time.

It was the tune Paralus had learned from celestial harps; and even after the last note floated away, Eudora seemed to hear the well remembered words:
Come hither, kindred spirit, come!
Hail to the mystic two in one!

CHAPTER XVIII.

Take courage I no vain dream hast thou beheld,
But in thy sleep a truth.
                    HOMER.

At the time of Philothea's death, Pandænus, the nephew of Phidias, was in Athens, intending soon to return to Elis, in company with an ambassador bound to Lacedæmon; and Eudora resolved to avail herself of this opportunity to follow the farewell advice of her friend. As the time for departure was near at hand, no change was made in household arrangements; and though the desolate maiden at times experienced sensations of extreme loneliness, the near vicinity of Clinias and Phoenarete left her no fears concerning adequate protection.

This confidence seemed well grounded; yet not many days after the funeral solemnities, Eudora suddenly disappeared. She had gone out, as usual, to gather flowers for the tomb of the beloved sleeper; and not rinding sufficient variety in the garden, had wandered into a small field adjoining. Milza was the first to observe that her absence was unusually protracted. She mentioned her anxiety to Geta, who immediately went out in search of his young mistress; but soon returned, saying she was neither in the house of Clinias, nor in the neighbouring fields, nor at the Fountain of Callirhöe.

The faithful attendants at once suspected treachery in Alcibiades. "I never rightly understood what was the difficulty, when Eudora was locked up in her chamber, and Lucos chained to the door," said Geta; "but from what I could hear, I know that Phidias was very angry with Alcibiades. Many a time I've heard him say that he would always have his own way, either by a straight course or a crooked one."

"And my good old master used to say he had changed but little since he was a boy, when he made the wagoner turn back, by lying down in front of his horses," rejoined Milza: "I thought of that, when Alcibiades came and drank at the Fountain, while I was filling my urn. You remember I told you that he just tasted of the water, for a pretence, and then began to inquire where Eudora was, and whether she would remain in Athens."

After some further consultation, it was deemed best for Milza to request a private interview with Phoenarete, during which she freely expressed her fears. The wife of Clinias, though connected by marriage with the house of Alcibiades, was far from resenting the imputation, or pretending that she considered it groundless. Her feelings were at once excited for the lonely orphan girl, whose beauty, vivacity, and gentleness, had won upon her heart; and she readily promised assistance in any plan for her relief, provided it met the approbation of her husband.

There was in Salamis a large mansion built by Eurysaces, the ancestor of Alcibiades, by whom it had been lately purchased, and repaired for a summer residence. Report said that many a fair maiden had been decoyed within its walls, and retained a prisoner. This place was guarded by several powerful dogs, and vigilant servants were always stationed at the gates. Milza proposed to disguise herself as much as possible, and, with a basket on her head, go thither to offer fish for sale. Geta, being afraid to accompany her, hired an honest boatman to convey her to the island, and wait till she was ready to return to Athens.

As she approached the walls of the mansion, the dogs began to growl, but were soon silenced by the porters. Without answering the indecent jibes, with which they greeted her ears as she passed along, the little fish-woman balanced her basket on her head, and began carelessly to sing some snatches of a hymn to Amphitrite. It was a tune of which Eudora was particularly fond; and often when Milza was humming it over her work, her soft and sonorous voice had been heard responding from the inner apartment.

She had scarcely finished the first verse, ere the chorus was repeated by some one within the dwelling; and she recognized the half-suppressed growl of Hylax, as if his barking had been checked by some cautious hand. Afraid to attract attention by a prolonged stay, Milza passed along and entered the servants' apartment. Having sold a portion of her fish, and lingered as long as she dared in conversation with the cooks, she returned slowly in the same direction, singing as she went, and carefully observing everything around her. She was just beginning to fear the impossibility of obtaining any solution of her doubts, when she saw a leaf fluttering near the ground, as if its motions were impelled by some other cause than the wind. Approaching nearer, she perceived that it was let down from a grated opening in the wall above, by a small thread, with a little ball of wax attached to it for a weight. She examined the leaf, and discovered certain letters pricked upon it; and when the string was pulled gently, it immediately dropped upon her arm. At the same time, a voice, which she distinctly recognized as Eudora's, was heard singing:
On a rock, amid the roaring water,
Lies Cassiopea's gentle daughter.

Milza had just begun to sing, "Bold Perseus comes," when she perceived a servant crossing the court, and deemed it prudent to retire in silence. She carefully preserved the leaf, and immediately after her return hastened to the apartment of Phoenarete, to obtain an explanation. That matron, like most Grecian women, was ignorant of her own written language. The leaf was accordingly placed in a vessel of water, to preserve its freshness until Clinias returned from the Prytaneum. He easily distinguished the name of Pandænus joined with his own; and having heard the particulars of the story, had no difficulty in understanding that Milza was directed to apply to them for assistance. He readily promised to intercede with his profligate kinsman, and immediately sent messengers in search of Pandænus.

Geta awaited intelligence with extreme impatience. He was grateful for many an act of kindness from Eudora; and he could not forget that she had been the cherished favourite of his beloved and generous master.

At night, Clinias returned from a conference with Alcibiades, in which the latter denied all knowledge of Eudora; and it seemed hazardous to institute legal inquiries into the conduct of a man so powerful and so popular, without further evidence than had yet been obtained. Pandænus could not be found. At the house where he usually resided, no information could be obtained, except that he went out on the preceding evening, and had not returned as usual.

During that night, and part of the following day, the two faithful attendants remained in a state of melancholy indecision. At last, Geta said, "I will go once more in search of Pandænus; and if he has not yet returned, I have resolved what to do. To-day I saw one of the slaves of Artaphernes buying olives; and he said he must have the very best, because his master was to give a feast to-night. Among other guests, he spoke of Alcibiades; and he is one that is always sure to stay late at his wine. While he is feasting, I will go to Salamis. His steward often bought anchovies of me at Phalerum. He is a countryman of mine; and I know he is as avaricious as an Odomantian. I think money will bribe him to carry a message to Eudora, and to place a ladder near the outer wall for her escape. He is intrusted with all the keys, and can do it if he will. And if he can get gold enough by it, I believe he will trust Hermes to help him settle with his master, as he has done many a time before this. I will be in readiness at the Triton's Cove, and bring her back to Athens as fast as oars can fly."

"Do so, dear Geta," replied Milza; "but disguise yourself from the other servants, and take with you the robe and veil that I wear to market. Then if Eudora could only walk a little more like a fish-woman, she might pass very well. But be sure you do not pay the steward till you have her at the boat's edge; for he that will play false games with his master, may do the same by you."

Necessary arrangements were speedily made. Geta resolved to offer the earnings of his whole life as a bribe, rather than intrust the secret of his bold expedition to any of the household of Clinias; and Milza, fearful that their own store would not prove a sufficient temptation, brought forth a sum of money found in Eudora's apartment, together with a valuable necklace, which had been a birth-day present from Phidias.

It was past midnight when three figures emerged from the shadow of the high wall surrounding the mansion of Alcibiades, and with cautious haste proceeded toward the cove. Before they could arrive at the beach, a large and gaily-trimmed boat was seen approaching the shore, from the direction of the Piræus. It was flaming with torches; and a band of musicians poured out upon the undulating waters a rich flood of melody, rendered more distinct and soft by the liquid element over which it floated. One of the fugitives immediately turned, and disappeared within the walls they had left; the other two concealed themselves in a thick grove, the darkness of which was deepened by the glare of torches along its borders. A man richly dressed, with several fillets on his head, and crowned with a garland of violets, ivy, and myrtle, stepped from the boat, supported by the arm of a slave. His countenance was flushed with wine, and as he reeled along, he sung aloud:

"Have I told you all my flames,
'Mong the amorous Syrian dames?

Have I numbered every one
Glowing under Egypt's sun!
Or the nymphs, who, blushing sweet,
Deck the shrine of Love in Crete—
Where the God, with festal play,
Holds eternal holiday?"

"Castor and Polydeuces!" whispered Geta, "there goes Alcibiades. He has returned from his wine earlier than usual; but so blinded by the merry god, that he would not have known us, if we had faced the glare of his torches."

"Oh, hasten! hasten!" said Eudora, weeping and trembling, as she spoke. "I beseech you do not let a moment be lost."

As Alcibiades and his train disappeared, they left the grove, and hurried toward their boat; keeping as much as possible within the shadow of the trees. They reached the cove in safety, and Geta rowed with unwonted energy; but he was single-handed, and Salamis was many stadia from Athens. Long before he arrived at the place were he had been accustomed to land, they heard the sound of distant oars plied with furious rapidity.

They landed, and with the utmost haste proceeded toward the city. Eudora, fearful of being overtaken, implored Geta to seek refuge behind the pillars of Poseidon's temple. Carefully concealing themselves in the dense shadow, they remained without speaking, and almost without breathing, until their pursuers had passed by. The moment these were out of hearing, they quitted their hiding-place, and walked swiftly along the Piræus. Intense fear imparted a degree of strength, which the maiden, under other circumstances, would have hardly deemed it possible to exert. She did not for a moment relax her speed, until they came within sight of the Areopagus, and heard noisy shouts, apparently not far distant. Eudora, sinking with fatigue and terror, entreated Geta not to attempt any approach to the house of Clinias, where her enemies would certainly be lying in wait for them. With uncertain steps they proceeded toward the great Gate of the Acropolis, until the helpless maiden, frightened at the approaching noise, stopped suddenly, and burst into a flood of tears.

"There is one place of safety, if you have courage to try it," said Geta: "We are nearly under the Propylæa; and close beside us is the grotto of Creüsa. Few dare to enter it in the day-time, and no profane steps will venture to pass the threshold after nightfall; for it is said the gods often visit it, and fill it with strange sights and sounds. Shall we enter?"

It was a windy night, and the clouds that occasionally passed over the face of the moon gave the earth a dreary aspect. The high wall under which they stood seemed to frown gloomily upon them, and the long flight of white marble steps, leading from the Propylæa, looked cold and cheerless beneath the fitful gleamings of the moon.

Eudora hesitated, and looked timidly around; but as the sound of riotous voices came nearer, she seized Geta's arm, and exclaimed, in hurried accents, "The gods protect me! Let us enter."

Within the grotto, all was total darkness. Having groped their way a short distance from the entrance, they found a large rock, on which they seated themselves. The voices approached nearer, and their discordant revelry had an awful sound amid the echoes of the grotto. These gradually died away in the distance, and were heard no more.

When all was perfectly still, Eudora, in whispered accents, informed Geta that she had been seized, as she stooped to gather flowers within sight of her own dwelling. Two men suddenly started up from behind a wall, and one covered her mouth, while the other bound her hands. They made a signal to a third, who came with two attendants and a curtained chariot, in which she was immediately conveyed to a solitary place on the seashore, and thence to Salamis. Two men sat beside her, and held her fast, so as to prevent any possibility of communication with the few people passing at that early hour.

Arrived at the place of destination, she was shut up in a large apartment, luxuriously furnished. Alcibiades soon visited her, with an affectation of the most scrupulous respect, urging the plea of ardent love as an excuse for his proceedings.

Aware that she was completely in his power, she concealed her indignation and contempt, and allowed him to indulge the hope that her affections might be obtained, if she were entirely convinced of his wish to atone for the treachery and violence with which she had been treated.

Milza's voice had been recognized the moment she began to sing; and she at once conjectured the object that led her thither. But when hour after hour passed without any tidings from Pandænus or Clinias, she was in a state of anxiety bordering on distraction; for she soon perceived sufficient indication that the smooth hypocrisy of Alcibiades was assumed but for a short period.

She had already determined on an effort to bribe the servants, when the steward came stealthily to her room, and offered to convey her to the Triton's Cove, provided she would promise to double the sum already offered by Geta. To this she eagerly assented, without even inquiring the amount; and he, fearful of detection, scarcely allowed time to throw Milza's robe and veil over her own.

Having thus far effected her escape, Eudora was extremely anxious that Pandænus and Clinias should be informed of her place of retreat, as soon as the morning dawned. When Geta told her that Pandænus had disappeared as suddenly as herself, and no one knew whither, she replied, "This, too, is the work of Alcibiades."

Their whispered conversation was stopped by the barking of a dog, to which the echoes of the cavern gave a frightful appearance of nearness. Each instinctively touched the other's arm, as a signal for silence. When all was again quiet, Geta whispered, "It is well for us they were not witty enough to bring Hylax with them; for the poor fellow would certainly have betrayed us." This circumstance warned them of the danger of listeners, and few more words were spoken.

The maiden, completely exhausted by the exertions she had made, laid her head on the shoulder of her attendant, and slept until the morning twilight became perceptible through the crevices of the rocks.

At the first approach of day, she implored Geta to hasten to the house of Clinias, and ask his protection: for she feared to venture herself abroad, without the presence of some one whose rank and influence would be respected by Alcibiades.

"Before I go," replied Geta, "let me find a secure hiding-place for you; for though I shall soon return, in the meantime those may enter whose presence may be dangerous."

"You forget that this is a sacred place," rejoined Eudora, in tones that betrayed fear struggling with her confidence.

"There are men, with whom nothing is sacred," answered Geta; "and many such are now in Athens."

The cavern was deep, and wide. As they passed along, the dawning light indistinctly revealed statues of Phoebus and Pan, with altars of pure white marble. At the farthest extremity, stood a trophy of shields, helmets, and spears, placed there by Miltiades, in commemoration of his victory at Marathon. It was so formed as to be hollow in the centre, and Geta proposed that the timid maiden should creep in at the side, and stand upright. She did so, and it proved an effectual screen from head to foot. Having taken this prudent precaution, the faithful attendant departed, with a promise to return as soon as possible. But hour after hour elapsed, and he came not. As Eudora peeped through the chinks of the trophy, she perceived from the entrance of the cave glowing streaks of light, that indicated approaching noon. Yet all remained still, save the echoed din of noises in the city; and no one came to her relief.

Not long after the sun had begun to decline from its meridian, two men entered, whom she recognized as among the individuals that had seized and conveyed her to Salamis. As they looked carefully all around the cave, Eudora held her breath, and her heart throbbed violently. Perceiving no one, they knelt for a moment before the altars, and hastily retreated, with indications of fear; for the accusations of guilty minds were added to the usual terrors of this subterranean abode of the gods.

The day was fading into twilight, when a feeble old man came, with a garland on his head, and invoked the blessing of Phoebus. He was accompanied by a boy, who laid his offering of flowers and fruit on the altar of Pan, with an expression of countenance that showed how much he was alarmed by the presence of that fear-inspiring deity.

After they had withdrawn, no other footsteps approached the sacred place. Anxiety of mind, and bodily weariness, more than once tempted Eudora to go out and mingle with the throng continually passing through the city. But the idea that Geta might arrive, and be perplexed by her absence, combined with the fear of lurking spies, kept her motionless, until the obscurity of the grotto gave indication that the shadows of twilight were deepening.

During the day, she had observed near the trophy a heap of withered laurel branches and wreaths, with which the altar and statue of Phoebus had been at various times adorned. Overcome with fatigue, and desirous to change a position, which from its uniformity had become extremely painful, she resolved to lie down upon the rugged rock, with the sacred garlands for a pillow. She shuddered to remember the lizards and other reptiles she had seen crawling, through the day; but the universal fear of entering Creüsa's grotto after nightfall, promised safety from human intrusion; and the desolate maiden laid herself down to repose, in such a state of mind that she would have welcomed a poisonous reptile, if it brought the slumbers of death. It seemed to her that she was utterly solitary and friendless; persecuted by men, and forsaken by the gods.

By degrees, all sounds died away, save the melancholy hooting of owls, mingled occasionally with the distant barking and howling of dogs. Alone, in stillness and total darkness, memory revealed herself with wonderful power. The scenes of her childhood; the chamber in which she had slept; figures she had embroidered and forgotten; tunes that had been silent for years; thoughts and feelings long buried; Philæmon's smile; the serene countenance of Philothea; the death-bed of Phidias; and a thousand other images of the past, came before her with all the vividness of present reality. Exhausted in mind and body, she could not long endure this tide of recollection. Covering her face with her hands, she sobbed convulsively, as she murmured, "Oh, Philothea! why didst thou leave me? My guide, my only friend! oh, where art thou!"

A gentle strain of music, scarcely audible, seemed to make reply. Eudora raised her head to listen—and lo! the whole grotto was filled with light; so brilliant that every feather in the arrow of Phoebus might be counted, and the gilded horns and star of Pan were radiant as the sun.

Her first thought was that she had slept until noon. She rubbed her eyes, and glanced at the pedestal of a statue, on which she distinctly read the inscription: "Here Miltiades placed me, Pan, the goat-footed god of Arcadia, who warred with the Athenians against the Medes."

Frightened at the possibility of having overslept herself, she started up, and was about to seek the shelter of the trophy, when Paralus and Philothea stood before her! They were clothed in bright garments, with garlands on their heads. His arm was about her waist, and hers rested on his shoulder. There was a holy beauty in their smile, from which a protecting influence seemed to emanate, that banished mortal fear.

In sweet, low tones, they both said, as if with one voice, "Seek Artaphernes, the Persian."

"Dearest Philothea, I scarcely know his countenance," replied the maiden.

Again the bright vision repeated, "Seek Artaphernes, nothing doubting."

The sounds ceased; the light began to fade; it grew more and more dim, till all was total darkness. For a long time, Eudora remained intensely wakeful, but inspired with a new feeling of confidence and hope, that rendered her oblivious of all earthly cares. Whence it came, she neither knew nor asked; for such states preclude all inquiry concerning their own nature and origin.

After awhile, she fell into a tranquil slumber, in which she dreamed of torrents crossed in safety, and of rugged, thorny paths, that ended in blooming gardens. She was awakened by the sound of a troubled, timid voice, saying, "Eudora! Eudora!"

She listened a moment, and answered, "Is it you, Milza?"

"Oh, blessed be the sound of your voice," replied the peasant. "Where are you? Let me take your hand; for I am afraid in this awful place."

"Don't be frightened, my good Milza. I have had joyful visions here," rejoined the maiden. She reached out her arms as she spoke, and perceived that her companion trembled exceedingly. "May the gods protect us!" whispered she; "but it is a fearful thing to come here in the night-time. All the gold of Croesus would not have tempted me, if Geta had not charged me to do it, to save you from starving."

"You are indeed kind friends," said Eudora; "and the only ones I have left in this world. If ever I get safely back to Elis, you shall be to me as brother and sister."

"Ah, dear lady," replied the peasant, "you have ever been a good friend to us;—and there is one that sleeps, who never spoke an ungentle word to any of us. When her strength was almost gone, she bade me love Eudora, even as I had loved her; and the gods know that for her sake Milza would have died. Phoebus protect me, but this is an awful place to speak of those who sleep. It must be near the dawn; but it is fearfully dark here. Where is your hand? I have brought some bread and figs, and this little arabyllus of water mixed with Lesbian wine. Eat; for you must be almost famished."

Eudora took the refreshment, but ere she tasted it, inquired, "Why did not Geta come, as he promised?" Milza began to weep.

"Has evil befallen him?" said Eudora, in tones of alarm.

The afflicted wife sobbed out, "Poor Geta! Poor, dear Geta! I dreaded to come into this cavern; but then I thought if I died, it would be well, if we could but die together."

"Do tell me what has happened," said Eudora: "Am I doomed to bring trouble upon all who love me? Tell me, I entreat you."

Milza, weeping as she spoke, then proceeded to say that Alcibiades had discovered Eudora's escape immediately after his return from the feast of Artaphernes. He was in a perfect storm of passion, and threatened every one of the servants with severe punishment, to extort confession. The steward received a few keen lashes, notwithstanding his protestations of innocence. But he threatened to appeal to the magistrates for another master; and Alcibiades, unwilling to lose the services of this bold and artful slave, restrained his anger, even when it was at its greatest height.

To appease his master's displeasure, the treacherous fellow acknowledged that Geta had been seen near the walls, and that his boat had been lying at the Triton's Cove.

In consequence of this information, men were instantly ordered in pursuit, with orders to lie in wait for the fugitives, if they could not be overtaken before morning. When Geta left Creüsa's Grotto, he was seized before he reached the house of Clinias.

Milza knew nothing of these proceedings, but had remained anxiously waiting till the day was half spent. Then she learned that Alcibiades had claimed Eudora and Geta as his slaves, by virtue of a debt due to him from Phidias, for a large quantity of ivory; and notwithstanding the efforts of Clinias in their favour, the Court of Forty Four, in the borough of Alcibiades, decided that he had a right to retain them, until the debt was paid, or until the heir appeared to show cause why it should not be paid. "The gods have blessed Clinias with abundant wealth," said Eudora; "Did he offer nothing to save the innocent?"

"Dear lady," replied Milza, "Alcibiades demands such an immense sum for the ivory, that he says he might as well undertake to build the wall of Hipparchus, as to pay it. But I have not told you the most cruel part of the story. Geta has been tied to a ladder, and shockingly whipped, to make him tell where you were concealed. He said he would not do it, if he died. I believe they had the will to kill him; but one of the young slaves, whose modesty Alcibiades had insulted, was resolved to make complaint to the magistrates, and demand another master. She helped Geta to escape: they have both taken refuge in the Temple of Theseus. Geta dared trust no one but me to carry a message to Clinias. I told him he supped with Pericles to-night; and he would not suffer me to go there, lest Alcibiades should be among the guests."

"I am glad he gave you that advice," said Eudora; "for though Pericles might be willing to serve me, for Philothea's sake, I fear if he once learned the secret, it would soon be in Aspasia's keeping."

"And that would be all the same as telling Alcibiades himself," rejoined Milza. "But I must tell you that I did not know of poor Geta's sufferings until many hours after they happened. Since he went to Salamis in search of you, I have not seen him until late this evening. He is afraid to leave the altar, lest he should fall into the hands of his enemies; and that is the reason he sent me to bring you food. He expects to be a slave again; but having been abused by Alcibiades, he claims the privilege of the law to be transferred to another master."

Eudora wept bitterly, to think she had no power to rescue her faithful attendant from a condition he dreaded worse than death.

Milza endeavoured, in her own artless way, to soothe the distress her words had excited. "In all Geta's troubles, he thinks more of you than he does of himself," said she. "He bade me convey you to the house of a wise woman from Thessalia, who lives near the Sacred Gate; for he says she can tell us what it is best to do. She has learned of magicians in foreign lands. They say she can compound potions that will turn hatred into love; and that the power of her enchantments is so great, she can draw the moon down from the sky."

"Nevertheless, I shall not seek her counsel," replied the maiden; "for I have heard a better oracle."

When she had given an account of the vision in the cave, the peasant asked, in a low and trembling voice, "Did it not make you afraid?"

"Not in the least," answered Eudora; "and therefore I am doubtful whether it were a vision or a dream. I spoke to Philothea just as I used to do; without remembering that she had died. She left me more composed and happy than I have been for many days. Even if it were a vision, I do not marvel that the spirit of one so pure and peaceful should be less terrific than the ghost of Medea or Clytemnestra."

"And the light shone all at once!" exclaimed Milza, eagerly. "Trust to it, dear lady—trust to it. A sudden brightness hath ever been a happy omen."

Two baskets, filled with Copaic eels and anchovies, had been deposited near the mouth of the cavern; and with the first blush of morning, the fugitives offered prayers to Phoebus and Pan, and went forth with the baskets on their heads, as if they sought the market. Eudora, in her haste, would have stepped across the springs that bubbled from the rocks; but Milza held her back, saying, "Did you never hear that these brooks are Creüsa's tears? When the unhappy daughter of Erectheus left her infant in this cave to perish, she wept as she departed; and Phoebus, her immortal lover, changed her tears to rills. For this reason, the water has ever been salt to the taste. It is a bad omen to wet the foot in these springs."

Thus warned, Eudora turned aside, and took a more circuitous path.

It happened, fortunately, that the residence of Artaphernes stood behind the temple of Asclepius, at a short distance from Creüsa's Grotto; and they felt assured that no one would think of searching for them within the dwelling of the Persian stranger. They arrived at the gate without question or hindrance; but found it fastened. To their anxious minds, the time they were obliged to wait seemed like an age; but at last the gate was opened, and they preferred a humble request to see Artaphernes. Eudora, being weary of her load, stooped to place the basket of fish on a bench, and her veil accidentally dropped. The porter touched her under the chin, and said, with a rude laugh, "Do you suppose, my pretty dolphin, that Artaphernes buys his own dinner?"

Eudora's eyes flashed fire at this familiarity; but checking her natural impetuosity, she replied, "It was not concerning the fish that I wished to speak to your master. We have business of importance."

The servant gave a significant glance, more insulting than his former freedom. "Oh, yes, business of importance, no doubt," said he; "but do you suppose, my little Nereid, that the servant of the Great King is himself a vender of fish, that he should leave his couch at an hour so early as this?"

Eudora slipped a ring from her finger, and putting it in his hand, said, in a confidential tone, "I am not a fish-woman. I am here in disguise. Go to your master, and conjure him, if he ever had a daughter that he loved, to hear the petition of an orphan, who is in great distress."

The man's deportment immediately changed; and as he walked away, he muttered to himself, "She don't look nor speak like one brought up at the gates; that's certain."

Eudora and Milza remained in the court for a long time, but with far less impatience than they had waited at the gate. At length the servant returned, saying his master was now ready to see them. Eudora followed, in extreme agitation, with her veil folded closely about her; and when they were ushered into the presence of Artaphernes, the embarrassment of her situation deprived her of the power of utterance. With much kindness of voice and manner, the venerable stranger said: "My servant told me that one of you was an orphan, and had somewhat to ask of me."

Eudora replied: "O Persian stranger, I am indeed a lonely orphan, in the power of mine enemies; and I have been warned by a vision to come hither for assistance."

Something in her words, or voice, seemed to excite surprise, mingled with deeper feelings; and the old man's countenance grew more troubled, as she continued: "Perhaps you may recollect a maiden that sung at Aspasia's house, to whom you afterwards sent a veil of shining texture?"

"Ah, yes," he replied, with a deep sigh: "I do recollect it. They told me she was Eudora, the daughter of Phidias."

"I am Eudora, the adopted daughter of Phidias," rejoined the maiden. "My benefactor is dead, and I am friendless."

"Who were your parents?" inquired the Persian.

"I never knew them," she replied. "I was stolen from the Ionian coast by Greek pirates. I was a mere infant when Phidias bought me."

In a voice almost suffocated with emotion, Artaphernes asked, "Were you *then* named Eudora?"

The maiden's heart began to flutter with a new and strange hope, as she replied, "No one knew my name. In my childish prattle, I called myself Baby Minta."

The old man started from his seat—his colour went and came—and every joint trembled. He seemed to make a strong effort to check some sudden impulse. After collecting himself for a moment, he said, "Maiden, you have the voice of one I dearly loved; and it has stirred the deepest fountains of my heart. I pray you, let me see your countenance."

As Eudora threw off the veil, her long glossy hair fell profusely over her neck and shoulders, and her beautiful face was flushed with eager expectation.

The venerable Persian gazed at her for an instant, and then clasped her to his bosom. The tears fell fast, as he exclaimed, "Artaminta! My daughter! My daughter! Image of thy blessed mother! I have sought for thee throughout the world, and at last I believed thee dead. My only child! My long-lost, my precious one! May the blessing of Oromasdes be upon thee."

CHAPTER XIX.

Whate'er thou givest, generous let it be.
EURIPIDES

When it was rumoured that Artaphernes had ransomed Eudora and Geta, by offering the entire sum demanded for the ivory, many a jest circulated in the agoras, at the expense of the old man who had given such an enormous price for a handsome slave; but when it became known, that he had, in some wonderful and mysterious manner, discovered a long-lost daughter, the tide of public feeling was changed.

Alcibiades at once remitted his claim, which in fact never had any foundation in justice; he having accepted two statues in payment for the ivory, previous to the death of Phidias. He likewise formally asked Eudora in marriage; humbly apologizing for the outrage he had committed, and urging the vehemence of his love as an extenuation of the fault.

Artaphernes had power to dispose of his daughter without even making any inquiry concerning the state of her affections; but the circumstances of his past life induced him to forbear the exercise of his power.

"My dear child," said he, "it was my own misfortune to suffer by an ill-assorted marriage. In early youth, my parents united me with Artaynta, a Persian lady, whose affections had been secretly bestowed upon a near kinsman. Her parents knew of this fact, but mine were ignorant of it. It ended in wretchedness and disgrace. To avoid the awful consequences of guilt, she and her lover eloped to some distant land, where I never attempted to follow them.

Some time after, the Great King was graciously pleased to appoint me Governor of the sea-coast in Asia Minor. I removed to Ephesus, where I saw and loved your blessed mother, the beautiful Antiope, daughter of Diophanes, priest of Zeus. I saw her accidentally at a fountain, and watched her unobserved, while she bathed the feet of her little sister. Though younger than myself, she reciprocated the love she had inspired. Her father consented to our union; and for a few years I enjoyed as great happiness as Oromasdes ever bestows on mortals. You were our only child; named Artaminta, in remembrance of my mother. You were scarcely two years old, when you and your nurse suddenly disappeared. As several other women and children were lost at the same time, we supposed that you were stolen by pirates. All efforts to ascertain your fate proved utterly fruitless. As moon after moon passed away, bringing no tidings of our lost treasure, Antiope grew more and more hopeless. She was a gentle, tender-hearted being, that complained little and suffered much. At last, she died broken-hearted."

After remaining in silent thoughtfulness for a few moments, he added: "Of my two sons by Artaynta, one died in childhood; the other was killed in battle, before I came to Athens. I had never ceased my exertions to discover you; but after I became childless, it was the cherished object of existence. Some information received from Phoenician sailors led to the conclusion that I owed my misfortune to Greek pirates; and when the Great King informed me that he had need of services in Athens, I cherfully undertook the mission."

"Having suffered severely in my own marriage, I would not willingly endanger your happiness by any unreasonable exercise of parental authority. Alcibiades is handsome, rich, and of high rank. How do you regard his proposal of marriage?"

The colour mounted high in Eudora's cheek, and she answered hastily, "As easily could I consent to be the wife of Tereus, after his brutal outrage on the helpless Philomela. I have nothing but contempt to bestow on the man who persecuted me when I was friendless, and flatters me when I have wealthy friends."

Artaphernes replied, "I knew not how far you might consider violent love an excuse for base proceedings; but I rejoice to see that you have pride becoming your noble birth. For another reason, it gives me happiness to find you ill-disposed toward this match; for duty will soon call me to Persia, and having just recovered you in a manner so miraculous, it would be a grievous sacrifice to relinquish you so soon. But am I so fortunate as to find you willing to return with me? Are there no strong ties that bind your heart to Athens?"

Perceiving that Eudora blushed deeply, he added, in an inquiring tone, "Clinias told me to-day, that Phidias wished to unite you with that gifted artist, his nephew Pandænus?"

The maiden replied, "I have many reasons to be grateful to Pandænus; and it was painful to refuse compliance with the wishes of my benefactor; but if Phidias had commanded me to obey him in this instance, my happiness would have been sacrificed. Of all countries in the world, there is none I so much wish to visit as Persia. Of that you may rest assured, my father."

The old man looked upon her affectionately, and his eyes filled with tears, as he exclaimed, "Oromasdes be praised, that I am once more permitted to hear that welcome sound! No music is so pleasant to my ears as that word—father. Zoroaster tells us that children are a bridge joining this earth to a heavenly paradise, filled with fresh springs and blooming gardens. Blessed indeed is the man who hears many gentle voices call him father! But, my daughter, why is it that the commands of Phidias would have made you unhappy? Speak frankly, Artaminta; lest hereafter there should be occasion to mourn that we misunderstood each other."

Eudora then told all the particulars of her attachment to Philæmon, and her brief infatuation with regard to Alcibiades. Artaphernes evinced no displeasure at the disclosure; but spoke of Philæmon with great respect and affection. He dwelt earnestly upon the mischievous effects of such free customs as Aspasia sought to introduce, and warmly eulogized the strictness and complete seclusion of Persian education. When Eudora expressed fears that she might never be able to regain Philæmon's love, he gazed on her beautiful countenance with fond admiration, and smiled incredulously as he turned away.

The proposal of Alcibiades was civilly declined; the promised sum paid to his faithless steward, and the necklace, given by Phidias, redeemed.

Hylax had been forcibly carried to Salamis with his young mistress, lest his sagacity should lead to a discovery of her prison. When Eudora escaped from the island, she had reluctantly left him in her apartment, in order to avoid the danger that might arise from any untimely noise; but as soon as her own safety was secured, her first thoughts were for the recovery of this favourite animal, the early gift of Philæmon. The little captive had pined and moaned continually, during their brief separation; and when he returned, it seemed as if his boisterous joy could not sufficiently manifest itself in gambols and caresses.

When Artaphernes was convinced that he had really found his long-lost child, the impulse of gratitude led to very early inquiries for Pandænus. The artist had not yet re-appeared; and all Athens was filled with conjectures concerning his fate. Eudora still suspected that Alcibiades had secreted him, for the same reason that he had claimed Geta as a slave; for it was sufficiently obvious that he had desired, as far as possible, to deprive her of all assistance and protection.

The event proved her suspicions well founded. On the fourth day after her escape from Salamis, Pandænus came to congratulate Artaphernes, and half in anger, half in laughter, told the particulars of his story. He had been seized as he returned home at night, and had been forcibly conveyed to the mansion of Eurysaces, where he was kept a close prisoner, with the promise of being released whenever he finished a picture, which Alcibiades had long desired to obtain. This was a representation of Europa, just entering the ocean on the back of the beautiful bull, which she and her unsuspecting companions had crowned with garlands.

At first, the artist resisted, and swore by Phoebus Apollo that he would not be thus forced into the service of any man; but an unexpected circumstance changed his resolution.

There was a long, airy gallery, in which he was allowed to take exercise any hour of the day. In some places, an open-work partition, richly and curiously wrought by the skilful hand of Callicrates, separated this gallery from the outer balustrade of the building. During his walks, Pandænus often heard sounds of violent grief from the other side of the screen. Curiosity induced him to listen, and inquire the cause. A sad, sweet voice answered, "I am Cleonica, daughter of a noble Spartan. Taken captive in war, and sold to Alcibiades, I weep for my dishonoured lot; for much I fear it will bring the gray hairs of my mother to an untimely grave."

This interview led to another, and another; and though the mode of communication was imperfect, the artist was enabled to perceive that the captive maiden was a tall, queenly figure, with a rich profusion of sunny hair, indicating a fair and fresh complexion. The result was a promise to paint the desired picture, provided he might have the Spartan slave as a recompense.

Alcibiades, equally solicitous to obtain the painting, and to prolong the seclusion of Pandænus, and being then eager in another pursuit, readily consented to the terms proposed. After Eudora's sudden change of fortune, being somewhat ashamed of the publicity of his conduct, and desirous not to lose entirely the good opinion of Artaphernes, he gave the artist his liberty, simply requiring the fulfilment of his promise.

"And what are your intentions with regard to this fair captive?" inquired the Persian, with a significant smile.

With some degree of embarrassment, Pandænus answered, "I came to ask your protection; and that Eudora might for the present consider her as a sister, until I can restore her to her family."

"It shall be so," replied Artaphernes; "but this is a very small part of the debt I owe the nephew of Phidias. Should you hereafter have a favour to ask of Cleonica's noble family, poverty shall be no obstruction to your wishes. I have already taken measures to purchase for you a large estate in Elis, and to remit yearly revenues, which will I trust be equal to your wishes. I have another favour to ask, in addition to the many claims you already have upon me. Among the magnificent pictures that adorn the Poecile, I have not observed the sculptor of your gods. I pray you exert your utmost skill in a painting of Phidias crowned by the Muses; that I may place it on those walls, a public monument of my gratitude to that illustrious man."

"Of his statues and drawings I have purchased all that can be bought in Athens. The weeping Panthea, covering the body of Abradates with her mantle, is destined for my royal and munificent master. By the kindness of Pericles, I have obtained for myself the beautiful group, representing my precious little Artaminta caressing the kid, in that graceful attitude which first attracted the attention of her benefactor. For the munificent Eleans, I have reserved the Graceful Three, which your countrymen have named the presiding deities over benevolent actions. All the other statues and drawings of your illustrious kinsman are at your disposal. Nay, do not thank me, young man. Mine is still the debt, and my heart will be ever grateful."

The exertions of Clinias, although they proved unavailing, were gratefully acknowledged by the present of a large silver bowl, on which the skilful artificer, Mys, had represented, with exquisite delicacy, the infant Dionysus watched by the nymphs of Naxos.

In the midst of this generosity, the services of Geta and Milza were not forgotten. The bribe given to the steward was doubled in the payment, and an offer made to establish them in any part of Greece or Persia, where they wished to reside.

A decided preference was given to Elis, as the only place where they could be secure from the ravages of war. A noble farm, in the neighbourhood of Proclus, was accordingly purchased for them, well stocked with herds and furnished with all agricultural and household conveniences. Geta, having thus become an owner of the soil, dropped the brief name by which he had been known in slavery, and assumed the more sonorous appellation of Philophidias.

Dione, old as she was, overcame her fear of perils by land and sea, and resolved to follow her young mistress into Persia.

Before a new moon had begun its course, Pandænus fulfilled his intention of returning to Olympia, in company with the Lacedæmonian ambassador and his train. Cleonica, attended by Geta and Milza, travelled under the same protection. Artaphernes sent to Proclus four noble horses and a Bactrian camel, together with seven minæ as a portion for Zoila. For Pterilaüs, likewise, was a sum of money sufficient to maintain him ten years in Athens, that he might gratify his ardent desire to become the disciple of Plato. Eudora sent her little playmate a living peacock, which proved even more acceptable than her flock of marble sheep with their painted shepherd. To Melissa was sent a long affectionate epistle, with the dying bequest of Philothea, and many a valuable token of Eudora's gratitude.

Although a brilliant future was opening before her, the maiden's heart was very sad, when she bade a last farewell to the honest and faithful attendants, who had been with her through so many changing scenes, and aided her in the hour of her utmost need. The next day after their departure was spent by the Persian in the worship of Mithras, and prayers to Oromasdes. Eudora, in remembrance of her vision, offered thanksgiving and sacrifice to Phoebus and Pan; and implored the deities of ocean to protect the Phoenician galley, in which they were about to depart from Athens.

These ceremonies being performed, Artaphernes and his weeping daughter visited the studio of Myron, who, in compliance with their orders, had just finished the design of a beautiful monument to Paralus and Philothea, on which were represented two doves sleeping upon garlands.

For the last time, Eudora poured oblations of milk and honey, and placed fragrant flowers, with ringlets of her hair, upon the sepulchre of her gentle friend; then, with many tears, she bade a long farewell to scenes rendered sacred by the remembrance of their mutual love.

CHAPTER XX.

Next arose
A well-towered city, by seven golden gates
Inclosed, that fitted to their lintels hung.
Then burst forth
Aloud the marriage song; and far and wide
Long splendors flashed from many a quivering torch.
HESIOD

When the galley arrived at the opulent city of Tyre, the noble Persian and his retinue joined a caravan of Phoenician merchants bound to Ecbatana, honoured at that season of the year with the residence of the royal family. Eudora travelled in a cedar carriage drawn by camels. The latticed windows were richly gilded, and hung with crimson curtains, which her father ordered to be closed at the slightest indication of approaching travellers. Dione, with six more youthful attendants, accompanied her, and exerted all their powers to make the time pass pleasantly; but all their stories of romantic love, of heroes mortal and immortal, combined with the charms of music, could not prevent her from feeling that the journey was exceedingly long and wearisome.

She recollected how her lively spirit had sometimes rebelled against the restraints imposed on Grecian women, and sighed to think of all she had heard concerning the far more rigid customs of Persia. Expressions of fatigue sometimes escaped her; and her indulgent parent consented that she should ride in the chariot with him, enveloped in a long, thick veil, that descended to her feet, with two small openings of net-work for the eyes.

As they passed through Persia, he pointed out to her the sacred groves, inhabited by the Magii: the entrance of the cave where Zoroaster penned his divine precepts; and the mountain on whose summit he was wont to hold midnight communication with the heavenly bodies.

Eudora remarked that she nowhere observed temples or altars; objects to which her eye had always been accustomed, and which imparted such a sacred and peculiar beauty to Grecian scenery.

Artaphernes replied, "It is because these things are contrary to the spirit of Persian theology. Zoroaster taught us that the temple of Oromasdes was infinite space—his altar, the air, the earth, and the heavens."

When the travellers arrived within sight of Ecbatana, the setting sun poured upon the noble city a flood of dazzling light. It was girdled by seven walls of seven different colours; one rising above the other, in all the hues of the rainbow. From the centre of the innermost, arose the light, graceful towers of the royal palace, glittering with gold. The city was surrounded by fertile, spacious plains, bounded on one side by Mount Orontes, and on the other by a stately forest, amid whose lofty trees might here and there be seen the magnificent villas of Persian nobles.

Eudora's heart beat violently, when her father pointed to the residence of Megabyzus, and told her that the gilded balls on its pinnacles could be discovered from their own dwelling; but maiden shame prevented her from inquiring whether Philæmon was still the instructor of his sons.

The morning after his arrival, Artaphernes had a private audience with his royal master. This conference lasted so long, that many of the courtiers supposed his mission in Greece related to matters of more political importance than the purchase of pictures and statues; and this conjecture was afterward confirmed by the favours lavished upon him.

It was soon known throughout the precincts of the court that the favourite noble had returned from Athens, bringing with him his long-lost daughter. The very next day, as Eudora walked round the terraces of her father's princely mansion, she saw the royal carriages approach, followed by a long train of attendants, remarkable for age and ugliness, and preceded by an armed guard, calling aloud to all men to retire before their presence, on pain of death. In obedience to these commands, Artaphernes immediately withdrew to his own apartment, closed the shutters, and there remained till the royal retinue departed.

The visiters consisted of Amestris, the mother of Artaxerxes; Arsinöe of Damascus, his favourite mistress; and Parysatis, his daughter; with their innumerable slaves. They examined Eudora with more than childish curiosity; pulled every article of her dress, to ascertain its colour and its texture; teased to see all her jewels; wanted to know the name of everything in Greek; requested her to sing Greek songs; were impatient to learn Ionian dances; conjured her to paint a black streak from the eyes to the ears; and were particularly anxious to ascertain what cosmetic the Grecian ladies used to stain the tips of their fingers.

When all these important matters were settled, by means of an interpreter, they began to discuss the merits of Grecian ladies; and loudly expressed their horror at the idea of appearing before brothers unveiled, and at the still grosser indelicacy of sometimes allowing the face to be seen by a betrothed lover. Then followed a repetition of all the gossip of the harem; particularly, a fresh piece of scandal concerning Apollonides of Cos, and their royal kinswoman, Amytis, the wife of Megabyzus. Eudora turned away to conceal her blushes; for the indelicacy of their language was such as seldom met the ear of a Grecian maiden.

The Queen mother was eloquent in praise of a young Lesbian girl, whom Artaphernes had bought to attend upon his daughter. This was equivalent to asking for the slave; and the captive herself evinced no unwillingness to join the royal household; it having been foretold by an oracle that she would one day be the mother of kings. Amestris accepted the beautiful Greek, with many thanks, casting a triumphant glance at Arsinöe and Parysatis, who lowered their brows, as if each had reasons of her own for being displeased with the arrangement.

The royal guests gave and received a variety of gifts; consisting principally of jewels, embroidered mantles, veils, tufts of peacock feathers with ivory handles, parrots, and golden boxes filled with roseate powder for the fingers, and black paint for the eyebrows. At length they departed, and Eudora's attendants showered perfumes on them as they went.

Eudora recalled to mind the pure and sublime discourse she had so often enjoyed with Philothea, and sighed as she compared it with this specimen of intercourse with high-born Persian ladies.

When the sun was setting, she again walked upon the terrace; and, forgetful of the customs of the country, threw back her veil, that she might enjoy more perfectly the beauty of the landscape. She stood thoughtfully gazing at the distant pinnacles, which marked the residence of Megabyzus, when the barking of Hylax attracted her attention, and looking into the garden, she perceived a richly dressed young man, with his eyes fixed earnestly upon her. She drew her veil hastily, and retired within the dwelling, indulging the secret hope that none of her attendants had witnessed an action, which Artaphernes would deem so imprudent.

On the following morning commenced the celebrated festival called, 'The Salutation of Mithras;' during which, forty days were set apart for thanksgiving and sacrifice. The procession formed long before the rising of the sun. First appeared a long train of the most distinguished Magii from all parts of the empire, led by their chief in scarlet robes, carrying the sacred fire upon a silver furnace. Next appeared an empty chariot consecrated to Oromasdes, decorated with garlands, and drawn by white steeds harnessed with gold. This was followed by a magnificent large horse, his forehead flaming with gems, in honour of Mithras. Then came the Band of Immortals, and the royal kindred, their Median vests blazing with embroidery and gold. Artaxerxes rode in an ivory chariot, richly inlaid with precious stones. He was followed by a long line of nobles, riding on camels splendidly caparisoned; and their countless attendants closed the train. This gorgeous retinue slowly ascended Mount Orontes. When they arrived upon its summit, the chief of the Magii assumed his tiara interwoven with myrtle, and hailed the first beams of the rising sun with sacrifice. Then each of the Magii in turns sung orisons to Oromasdes, by whose eternal power the radiant Mithras had been sent to gladden the earth, and preserve the principle of life. Finally, they all joined in one universal chorus, while king, princes, and nobles, prostrated themselves, and adored the Fountain of Light.

At that solemn moment, a tiger leaped from an adjoining thicket, and sprung toward the king. But ere the astonished courtiers had time to breathe, a javelin from some unknown hand passed through the ferocious animal, and laid him lifeless in the dust.

Eudora had watched the procession from the house-top; and at this moment she thought she perceived hurried and confused movements, of which her attendants could give no explanation.

The splendid concourse returned toward the palace in the same order that it had ascended the mountain. But next to the royal chariot there now appeared a young man on a noble steed, with a golden chain about his neck, and two heralds by his side, who ever and anon blew their trumpets, and proclaimed, "This is Philæmon of Athens, whom the king delighteth to honour?"

Eudora understood the proclamation imperfectly; but afar off, she recognized the person of her lover. As they passed the house, she saw Hylax running to and fro on the top of the wall, barking, and jumping, and wagging his tail, as if he too were conscious of the vicinity of some familiar friend. The dog evidently arrested Philæmon's attention; for he observed him closely, and long continued to look back and watch his movements.

A tide of sweet and bitter recollections oppressed the maiden's heart; a deadly paleness overspread her cheeks; a suffocating feeling choked her voice; and had it not been for a sudden gush of tears, she would have fallen.

When her father returned, he informed her that the life of Artaxerxes had been saved by the promptitude and boldness of Philæmon, who happened to perceive the tiger sooner than any other person at the festival. He added, "I saw Philæmon after the rescue, but we had brief opportunity to discourse together. I think his secluded habits have prevented him from hearing that I found a daughter in Athens. He told me he intended soon to return to his native country, and promised to be my guest for a few days before he departed. Furthermore, my child, the Great King, in the fulness of his regal bounty, last night sent a messenger to demand you in marriage for his son Xerxes."

He watched her countenance, as he spoke; but seemed doubtful how to understand the fluctuating colour. Still keeping his scrutinizing gaze fixed upon her, he continued, "Artaminta, this is an honour not to be lightly rejected; to be princess of Persia now, and hereafter perhaps its queen."

In some confusion, the maiden answered, "Perhaps the prince may not approve his father's choice."

"No, Artaminta; the prince has chosen for himself. He sent his sister to obtain a view of my newly discovered daughter; and he himself saw you, as you stood on the terrace unveiled."

In an agitated voice, Eudora asked, "And must I be compelled to obey the commands of the king?"

"Unless it should be his gracious pleasure to dispense with obedience," replied Artaphernes. "I and all my household are his servants. I pray Oromasdes that you may never have greater troubles than the fear of becoming a princess."

"But you forget, my dear father, that Parysatis told me her brother Xerxes was effeminate and capricious, and had a new idol with every change of the moon. Some fairer face would soon find favour in his sight; and I should perhaps be shut up with hundreds of forgotten favourites, in the old harem, among silly women and ugly slaves."

Her father answered, in an excited tone, "Artaminta, if you had been brought up with more becoming seclusion, like those silly Persian women, you would perhaps have known, better than you now seem to do, that a woman's whole duty is submission."

Eudora had never heard him speak so harshly. She perceived that his parental ambition was roused, and that her indifference to the royal proposal displeased him. The tears fell fast, as she replied, "Dear father, I will obey you, even if you ask me to sacrifice my life, at the command of the king."

Her tears touched the feelings of the kind old man. He embraced her affectionately, saying, "Do not weep, daughter of my beloved Antiope. It would indeed gratify my heart to see you Queen of Persia; but you shall not be made wretched, if my interest with the Great King can prevent it. All men praise his justice and moderation; and he has pledged his royal word to grant anything I ask, in recompense for services rendered in Greece. The man who has just saved his life can no doubt obtain any favour. But reflect upon it well, my daughter. Xerxes has no son; and should you give birth to a boy, no new favourite could exclude you from the throne. Perhaps Philæmon was silent from other causes than ignorance of your arrival in Persia; and if this be the case, you may repent a too hasty rejection of princely love."

Eudora blushed like crimson, and appeared deeply pained by this suggestion; but she made no answer. Artaphernes departed, promising to seek a private audience with the king; and she saw him no more that night. When she laid her head upon the pillow, a mind troubled with many anxious thoughts for a long time prevented repose; and when she did sink to sleep, it was with a confused medley of ideas, in which the remembrance of Philæmon's love was mixed up with floating visions of regal grandeur, and proud thoughts of a triumphant marriage, now placed within her power, should he indeed prove as unforgiving and indifferent, as her father had suggested.

In her sleep, she saw Philothea; but a swift and turbid stream appeared to roll between them; and her friend said, in melancholy tones, "You have left me, Eudora; and I cannot come to you, now. Whence are these dark and restless waters, which separate our souls?"

Then a variety of strange scenes rapidly succeeded each other—all cheerless, perturbed, and chaotic. At last, she seemed to be standing under the old grape-vine, that shaded the dwelling of Anaxagoras, and Philæmon crowned her with a wreath of myrtle. In the morning, soon after she had risen from her couch, Artaphernes came to her apartment, and mildly asked if she still wished to decline the royal alliance. He evinced no displeasure when she answered in the affirmative; but quietly replied, "It may be that you have chosen a wise part, my child; for true it is, that safety and contentment rarely take up their abode with princes. But now go and adorn yourself with your richest apparel; for the Great King requires me to present you at the palace, before the hour of noon. Let your Greek costume be laid aside; for I would not have my daughter appear like a foreigner, in the presence of her king."

With a palpitating heart, Eudora resigned herself into the hands of her Persian tire-women, who so loaded her with embroidery and gems, that she could scarcely support their weight.

She was conveyed to the palace in a cedar carriage, carefully screened from observation. Her father rode by her side, and a numerous train of attendants followed. Through gates of burnished brass, they entered a small court with a tesselated pavement of black and white marble. Thence they passed into a long apartment, with walls of black marble, and cornices heavily gilded. The marble was so highly polished, that Eudora saw the light of her jewels everywhere reflected like sunbeams. Surprised by the multiplied images of herself and attendants, she did not at first perceive, through the net-work of her veil, that a young man stood leaning against the wall, with his arms folded. This well-remembered attitude attracted her attention, and she scarcely needed a glance to assure her it was Philæmon.

It being contrary to Persian etiquette to speak without license within hearing of the royal apartments, the Athenian merely smiled, and bowed gracefully to Artaphernes; but an audible sigh escaped him, as he glanced at the Greek attendants. Eudora hastily turned away her head, when he looked toward her; but her heart throbbed so violently that every fold of her veil trembled. They continued thus in each other's presence many minutes; one in a state of perfect unconsciousness, the other suffering an intensity of feeling, that seemed like the condensed excitement of years. At last a herald came to say it was now the pleasure of the Great King to receive them in the private court, opening into the royal gardens.

The pavement of this court was of porphyry inlaid with costly marbles, in various hieroglyphics. The side connected with the palace was adorned with carved open-work, richly painted and gilded, and with jasper tablets, alternately surmounted by a golden ram and a winged lion; one the royal ensign of Persia, the other emblematic of the Assyrian empire conquered by Cyrus. The throne was placed in the centre, under a canopy of crimson, yellow, and blue silk, tastefully intermingled and embroidered with silver and gold. Above this was an image of the sun, with rays so brilliant, that it dazzled the eyes of those who looked upon it.

The monarch seemed scarcely beyond the middle age, with long flowing hair, and a countenance mild and dignified. On his right hand stood Xerxes—on his left, Darius and Sogdianus; and around him were a numerous band of younger sons; all wearing white robes, with jewelled vests of Tyrian purple.

As they entered, the active buzzing of female voices was heard behind the gilded open-work of the wall; but this was speedily silenced by a signal from the herald. Artaphernes prostrated himself, till his forehead touched the pavement; Eudora copied his example; but Philæmon merely bowed low, after the manner of the Athenians. Artaxerxes bade them arise, and said, in a stern tone, "Artaphernes, has thy daughter prepared herself to obey our royal mandate? Or is she still contemptuous of our kingly bounty?"

Eudora trembled; and her father again prostrated himself, as he replied: "O great and benignant king! mayest thou live forever. May Oromandes bless thee with a prosperous reign, and forever avert from thee the malignant influence of Arimanius. I and my household are among the least of thy servants. May the hand that offends thee be cut off, and cast to unclean dogs."

"Arise, Artaphernes!" said the monarch: "Thy daughter has permission to speak."

Eudora, awed by the despotic power and august presence of Artaxerxes, spoke to her father, in a low and tremulous voice, and reminded him of the royal promise to grant whatever he might ask."

Philæmon turned eagerly, and a sudden flush mantled his cheeks, when he heard the pure Attic dialect, "with its lovely marriage of sweet sounds."

"What does the maiden say?" inquired the king. Artaphernes again paid homage, and answered; "O Light of the World! Look in mercy upon the daughter of thy servant, and grant that her petition may find favour in thy sight. As yet, she hath not gained a ready utterance of the Persian language—honoured and blessed above all languages, in being the messenger of thy thoughts, O king. Therefore she spoke in the Greek tongue, concerning thy gracious promise to grant unto the humblest of thy servants whatsoever he might ask at thy hands."

Then the monarch held forth his golden sceptre, and replied, "Be it unto thee, as I have said. I have sought thy daughter in marriage for Xerxes, prince of the empire. What other boon does Artaphernes ask of the king?"

The Persian approached, and reverently touching the point of the sceptre, answered: "O King of kings! before whom the nations of the earth do tremble. Thy bounty is like the overflowing Nilus, and thy mercy refreshing as dew upon the parched earth. If it be thy pleasure, O King, forgive Artaminta, my daughter, if she begs that the favour of the prince, like the blessed rays of Mithras, may fall upon some fairer damsel. I pray thee have her excused."

Xerxes looked up with an angry frown; but his royal father replied, "The word of the king is sacred; and his decree changeth not. Be it unto thee even as thou wilt."

Then turning to Philæmon, he said: "Athenian stranger, our royal life preserved by thy hand deserves a kingly boon. Since our well beloved son cannot find favour in the eyes of this damsel, we bestow her upon thee. Her father is one of the illustrious Pasargadæ, and her ancestors were not unremotely connected with the princes of Media. We have never looked upon her countenance—deeming it wise to copy the prudent example of our cousin Cyrus; but report describes her beautiful as Panthea."

Eudora shrunk from being thus bestowed upon Philæmon; and she would have said this to her father, had he not checked the first half-uttered word by a private signal.

With extreme confusion, the Athenian bowed low, and answered, "Pardon me, O King, and deem me not insensible of thy royal munificence. I pray thee bestow the daughter of the princely Artaphernes upon one more worthy than thy servant."

"Now, by the memory of Cyrus!" exclaimed Artaxerxes, "The king's favours shall this day be likened unto a beggar, whose petitions are rejected at every gate."

Then, turning to his courtiers, he added: "A proud nation are these Greeks! When the plague ravaged all Persia and Media, Hippocrates of Cos refused our entreaties, and scorned our royal bounty; saying he was born to serve his own countrymen, and not foreigners. Themistocles, on whom our mighty father bestowed the revenues of cities, died, rather than fight for him against Athens; and lo! here is a young Athenian, who refuses a maiden sought by the Persian prince, with a dowry richer than Pactolus.

Philæmon bowed himself reverently, and replied: "Deem not, O king, that I am moved by Grecian pride; for well I know that I am all unworthy of this princely alliance. An epistle lately received from Olympia makes it necessary for me to return to Greece; where, O king, I seek a beloved maiden, to whom I was betrothed before my exile."

Eudora had trembled violently, and her convulsive breathing was audible, while Philæmon spoke; but when he uttered the last words, forgetful of the reverence required of those who stood in the presence of majesty, she murmured, "Oh, Philothea!" and sunk into the arms of her father.

The young man started; for now, not only the language, but the tones were familiar to his heart. As the senseless form was carried into the garden, he gazed upon it with an excited and bewildered expression.

Artaxerxes smiled, as he said: "Athenian stranger, the daughter of Artaphernes, lost on the coast of Ionia, was discovered in the household of Phidias, and the Greeks called her Eudora."

Philæmon instantly knelt at the monarch's feet, and said, "Pardon me, O king. I was ignorant of all this. I ———"

He would have explained more fully; but Artaxerxes interrupted him; "We know it all, Athenian stranger—we know it all. You have refused Artaminta, and now we bestow upon you Eudora, with the revenues of Magnesia and Lampsacus for her dowry."

Before the next moon had waned, a magnificent marriage was celebrated in the court of audience, opening into the royal gardens. On a shining throne, in the midst of a stately pavilion, was seated Artaxerxes, surrounded by the princes of the empire. Near the throne stood Philæmon and Eudora. Artaphernes placed the right hand of the bride within the right hand of the bridegroom, saying, "Philæmon of Athens, I bestow upon thee, Artaminta, my daughter, with my estates in Pasagarda, and five thousand darics as her dowry."

The chief of the Magii bore sacred fire on a silver censer, and the bridal couple passed slowly around it three times, bowing reverently to the sacred emblem of Mithras. Then the bridegroom fastened a golden jewel about the bride's neck, and they repeated certain words, promising fidelity to each other. The nuptial hymn was sung by six handsome youths, and as many maidens, clothed in white garments, with a purple edge.

Numerous lamps were lighted in the trees, making the gardens bright as noon. Women belonging to the royal household, and to the most favoured of the nobility, rode through the groves and lawns, in rich pavilions, on the backs of camels and white elephants. As the huge animals were led along, fireworks burst from under their feet, and playing for a moment in the air, with undulating movements, fell in a sparkling shower.

Artaxerxes gave a luxurious feast, which lasted seven days; during which time the Queen entertained her guests with equal splendour, in the apartments of the women.

The Athenian decree against those of foreign parentage had been repealed in favour of young Pericles; but in that country everything was in a troubled and unsettled state; and Artaphernes pleaded hard to have his daughter remain in Persia.

It was therefore decided that the young couple should reside at Pasagarda, situated in a fertile valley, called the Queen's Girdle, because its revenues were appropriated to that costly article of the royal wardrobe. This pleasant city had once been the favourite residence of Cyrus the Great, and a plain obelisk in the royal gardens marked his burial-place. The adjacent promontory of Taoces afforded a convenient harbour for Tyrian merchants, and thus brought in the luxuries of Phoenicia, while it afforded opportunities for literary communication between the East and the West. Here were celebrated schools under the direction of the Magii, frequently visited by learned men from Greece, Ethiopia, and Egypt.

Philæmon devoted himself to the quiet pursuits of literature; and Eudora, happy in her father, husband and children, thankfully acknowledged the blessings of her lot.

Her only daughter, a gentle maiden, with plaintive voice and earnest eyes, bore the beloved name of Philothea.

APPENDIX

Zeus—The Jupiter of the Romans.

Zeus Xenius—Jupiter the Hospitable.

Hera—Juno.

Pallas—Minerva.

Pallas Athena—An ancient appellation of Minerva, from which Athens took its name.

Pallas Parthenia—Pallas the Virgin.

Pallas Promachos—Pallas the Defender.

Phoebus—The Apollo of the Romans; the Sun.

Phoebus Apollo—Phoebus the Destroyer, or the Purifier.

Phoebe—Diana; the Moon.

Artemis—Diana.

Agrotera—Diana the Huntress.

Orthia—Name of Diana among the Spartans.

Poseidon—Neptune.

Aphrodite—Venus.

Urania—The Heavenly Venus. The same name was applied to the Muse of Astronomy.

Eros—Cupid.

Hermes—Mercury.

Demeter—Ceres.

Persephone—Proserpine.

Dionysus—Bacchus.

Pandamator—A name of Vulcan, signifying the All-subduing.

Mnemosyne—Goddess of Memory.

Chloris—Flora.

Asclepius—Esculapius.

Rhamnusia—Name of a statue of Nemesis, goddess of Vengeance; so called because it was in the town of Rhamnus.

Polydeuces—Pollux.

Leto—Latona.

Taraxippus—A deity whose protection was implored at Elis, that no harm might happen to the horses.

Erinnys—The Eumenides, or Furies.

Naiades—Nymphs of Rivers, Springs, and Fountains.

Nereides—Nymphs of the Sea.

Oreades—Nymphs of the Mountains.

Dryades—Nymphs of the Woods.

Oromasdes—Persian name for the Principle of Good.

Mithras—Persian name for the Sun.

Arimanius—Persian name for the Principle of Evil.

Odysseus—Ulysses.

Achilleus-Achilles.

Cordax—An immodest comic dance.

Agora—A Market House.

Prytaneum—The Town House.

Deigma—A place in the Piræus, corresponding to the modern Exchange.

Clepsydra—A Water-dial.

Cotylæ—A measure. Some writers say one third of a quart; others much less.

Arytana—A small cup.

Arabyllus—A vase, wide at bottom and narrow at top.

Archons—Chief Magistrates of Athens.

Prytanes—Magistrates who presided over the Senate.

Phylarchi—Sheriffs.

Epistates—Chairman, or speaker.

Hippodrome—The Horse-course.

Stadium—Thirty-six and a half rods.

Obulus, (plural *Oboli*)—A small coin, about the value of a penny.

Drachma, (plural *Drachmæ*)—About ten-pence sterling.

Mina, (plural *Minæ*)—Four pounds, three shillings, four pence.

Stater—A gold coin; estimated at about twelve shillings, three pence.

Daric—A Persian gold coin, valued one pound, twelve shillings, three pence.

(All the above coins are estimated very differently by different writers.)

In some unimportant matters, I have not adhered strictly to dates; deeming this an allowable freedom in a work so purely romantic, relating to times so ancient.

I am aware that the Christian spirit is sometimes infused into a Grecian form; and in nothing is this more conspicuous than the representation of love as a pure sentiment rather than a gross passion.

Greek names for the deities were used in preference to the Roman, because the latter have become familiarized by common and vulgar use.

If there be errors in the application of Greek names and phrases, my excuse must be an entire want of knowledge in the classic languages. But, like the ignoramus in the Old Drama, I can boast, "Though I *speak* no Greek, I love the *sound* on't."

Echo Library

www.echo-library.com

Echo Library uses advanced digital print-on-demand technology to build and preserve an exciting world class collection of rare and out-of-print books, making them readily available for everyone to enjoy.

Situated just yards from Teddington Lock on the River Thames, Echo Library was founded in 2005 by Tom Cherrington, a specialist dealer in rare and antiquarian books with a passion for literature.

Please visit our website for a complete catalogue of our books, which includes foreign language titles.

The Right to Read

Echo Library actively supports the Royal National Institute of the Blind's Right to Read initiative by publishing a comprehensive range of large print and clear print titles.

Large Print titles are in 16 point Tiresias font as recommended by the RNIB.

Clear Print titles are in 13 point Tiresias font and designed for those who find standard print difficult to read.

Customer Service

If there is a serious error in the text or layout please send details to feedback@echo-library.com and we will supply a corrected copy. If there is a printing fault or the book is damaged please refer to your supplier.

CPSIA information can be obtained at www.ICGtesting.com
Printed in the USA
LVOW08s0429250714

395891LV00001B/39/P